FOX
SNARE

Also by Yoon Ha Lee

DRAGON PEARL

★ "Lee skillfully weaves Korean folklore into this space opera narrative, creating dynamic and relatable characters. With ghosts, pirates, and a rollicking space adventure, there's a little something for everyone here."
—*School Library Journal* (starred review)

★ "A high-octane, science-fiction thriller painted with a Korean brush and a brilliant example of how different cultures can have unique but accessible cosmology and universal appeal."
—*Kirkus Reviews* (starred review)

★ "Lee offers a perfect balance of space opera and Korean mythology with enough complexity to appeal to teens."
—*Publishers Weekly* (starred review)

"*Dragon Pearl* is a clever mash-up of Korean mythology and science-fiction tropes. With crisp dialogue, a winning protagonist and a propulsive plot, the tale is enormously entertaining."
—*New York Times Book Review*

A *New York Times* Best Seller

Locus Award Winner for Best Young Adult Novel 2020

Mythopoeic Scholarship Award for Children's Literature Winner 2020

Kirkus Reviews' Best Children's Books of 2019

Chicago Public Library's Best of the Best Books of 2019

A Junior Library Guild Selection

TIGER HONOR

"The question of honor versus family loyalty plays out in a thrilling Korean-inspired space opera. Throughout, Lee develops an important thread that examines hard decisions when family tradition and personal integrity clash, an emotional dilemma that will resonate with many readers. The Thousand Worlds universe continues to thrill with the lure of Korean mythology, the action of space battle, and the personal struggle to act with honor. Fans will demand more. Weaves together science fiction and cultural elements with tremendous appeal."

—*Kirkus Reviews*

"With a delightful mix of Korean mythology and science fiction, Lee expands on the intriguing world of his previous novel to create another exhilarating adventure with a new precocious protagonist. Fans of *Dragon Pearl* will enjoy this dive back into the Thousand Worlds universe."

—*Booklist*

"Themes of personal integrity, courage, friendship, and loyalty are delivered in a fast-paced plot filled with engaging twists, turns, and near-misses. . . . Nonbinary characters and women in positions of military power are refreshingly commonplace in this original space opera interwoven with Korean mythology."

—*School Library Journal*

Selected for the 2023 Eleanor Cameron Notable Middle Grade Books List by the American Library Association's Core Committee Recognizing Excellence in Children's and Young Adult Science Fiction

Named to the 2023 Rainbow List by the Rainbow Round Table of the American Library Association

FOX SNARE

YOON HA LEE

A THOUSAND WORLDS NOVEL

RICK RIORDAN PRESENTS

Disney • HYPERION   LOS ANGELES   NEW YORK

First Edition, October 2023
1 3 5 7 9 10 8 6 4 2
FAC-004510-23236
Printed in the United States of America

This book is set in Janson MT Pro, Carlin Script LT Std/
Monotype; Penumbra Std, Goudy Trajan Pro/Fontspring
Designed by Tyler Nevins

Library of Congress Cataloging-in-Publication Data
Names: Lee, Yoon Ha, author. • To, Vivienne, illustrator. Title:
Fox snare / Yoon Ha Lee; [illustrations by Vivienne To].
Description: First edition. • Los Angeles : Disney Hyperion, 2023. • Series: A
Thousand Worlds novel; book 3 • "Rick Riordan Presents." • Audience: Ages 8–12. •
Audience: Grades 4–6. • Summary: "When Min the fox spirit and her ghost brother
Jun are sent on a goodwill mission to prevent war from breaking out, they end up
getting stranded on a death planet behind enemy lines"—Provided by publisher.
Identifiers: LCCN 2022037961 • ISBN 9781368081818 (hardcover) • ISBN 9781368081924 (ebk)
Subjects: CYAC: Space flight—Fiction. • Magic—Fiction. • Brothers
and sisters—Fiction. • Adventure and adventurers—Fiction. •
Science fiction. • LCGFT: Science fiction. • Novels.
Classification: LCC PZ7.1.L4414 Fo 2023 • DDC [Fic]—dc23
LC record available at https://lccn.loc.gov/2022037961

Reinforced binding
Visit www.DisneyBooks.com
Follow @ReadRiordan

For Seth Fishman, agent extraordinaire.
Thank you for all your support, savviness, and kindness.

ONE

Min

The best thing in the world is a party, except when you're the youngest person there and everyone wishes you would go away.

It's one thing to be the youngest at a party that's for you, when you're expecting gifts and a good time. For a day you can forget that the dome that protects your shabby house from the dusty atmosphere needs repair, that your helper robot has broken down again, that your mean cousin Bora messed up the household digi-slate so no one can watch holo shows. For my family, that day used to be New Year's, when everyone added a year to their age. We'd always exchange gifts, however small: hand-sewn needle minders, or a pin to hold up our hair, or a solar-powered toy blaster that actually lit up.

That was back on my old home on the steader world of Jinju. We were poor, but we had each other. Something I hadn't appreciated at the time.

Today's party was on the space station of Ssangyong—the name means *twin dragons*—and at times I thought it was bigger than the biggest city on Jinju. My obnoxious cousin Bora wouldn't be attending this celebration, but that was the only good thing about it. I lurked by the trays of food, trying not to look like the only thing I cared about was the mandu dumplings, stuffed with seasoned pork and green onion. They'd invited me here as Bearer of the Dragon Pearl, a magical artifact that could transform whole worlds. An artifact that might be the key to peace between the Thousand Worlds (my nation) and the Sun Clans, with whom we'd been at war for years. Spoiler alert: The only thing I *wanted* to care about was the mandu. Too bad it would cause a diplomatic incident if I chowed down before the real guests arrived.

I had to admit the place looked great. The officials, or more accurately, their peons, had decorated it for the occasion. The Thousand Worlds' symbols were everywhere, as if to remind any guests that we were at the heart of our influence.

The banners showed everything from the mugunghwa flower with its pink and magenta petals to paintings of entwined dragons in their native serpentine form, coiling around stylized clouds that reached up to the starry skies. People were dressed in gold-embroidered silk and stiff brocades, rich in the bold colors that the people of the Thousand Worlds loved so much. Instead of the plain, functional pronoun pins that the Space Forces used, people had fancy ones, often sporting jewels or elaborate enamel designs. Even I'd consented to wear a hanbok in bright red and blue and have my hair braided with matching ribbons. It almost made me fit in.

I was in the form of an older teen, the sixteen-year-old guise I wore for the sake of convenience. But while I may have looked like just another one of the young women in the room, I was an impostor. I was a gumiho, a shape-shifting fox, and if the other guests knew the truth, they would never trust me again. A few of the higher-ranking officials were in on the secret, but people would be even more appalled by the presence of an untrustworthy fox than by my true age of fourteen.

They would be especially offended by the fact that a *fox* was the Bearer of the Dragon Pearl. The orb, a comforting presence the size of my fist, rested snugly in a silken pouch at my waist. I thought I could even hear its murmuration, as of a vanished sea. It was the most coveted object in the Thousand Worlds, and it had chosen me to carry it after I'd recovered it from the Ghost Sector last year.

Funny thing: I'd once asked my handler, Seok, if the Thousand Worlds literally included a thousand worlds, and he'd looked at me like I'd admitted that I couldn't count to four. "What do you mean by 'world'?" he asked. "Is a moon a 'world'? How about a really big starbase?" It wasn't until he'd left the room that I realized he'd never answered the question.

When I was growing up in a backward steader household on Jinju, I'd always imagined that the Thousand Worlds were the breadth and width of the universe. I'd never thought about the worlds that lay beyond our borders, our diplomatic reach— or the shadow of war.

I spotted my bodyguard, a lean woman in drab clothes, lurking at the edge of the party, not too close and not too far. I winked at her. Her face went carefully blank.

I'd asked for her name when we first met. She called herself Silhouette, which was exactly the kind of code name I imagined a former spy would have. Seok hadn't coughed up her actual name, either, so Silhouette it was. Mostly I thought of her as "the bodyguard," which at least described her function.

I could only waste so much time teasing her, though. We'd been through the wink-and-ignore routine a dozen times already during the course of this party.

"Where are they?" I grumbled, confident that even other supernaturals, such as tiger spirits or goblins, couldn't overhear me over the hubbub of chatter and gossip. "If the Sun Clans ambassador is any later, I'm going to turn into a fox and make off with that ginseng-stuffed chicken."

"Please don't," murmured my sensible older brother, Jun.

Jun was even less noticeable than I was. People overlooked him most of the time, not because of his retiring demeanor, but because he was a ghost. He usually faded into the background so he wouldn't spook anyone. Ghosts generated bad luck, and if the attendees found out he had accompanied me here, they'd probably get one of the shamans present to exorcise him on the spot, which I couldn't allow. Not after all the things we'd both been through.

Besides, if they got rid of Jun, who would protect me from my worst impulses?

I cast an eye around the milling group of officials, diplomats, and guards. Once I would have been thrilled to be in such august company. Today, though, all I could think were catty things like *Do you really think that hairdo does your face any favors?* and *Maybe go lighter on the cologne next time?* The latter, at least, was unfair—humans had less acute senses of smell than foxes did.

An older man, his hair lightly streaked with gray, sidled over to the food tables and began sneaking a bun decorated with edible flowers. I cleared my throat. If I couldn't eat yet, no one else would, either.

"Why, hello there, young lady!" he said, suavely replacing the bun. "You wouldn't let one of your elders collapse of hunger, would you? My doctors say I need to eat to keep up my strength."

I forced myself to smile. The older man, besides being dressed in robes that must have cost as much as my family's yearly allowance for food, had clear skin, great teeth, and a sturdy frame. His smell did hint that he was indeed ill, but I doubted he'd ever known hunger or shared expired ration bars because the hydroponics had malfunctioned and there was a poor harvest.

I couldn't say any of that to him, though. No one was supposed to know that Kim Min, Bearer of the Dragon Pearl, had come from such a hardscrabble background. Seok hadn't even wanted me to use my real name, but that was something I'd insisted on holding on to, especially since it was a pretty common name. After so much shape-shifting, I wasn't sure I remembered my native form, that of a small fox, let alone the default human one I'd used back home. My name—my real name—gave me an anchor to my identity.

The man's eyes narrowed as he studied me, and my unease grew. I didn't want to stand out too much, despite my so-called vital role in the ceremonial meeting. The meeting that our guests from a rival nation, the Sun Clans, were almost half an hour late for.

My stomach settled the matter by growling loudly. I blushed.

Best to distract him. "I'm Kim Min," I said with a deep bow, as befitted the man's age. "Pleased to meet you."

"That's better," Jun said in his ghostly whisper.

"Ah, the Dragon Pearl's guardian," said the man with a firm nod, as if he'd won a bet with himself. "Forgive me, my dear. I'd expected you to be taller, or maybe broader."

If only you knew, I thought, hiding a grin. My shape-shifting had limits. I couldn't become very tall, or very broad, because as a fox I wasn't all that big. But I could stretch things if I had to, and as my power grew, so did my ability to expand.

The man hadn't finished speaking. "Of course, people say the same thing to me." He smiled wryly. "I'm the minister of defense, so people expect me to have the build of a taekwondo champion or a wrestler."

Now he had my attention. Minister Baik. I'd seen him in the news holos, but he'd been a tiny speck of a figure then, so I hadn't recognized him in the flesh.

I should have taken a closer look at the guest list when Seok was going over the mission brief with me, but my eyes had glazed over after the umpteenth assistant to the assistant to the aide of the dog-walker to the . . . You get the idea. Many of the high-and-mighty people hadn't been able to make it in person, and a bunch of them had sent their aides, assistants, and so forth.

On the other hand, it made sense that the minister of defense had come. Seok had informed me that the Thousand Worlds and Sun Clans had a history of warfare going back to their founding and beyond, even back to the misty days when they'd both been small nations on the Old World, our origin planet. We'd lost the Old World in some crisis I didn't know the details of, and the ancient rivalries had followed us into space.

It was my turn to study the elderly man, although I had to do so without looking him straight in the eye, which would have been disrespectful, not just on account of his greater age, but also his position. "Sounds like a stressful job," I offered.

"This could be the turning point," Minister Baik said wistfully. "Peace between the Sun Clans and the Thousand Worlds. The Space Forces could stand down. I'd go to the final ceremony on the world of Jasujeong myself, but my doctors recommend against it. . . . Good thing I can rely on my assistant to represent the ministry in these matters, and work for peace."

I blinked. Not a sentiment I would have expected from the minister of *defense*. I wasn't super clear on the intricacies of the Thousand Worlds' government, other than the fact that steaders didn't get much say in matters of interstellar policy. But I did know that the minister of defense was in charge of the Space Forces. A better name for his position might have been the minister of war.

"I can see what you're thinking," Minister Baik said.

I winced and wished I had hidden my expression better.

"You've probably lost friends or family to marauders, or pirates, or Sun Clans raiders," he went on.

I nodded like I had some idea what he was talking about. I'd *encountered* pirates, but that was after I'd run away from home. Another story I didn't want to get into. On Jinju, we'd kept a low profile, and the neighbors had looked out for us. Once I would have killed for a nice, exciting raid to interrupt my boring chore of scrubbing vegetables. Now I knew better.

"The prospect of war is one thing," Minister Baik said. "The parades, the medals, the fancy machines and starships . . . But the reality is another." He shook his head. "I am haunted by my share of ghosts."

I startled. Had he spotted Jun? No, he must have been

talking metaphorically. I couldn't imagine the authorities would let someone hold government office if they thought he was actually being haunted.

Jun manifested as a chiaroscuro of light and dark just to my left, not coincidentally near the coveted pork mandu. I raised an eyebrow at him, then nodded toward the brooding minister. Jun shrugged, his long hair hanging down around his face, and shook his head. The ragged hair was one thing that gave away Jun's spectral status, along with his transparency. Otherwise, if you weren't paying close attention, he looked like any other Space Forces cadet, complete with blue uniform.

I was trying to think of a way to extricate myself from this depressing conversation, which was way over my head, when a ripple passed through the crowd. Minister Baik straightened as though someone had slapped him. Excited murmurs began, then quieted.

The Sun Clans ambassador and her entourage had finally arrived.

She would have stuck out anywhere in the Thousand Worlds. Even before Seok gave me the briefing (it was always briefings with him), I'd have identified her as *not from here*. The ambassador wasn't tall, but she radiated authority like a star. Several layers of robes draped her slight form, arranged so you could see just a peek of each color, from white to orange to red. Ruby-studded gold pins stuck out from her elaborate updo. I wondered morbidly if the pins were backup weapons.

She also came with bodyguards, because important people always had bodyguards. Even *I* had one. (*Why didn't Minister Baik?* I wondered much later.) The ambassador's came in a matched pair, each taller by a head, although their deferential bearing made it clear she was *definitely* the one in charge. I took more interest in their weapons: sheathed curved swords, one long and one short.

"Purely ceremonial," Minister Baik assured me when he saw me staring. "Nobody uses the katana and wakizashi in combat anymore. They probably don't even have edges."

"Still, either would make one heck of a club," I muttered. Getting walloped with even an unsharpened katana would suck. I noticed that the minister wasn't carrying any visible weapon. I hadn't seen one on Silhouette, either. I hoped she had something hidden on her person.

"Min," Jun said in that *Oh no you didn't* tone I'd gotten to know so well. "Let's hope he didn't hear you."

Minister Baik glanced in his direction, frowning. "I thought I heard . . . Never mind."

I glared at where Jun had been a second ago. He'd at least had the sense to fade out of sight. *Don't give yourself away,* I mouthed. You'd think that after everything we'd been through together, we'd have this down to a routine. Too bad fox spirits were notoriously bad at routines and order. And, thanks to the bad luck that Jun and I shared, things were always going topsy-turvy around me whether I wanted them to or not.

Distracted as I'd been by the food and the minister of defense, I'd forgotten that I was supposed to be up on the dais greeting the Sun Clans ambassador.

"Ah, I have pulled you away from your duty," Minister Baik said in a low voice. "Allow me." He beckoned me to follow.

I trudged behind him, chastened, while Silhouette drifted spookily along the wall to keep me in sight. I'd promised Seok that I'd do my duty so as not to risk an international incident, and what had happened? I'd allowed my weakness for mandu to sidetrack me.

Fortunately for me, they were still making official introductions up on the dais. Minister of This, Councilor That, Magician So-and-So. It's funny how important people sprout like mushrooms when there's a chance to show off fancy clothes and, let's face it, eat *free food*. I was sad that Seok had made me promise not to drink any of the rice wine on offer and to stick to tea instead. I'd had to swear it on the nine tails of my ancestors. Regardless, Jun would rat me out if I broke the promise.

At last, Minister Baik bustled his way to the front and bowed respectfully before the ambassador. He gestured, and an elegantly coiffed aide appeared bearing a coronet woven out of flowering branches. "Greetings, Ambassador Tanaka," he said, addressing her in Hangeul, the common language of the Thousand Worlds. "Please accept this small gesture of our appreciation for the long journey you've made here. Made with cherry blossoms in honor of your name."

Ambassador Tanaka shot him a jaundiced look. "Did you know," she returned in perfect Hangeul, "that every other woman in the Sun Clans is named Sakura? Cherry blossom hairpins. Cherry blossom kimonos. Cherry blossom stationery. Even cherry blossom guns. Rest assured, Minister of Defense, I've seen it all before."

I couldn't help it—I liked her already. I hadn't expected her to be such an undiplomatic diplomat.

"Maybe you're hungry?" I said into the appalled silence that followed. "I don't know about you, but the mandu smell really good."

Ambassador Tanaka turned toward me with a smile that

might have been real. "At last, someone with sense. I don't believe we've met before?"

Oh, that was right—there had to have been diplomatic exchanges between the Thousand Worlds and the Sun Clans before, so these people all knew each other. Jun and I were the odd ones out. Not that I minded. Sometimes it was nice not to have any reputation.

"I'm Kim Min, Bearer of the Dragon Pearl," I said, bowing more deeply than the minister had. Seok had given me a whole series of deportment lessons so I wouldn't bow to the wrong degree, or at the wrong time, and cause an international incident. (That was the theme of the month.)

The ambassador's gaze sharpened like she was an arrow and I was her target. "Indeed," she said, and this time her smile was definitely more guarded. "I'd expected you to be taller, or maybe broader." And she smiled at the minister of defense.

"Oh, you say that to everyone you meet," Minister Baik said.

"Because I learned it from you, you unimaginative old man."

This time I must have done a better job of concealing my astonishment, because no one looked at me. How long had they known each other? And, more important, did their years of acquaintance mean that peace actually had a chance after all?

I wished that were true. After all, I'd known Cousin Bora all her life and still couldn't stand her. There was a lesson in there, if I were the philosophical type.

"Lead the way to the mandu, Bearer of the Dragon Pearl," the ambassador said, addressing me far more formally than I was used to.

It made me feel weird. I didn't know whether the Sun Clans had shape-shifters of their own, a question that Seok had assured me was of great interest to our spies, but regardless, there was no way fourteen-year-old me (even in disguise as a sixteen-year-old) merited such stiff honorifics from a grown woman, especially one in a position of power.

"Please, just call me Min," I said.

Minister Baik shot me a sharp glance, and I realized, too late, that the degree of familiarity had political implications. But he was too savvy to call further attention to my slipup. "Come now, the cooks will be delighted to hear what you think of the food."

The ambassador had told me to lead, so I led. I kept my drooling at bay, but only just. I was so hungry! If only I'd listened to Jun and eaten a snack before the banquet, but I'd been holding out for *free food*.

Once we reached the platter-covered tables, we watched enviously while she took her first bite of a dumpling. "Excellent," she pronounced after she'd chewed and swallowed. "Even the gyoza back home aren't this good."

At least the ambassador had *some* diplomacy in her. She definitely smelled like she was stretching the truth for our benefit. Normally I would have asked her for more details, but just then I caught a whiff of a completely different scent—one that didn't belong—from the people crowding around us. A scent that I knew better than anyone else there.

Jun and I weren't the only foxes in the room.

TWO
Sebin

"**O**nly the biggest diplomatic mission in the last ten years and we're running late," gray-haired Captain Chaewon grumbled from her seat in her office. She was looking at her slate and not at me, despite having summoned me five minutes ago.

It was an impressive office, the only one of its type I'd ever seen. Shelves bolted to the wall contained rows and rows of succulents, ranging in color from glossy green to deep red or purple. Plaques commemorating past battles and honors mingled with tacky tourist banners. I loved everything about it.

But the captain had summoned me for a reason—hadn't she?

I shifted my weight, trying not to look like I had to use the head (what the restroom is called on a ship). She'd been muttering the same statement over and over for the last three days, something I knew because I'd been assigned bridge duty.

I'd worked hard for this. I was no longer the battle cruiser *Haetae*'s youngest cadet, but people remembered what had happened on my first tour of duty. A hijacking tends to leave a strong impression, even if it hadn't technically been my fault.

"Sir," I ventured, still standing at attention, although maybe a lowly cadet shouldn't interrupt a captain. "You wanted to brief me on the mission?"

I couldn't hide my curiosity. The captain wasn't a full-blown tiger spirit like myself, but she had some of that heritage, and it gave her a keener sense of smell than if she'd been fully human. That meant she could pick up my feelings even if I tried to disguise them.

Mostly, I wanted to know *why me?* I was only a cadet, after all. Maybe it was something that concerned cadets, and she wanted to see how we were doing, but in that case, she would have summoned Cadet Jee as well. Jee and I had begun our service on the *Haetae* at the same time, and I longed for his friendly presence now.

Captain Chaewon finally looked up from her slate and shoved it aside, focusing on me. "At ease, Cadet Sebin. You're here because we'll be conveying a diplomatic mission from Station Ssangyong to border territory."

I kept from bouncing on my toes with eagerness. Finally, some action! My family would have looked disapprovingly on my enthusiasm, preferring discipline and dignity at all times . . . but I had left my relatives behind. I had to take my joy where I could find it.

A smile warmed the captain's face. "You've heard that much, I'm sure."

I nodded. In theory, starship crew members weren't supposed to gossip, but in reality? We gossiped. Especially after completing what had been a dull, uneventful run escorting some freighters. We wanted to know what the next assignment was.

"You're here," Captain Chaewon went on, "because you

were specifically recommended by Special Investigator Yi." Her mouth quirked in a rueful smile. "We will be working with someone you've met before."

"The investigator, sir?"

"Not this time. Rather, Kim Min will be a guest aboard this starship, in her capacity as the Bearer of the Dragon Pearl."

I blinked. A great roaring filled my ears. The captain kept speaking, but I didn't hear a word she said.

The Thousand Worlds had recovered the Dragon Pearl after its long absence. It was a powerful artifact, able to terraform entire planets, turning them into garden worlds or desolate wastelands. Powerful—and lost for generations, until someone had recovered it.

Beyond that, however, the Dragon Pearl had a *personal* meaning for me. Not because I wanted it to terraform my old home. My family, the Juhwang Clan, had disowned me, which was just as well because they had gone on the run. I would never see the gardens and trees of the Juhwang Estate again.

But my uncle, the once feared and respected Captain Hwan, had committed treason by attempting to seize the Pearl for his own purposes. For the *family's* good, not that of the Thousand Worlds.

"Cadet!"

I blinked and saluted sharply.

"Cadet," Captain Chaewon said, more quietly. "Is there something I need to know?"

I hated it when she was solicitous. A captain shouldn't have to treat one of her cadets like they were made of glass. Yet that was exactly how everyone had handled me since the hijacking incident.

What could I say? That I'd thought Min was my friend,

but she'd kept this secret from me? The *biggest* secret? It would sound petty and immature, and I couldn't afford for the captain to think of me like that. Not if I wanted to be a captain myself someday.

It stung that Min hadn't told me, yet to be honest, I couldn't blame her. We'd gotten off on the wrong foot when we'd first met on our last voyage together. All right, that was an understatement—we'd been on opposite sides. But we'd come to work together, and trust each other. Or so I'd thought.

At the same time, she and I hadn't exactly had much time to sit around and chat during the hijacking. We'd been busy trying to stop my uncle from carrying out his treasonous plot. So perhaps I shouldn't hold it against Min that this little detail hadn't come up.

The captain resumed her briefing. I had to pay attention, something I should have been doing from the beginning.

"First we'll be picking up a member of the Dragon Council and their apprentice," Captain Chaewon said. "Then we'll head straight to Station Ssangyong, where the talks are taking place. It will be an opportunity for a little R&R."

The last thing I wanted after a (blessedly) dull, routine supply run was rest and relaxation. I wanted action and a chance to show my value to the crew. I might be young, but a young tiger was stronger than the average human, and it was never too early to demonstrate fighting spirit.

"You'll have a chance to socialize with the apprentice, who is close to your age," the captain added. "Her name is Haneul, and I'd like you to keep an eye on her."

My nose prickled at the smell of unease wafting off the captain. Was she asking me to be a *spy*? Something rotten was afoot, and I wasn't sure I liked it.

"Will she be serving as part of the crew, sir?" It wasn't like I had a choice, since orders were orders, but I could at least try to obtain some information.

Captain Chaewon sighed. "It's unclear whose jurisdiction Cadet Haneul falls under. As you will have surmised, she's a Space Forces cadet. At the same time, her family holds a great deal of influence on the Dragon Council. While I have every reason to believe that Haneul is a competent cadet, we can't afford for anything to happen to her. Especially since the Dragon Council and Space Forces have been at odds of late."

I understood now. "In other words, sir, it would look weird for you to assign her a grown bodyguard, but having another cadet in the role shouldn't raise any eyebrows."

The captain winced. "Crudely put, yes."

I wondered how much I'd see of Min once she came aboard, given my new bodyguard duty. At least that explained why the captain hadn't asked for Jee as well. "And if I need backup, sir?"

The captain straightened and arched an eyebrow at me. "Ideally, you should handle matters in a way that backup isn't needed."

I should have seen that coming. I nodded, trying to look prepared for anything.

"But in case matters become contentious, your contact is Ensign Hak. She'll know if further intervention is warranted."

I relaxed minutely. Ensign Hak had been in charge of my orientation when I first came aboard the *Haetae*. I could trust her.

"Any other questions, Cadet?"

"No, sir."

"Dismissed, then."

I exited the captain's office, palms sweating. I wondered

what Haneul would be like. The *Haetae* had some dragon crew members, who went around in human form like all supernaturals, since it was simply easier to design ships for humans. Among other things, humans were *smaller* than dragons. But I didn't know much about dragons in general beyond what my family had told me. And, as I'd found out the hard way, my family's information hadn't always been reliable.

Would Haneul be stuck-up and stand on privilege? After all, dragons controlled weather magic, and the Dragon Council was in charge of terraforming and its regulations. During those centuries when the Dragon Pearl had been lost, they'd been the ones to decide which planets received improvements and which planets languished. There were only so many dragons trained in the terraforming arts, and not everyone could benefit from their magic.

I shouldn't judge her before I meet her, I thought. But I was still lost in speculation when I reached hydroponics and almost collided with Jee. So much for situational awareness.

"Sorry!" Jee exclaimed. "You okay?"

That was Jee for you. He was the nicest person I'd ever met. Even though I'd invaded his personal space, he was worried that he'd hurt *me* in the collision. He was short and skinny, with a beaky nose too big for his face, and he always had a smile and a kind word for everyone.

"Sorry about that," I said. I looked around at the rows and rows of plants and thought of the captain's collection of succulents. "Are *you* looking forward to R&R?"

"You know me," Jee said with a grin. "I always look forward to R&R."

I debated whether to tell him about my assignment. The captain hadn't *said* anything about keeping it a secret, but I

doubted she wanted me to shout the assignment to every corner of the battle cruiser, either. Among other things, it would
suck if Haneul figured out I was hovering around to *spy* on her.

On the other hand, I didn't think the captain intended
to hide the presence of a Dragon Council member and their
apprentice. I assumed that the captain would want some sort
of cover story to explain the spying.

Quickly, as we walked to our stations in hydroponics, I
filled Jee in on the starship's guests. I told him that the captain
had selected me to escort Haneul and keep her entertained.
"It'll be boring," I said, hoping to make Jee feel less left out.
"She's probably going to want to talk about dull things like
chemistry."

"Chemistry's fun," Jee protested. "Not as fun as computers, but . . ."

I suppressed a groan. I did well enough in my studies, but
science and computers were things I did because I had to, not
because I loved them, like he did. I looked dubiously at the
tangles of green sprouts and decided to change the subject.
"Should these be brown?"

Jee peered at the mung bean sprouts. "No, they should definitely not look like that. We'd better clean them out before they
start rotting and foul up the water circulation."

I wasn't a scientist, but even I knew that leaving dead
brown sprouts in a more or less closed system would cause the
whole system to putrefy. Fortunately, or maybe not so fortunately, whoever had designed the hydroponics system knew
that things could go wrong (it seemed like things went wrong
every week) and had allowed for frequent disassembly of the
tubes and pipes.

Though Space Forces starships resupplied every time they

stopped at a starbase, space station, or planetary base, some higher-up had decided that we needed fresh vegetables to go with our vat-grown protein strips and jars of gimchi and marinated anchovies. You'd think this would result in something more exciting to eat than mung bean sprouts and spinach. But no, 80 percent of what we grew was mung bean sprouts and spinach.

Jee and I had both spent long, stultifying hours being trained in the maintenance of the pipes that supplied nutrient-filled water and the plasti-steel containers where the plants grew beneath carefully calibrated sun lamps. The warrant officer in charge of the system checked our work every so often, but by this point we were trusted to spot any dead sprouts, or mold, or changes in the water's acidity, all of which required decisive intervention.

I'd grown up on a properly terraformed planet, the world of Yonggi, on an estate surrounded by beautiful gardens and landscaping. In my dreams I still smelled the bamboo and azaleas of my grandmother's property. Hydroponics contained greenery, but it was a far cry from the lush flowers and trees of a planet.

Jee and I soon finished cleaning out the problem sprouts. The rest of our shift in hydroponics was reassuringly dull.

The next few days passed in a blur of more dullness. I'd once imagined that life in the Space Forces meant nonstop action. You know, fighting off pirates and enemy starships. But the truth was that even a mission as important as this one was unlikely to result in as much excitement as my first cruise. I mean, how do you top having your battle cruiser hijacked by your own uncle?

Jee and I were both summoned by Ensign Hak when the

Haetae made its stop at a starport to pick up Dragon Councilor Gwan and Haneul. The ensign, a woman whose no-nonsense manner and efficiency I'd come to appreciate, gave us an extra-thorough looking over before leading us to the docking bay.

I had assumed that this would be a routine escort job, but the sight of Captain Chaewon in her fanciest dress uniform put an end to *that* idea. She awaited us in the bay, straight-backed, her iron-gray hair immaculate. Ensign Hak fell in behind the captain, and Jee and I fell in behind Hak.

The gravity of the situation finally impressed itself on me. We weren't just playing host to two dragon spirits, respected throughout the Thousand Worlds for their affinity for water and their control over the weather. Our guests were *important* dragon spirits, the kind of people who decided which planets received assistance when there was a drought or the climate engineering failed.

Our guests came on board as humans—but I knew better. Even Jee, a human without an acute sense of smell, straightened and sniffed the air. I'd never been to the sea, but that wild saltwater smell couldn't be anything but a dragon's water magic.

The elder of the two looked disarmingly normal, with their black hair in an asymmetrical style similar to mine. Their jacket looked stylishly cut, as did their slacks, but otherwise I wouldn't have pegged them as anyone special. Not by their looks, anyway. The aura of storm-and-sea power that sizzled around them, on the other hand—*that* told me they were not someone to cross.

The younger one, Haneul, appeared maybe fifteen years old. She had her blue hair pinned back so it wouldn't get in the way, just as Space Forces regulations required. She was almost as tall as I was, and a similar sense of brewing storms wafted off her, although not as powerfully.

I instantly felt sorry for her, not because of her draconic heritage—the only thing better is being a tiger—but because of her clothes. Specifically, someone had dressed her in a standard Space Forces cadet uniform like the ones that Jee and I wore . . . then spruced it up with a fancy embroidered jacket in traditional-style stripes of bright color, plus a smattering of knotted charms and talismans. She was caught between the world of dragon magicians and the more prosaic world of a Space Forces cadet.

Captain Chaewon and Ensign Hak bowed, so Jee and I did, too, as deeply as we could manage without falling over. It felt odd not to salute after our tour of duty, but saluting was for other military personnel, and the dragon elder was clearly a civilian, if one who wielded authority. The dragon elder nodded calmly, accepting this as their due.

Haneul was another story. She went to salute, then started to bow before stopping halfway, confusion clear on her face. After an extremely awkward silence, she bobbed quickly, her eyes scrunched up and unhappy.

"Councilor Gwan," the captain said, tactfully ignoring Haneul's gaffe, "we're honored to have you on board. We're here to escort you to your quarters."

"Oh, come now, Captain," the councilor said, looking around themself with bright eyes. "I haven't been on a starship in ages. It's got that new-ship smell and everything."

Captain Chaewon smiled as though she wasn't sure she'd heard the dragon correctly. "You're kind to notice how well kept the ship is. The *Haetae* has actually been in service for many years."

"Of course, of course." Councilor Gwan beamed at her. "I'd love a tour of the bridge."

Naturally she would. Who *wouldn't* want to see the bridge as opposed to being shut up in a cabin, even the nicer ones reserved for important guests?

The captain nodded. "I'll be happy to show you around, Councilor."

"Good, good." The councilor beamed again. "Haneul, you go with your fellow cadets and prepare my cabin."

This was insulting, mainly the implication that a guest's cabin wouldn't be perfectly set up before their arrival. But Captain Chaewon didn't show any sign of taking offense, so I couldn't, either. I sensed that this wouldn't be the first power play ahead.

"Ensign, you're with me," Captain Chaewon said. "Cadets, the councilor and their apprentice will be staying in Cabins Seven and Eight."

"Have fun!" the councilor said with a cheery wave as they took the captain's arm and strolled off with her, for all the world looking like they had found a shopping cart full of chocolate in an otherwise empty supermarket.

Haneul bowed just as deeply as Jee and I had. "Of course, Councilor." Then she turned to us with unseemly haste. "Let's go!"

Had I imagined the whiff of pure, unadulterated relief that came from Haneul? What did she know about the councilor that we didn't?

THREE

Min

It took me a good ten minutes to extricate myself from the minister of defense and the ambassador. "But you simply must try one of these, too," the minister insisted every time I hinted that I had an urgent need to attend to. And the ambassador looked at me as though she smelled a fox in the henhouse.

The Dragon Pearl remained in its pouch at my waist, concealed so its glow wouldn't escape. I could tell the ambassador was looking for traces of its power on me. Did she expect me to parade around with it on the top of my head? It would make an amazing tiara, but if I tried that, I'd be grounded for the rest of my life.

At last my intermittent sneezing convinced the minister that I should get away from the food before I contaminated it all. "You should retire early, get some chicken soup into yourself," he said very seriously, as though what ailed me was as simple as a winter cold. "Chicken soup with ginseng is what my gran always made for me."

I mumbled something that I hoped sounded appropriately appreciative. Imagine having *real chicken* whenever you got sick! I'd only gotten *real chicken* on New Year's. My mother and aunties had scrimped and saved for it, and we'd all had to share the treat. Fortunately, fox spirits don't come down with regular ailments as easily as humans do, but I couldn't imagine taking real meat, from a real chicken, for granted. The one time we'd had a neighbor with chickens, they'd been kept for the eggs, not the meat. And too soon they'd all sickened and died.

I stifled sneezes all the way to the edge of the hall, but my affliction had nothing to do with colds or sickness. I was picking up fox magic. People dread fox spirits because humans can't ordinarily detect our special abilities. I'd learned since leaving home that shamans and magicians can manage it if they come prepared. But the rest of the time, the only ones who can detect a fox . . . are other foxes.

It didn't take me long to locate my target and ease my way closer to her. I grabbed a napkin off a table where people were too busy arguing to notice and did my desperate best to mask the sneezes. Too bad I couldn't wear the napkin like a veil, though it was certainly large enough to do the job.

Who are you? I wondered as I slunk among the councilors and aides and diplomats, the waiters circulating with drinks I wasn't allowed to have along with the boring green tea that I was. Kidding—green tea is also a luxury on Jinju, even if it is a boring luxury. Under other circumstances I would have gulped down whole liters of the stuff just to bask in the grassy taste and soothing aroma.

My bodyguard slunk along with me, looking like she wished she understood what I was up to. I felt somewhat bad for her, but this was important, and I wasn't going to let a little thing like a babysitter get in my way.

Fox Two (as I had started thinking of my target) held a cup of tea as though she'd trained all her life for it. She stood tall, but not too tall, and if I hadn't been a fox myself, I wouldn't have been able to look away from her face with its pointed features and red lips. She didn't wear her hair long or pinned up in a bun, in the traditional styles affected by many of the female councilors, but had it cut short in a sleek pageboy. Likewise, instead of a hanbok with either a dress or trousers, she was sheathed in modern clothes, a chic satin version of a spacefarer's outfit, all minimalist black angles and curves. When I looked more closely, I spotted the subtle black embroidery that embellished her collar and cuffs.

People thronged around her, smiling at her and laughing at her jokes. I couldn't tell what was so funny, and maybe that was the point—that her Charm, the ability that all fox spirits shared, made people think she was more interesting than she actually was. Either that or adults really did like listening to stories about paperwork and taxes.

The only thing that wasn't smooth and polished about Fox Two was the way she sneezed periodically into her elbow. "Excuse me," I overheard her saying to one of the hangers-on. "I've always had problems with allergies, even on space stations. Something about the air filters."

My heart squeezed with dread. Did she suspect another fox was nearby? Or did she really have allergies as she'd claimed?

As I approached her more closely, Fox Two smoothly excused herself and headed for the restroom. From the snatches of conversation around her, I finally learned her name, or the name she was using: Assistant Minister Yang Miho.

I refrained from rolling my eyes as I sidled through the

crowd after her. Yang was a common enough family name—face it, there aren't that many family names to go around despite the size of the Thousand Worlds, and somewhere out there is probably a whole legion of Kim Mins like myself. But Miho was perilously close to *gumiho*, the word for fox spirit. *Gumiho* literally means *nine-tailed fox*, although only the oldest and most powerful of us have the full complement of tails. I only have a single one myself.

Assistant Minister Yang and I weren't the only ones headed for the restrooms, which were open to any gender. There were other folks going in and coming out. It was a fancy setup, with a powder room for people to fix their outfits or just have a quiet space away from the hubbub of the reception.

Silhouette followed me in, because of course she did. Awkward, but if it didn't bother her, I wasn't going to let it bother me.

I parked myself in front of a floor-length mirror and fussed with my hair, which would have made my cousin Bora sneer if she'd caught me at it. No self-respecting fox needs a *mirror* to fix their appearance. Our shape-shifting magic provides everything from appropriate clothes to ID badges. But aside from disguising my age, I didn't want to shape-shift in public, and appearances mattered in surroundings like these.

I'd grown up doing everything the hard way, from taming my hair to mending my clothes. Mom and my aunties, fearing reprisal from prejudiced humans, hadn't allowed us to use even the slightest wisp of Charm to hide the twice-handed-down shabbiness of our outfits, or patch holes, or add some sparkle to our hairpins.

Judging from my urge to sneeze over and over, the assistant minister wasn't feeling any compunction about using Charm.

I'd expect someone in her position to be able to afford *actual* fancy clothes instead of having to magic them up, but maybe she'd bought something off the rack and was using Charm to tailor it.

Yang Miho caught my eye, even though I'd tried to be subtle in keeping tabs on her. "Hello there!" she said in her low, husky voice, as though she'd encountered a long-lost friend. The very warmth of her tone set me on edge. "I promise your petition regarding tax breaks is the very next thing on the docket. Why don't we go discuss it in—"

I assumed this was some kind of pretense to get us out of the powder room. While it wasn't quite public, the place wasn't private, either, with people constantly coming and going, and one annoying person next to me kept humming under their breath while fussing with a calculator. What sort of killjoy brought a calculator to a party?

"Steady," Jun whispered in my ear. He always accompanied me, even to the restroom, although he faded out for privacy's sake.

I breathed slowly, carefully. I wondered if Miho knew *I* was a fox. Either way, I had no guarantee of her friendliness.

"I'm the Bearer of the Dragon Pearl," I said.

Miho's eyes widened, then narrowed in interest.

"I was hoping to talk to you about terraforming allocations," I went on.

"Excuse us," Miho said to the calculator person, who had stopped fussing long enough to stare at us. Then the assistant minister grabbed my shoulder and started to hustle me out.

My bodyguard shifted, and I could tell she was about to intervene. I frantically signaled her with a headshake that everything was fine. Miho might be rude, but I didn't think she planned to attack me.

People should have noticed that Miho was manhandling me—not the sort of behavior you should see in a fancy setting like this one. My nose tickled again, and I clenched my teeth against another sneeze. At a guess, she was Charming people to think nothing untoward was going on.

Definitely a far cry from the *don't attract attention, never use your powers* stance my mom and aunties had taken.

I was more curious than alarmed—maybe not the best reaction to have. But we were fellow foxes, even if she didn't know it yet, and she didn't smell angry, just perplexed. Then again, I reminded myself, as a fox of unknown power, she might have the ability to mask her emotions. For the millionth time I wished that my family had taught me the full extent of fox magic instead of keeping everything hush-hush.

Yang Miho and I ended up in a small, dim office, far less grand than the banquet hall we'd left behind. She even managed to lock out my bodyguard, which worried me. I looked at the gray desk, enlivened only by a framed photo of a black cat and a white cat curled around each other yin-yang fashion, so perfect that I thought it must have been digital art rather than the real deal. Cute as the pic was, the office smelled of drudgery and breath mints.

"No one will bother us in here," the assistant minister said, hopping up to sit on the edge of the desk. She didn't belong in there any more than a crown of gold and jade belonged in a farmer's field. For that matter . . .

"How did you pick the lock?" I asked, frowning and trying to look stern.

"Oh, don't be like that," she said with a laugh that would have been much more charming if I hadn't been so wary of her. "They keep a few small offices open for impromptu meetings. I thought that you and I needed to have a heart-to-heart."

I hesitated for only a moment. "You hold a lot of *influence*," I said, emphasizing the last word slightly. I didn't know if it was true, but it couldn't hurt to open with flattery—and a veiled threat. To hint that I knew about her true identity.

"Careful . . ." Jun murmured. His chill radiated toward me, and I felt it all the way down to my bones, a sign of how perturbed he was.

Small consolation: Fox Two didn't show any sign that she could see him, and I wanted to keep it that way. As much as I was eager to ply her with questions, our shared heritage didn't automatically make us friends or allies. Even a fellow fox might not understand why one of her kind was hanging out with a ghost.

No, my original plan was the best one. I resolved not to let her figure out that I was a fox. If that were even possible.

For her part, Fox Two, Yang Miho, whoever, regarded me with slitted eyes. "What do you mean by that?"

Time to come out and say it. "How did a gumiho rise so high in the government?"

I've got to give her credit—she played it cool. I bit the inside of my cheek to suppress a sneeze as she exerted her Charm in my direction, presumably to make me favorably inclined toward her, or perhaps to muddle my memory. Who knew the limits of a fox's Charm?

But it seemed I had some natural resistance to her magic. I gave her a chilly smile.

"So, you're a magician," Miho spat, drawing exactly the wrong conclusion.

I wished! Was it possible to be both a magician *and* a fox spirit? I knew magicians existed, but this event was the closest I'd ever been to any. They were even rarer than shamans and kept to themselves. I'd heard that they achieved their supernatural powers through study, rather than being born with their powers. Some of them told fortunes using number magic or cards, while others could teleport. Abilities I lacked, unluckily.

Still, I wondered why Miho didn't suspect me of being one of her kind. Maybe years of sneezing from allergies had caused her to dismiss the possibility of anyone using Charm around her.

When I neither confirmed nor denied her guess, the assistant minister asked, "You have divined my secret. What can I offer you to keep it?"

Recklessly, I blurted out, "Show yourself." I longed to see a fellow fox in her true form.

I didn't think she'd actually do it. But with a swirl of magic that made my nose itch more ferociously than ever, Miho transformed. The damp smells of mist and decaying pine needles, the richness of loam and moss, wafted to my nostrils. In spite of myself, I inhaled more deeply, struck by an atavistic homesickness.

What *should* have made me homesick, of course, was dust and dry winds. If I'd run into those things, maybe I would have been swept away by nostalgia for our dome house on Jinju. But the inner heart of me, the part that went back to the Old World, thrilled to the intimation of a bygone forest.

Miho condensed into an elegant vixen, a queen of foxes if foxes had queens. Her coat was sleek and red, accented by black ears and black legs, although regal silver tufts of fur embellished the black. Her eyes shone the amber of a harvest moon.

I couldn't contain my gasp, however, when I beheld her tails. She had nine of them, russet, tipped with more of that coin-bright silver rather than pure white. Even in my family, my late great-grandmother had only possessed three.

"I am a fox of the Baektusan lineage," Miho said. "Perhaps we can come to an . . . understanding."

"Baektusan?" I asked, attempting (probably unsuccessfully) to conceal my awe. "I've never heard of that lineage."

"Foxes are territorial," Fox Two said. "Even fox spirits. My clan used to hunt on a legendary mountain called Baektusan, in the old country."

Once again I cursed the fact that Mom and the aunties had always been so close-lipped. "You still haven't explained what a fox is doing as an *assistant minister.*"

"You're slipping up on formality," Jun warned me.

He was right. I'd addressed Miho—this glorious fox with nine actual tails—as though she were family, rather than an important political figure.

Luckily for both of us, Fox Two didn't seem to take offense. The air shimmered around her, and she resumed her human form. This time she was, if possible, even more beautiful than before. Maybe it was the fox equivalent of touching up your makeup or sharpening your sword—preparation for different kinds of warfare.

"Min—may I call you Min?"

As my elder, she didn't need my permission. I nodded anyway, not wanting to offend her. Not until I learned more about what she was up to.

"In private, you should call me Miho," Fox Two went on with a confiding warmth.

I should have been flattered, except the one other time I'd met a fox spirit off Jinju, albeit one who had connections to my family, she hadn't exactly been looking out for my best interests. The fact that Miho wanted to be on first-name terms so quickly was a red flag. "If you insist . . . Miho," I said, smiling back so she didn't notice how wary I was.

"You asked what I was doing in politics." Miho's expression betrayed her fatigue, and the hint of vulnerability made me wonder what her job was like. "Min, if you know the lore about foxes from your studies as a magician, you can probably guess what it's been like for me. People talking about how foxes couldn't be trusted, how it's a good thing we're extinct, how foxes were a menace to society. As though all foxes were terrible, when the truth is that foxes were all individuals, the way goblins and celestials and humans are all individuals. I want to be accepted as a citizen of the Thousand Worlds, too."

As much as I agreed with the sentiment, I couldn't help pointing out a flaw in her logic. "Isn't posing as a human only going to make people *more* suspicious, not less, when they find out the truth?"

Foxes' ability to mimic other creatures, especially humans, especially *individuals*, was one of the main reasons people feared us so much. Not for the first time I understood why my family had been so secretive about our heritage.

Miho sighed and inspected her long, gleaming fingernails. "That may be the case, but if the alternative is sitting in some forest doing nothing, well . . . it's a risk I have to take."

It was a good story. I wanted so badly to believe it. The possibility that my family might have a secret ally among the rulers of the Thousand Worlds lifted my spirits.

All the same, I knew our kind's reputation wasn't entirely undeserved. I'd done my own share of trickery and deception, and I'd learned what it was like to lose friends and allies over it. What if Miho was making a terrible mistake?

And if she was, would she listen to a mere single-tailed fox's warning? Even one she thought was a magician?

"At least give me a chance to show you the things I've accomplished as Minister Baik's assistant," Miho said, fixing me with an intent stare.

I startled. "The minister of defense?" Or was it some other Baik?

"The very same," Miho said with a smile. "He's done so much to—"

I never got to hear about his accomplishments because someone rapped on the door. "You there!" snapped Silhouette's voice. "Did you kidnap the Bearer of the Dragon Pearl?" The doorknob rattled.

Oh no! Had I missed some ceremonial duty that Seok had forgotten to brief me on?

"Excuse me," Miho called out, her tone smooth and assured. "I'll be done in just a moment."

I choked back another sneeze at the rush of Charm that poured out from her.

"Oh, of course," said the bodyguard, sounding much more respectful. "Take your time. It's no big deal."

I must not have succeeded in suppressing my judgy look, because Miho's mouth twisted as she regarded me. "I see you think I should lie low and be content with the scraps the Thousand Worlds offer me. But I could have so much more. Just imagine, Min"—her voice warmed again, and I didn't think she was conscious that she was doing it—"think of the things we could accomplish together. With your control over the Dragon Pearl . . . and my influence in the Ministry of Defense."

I hesitated. It sounded good . . . too good. I wondered what my mother would think of this nine-tailed fox, a true nine-tailed fox, flaunting her magic in the heart of government.

"At least give me a chance," Miho said, speaking a little more rapidly. So maybe she wasn't as confident as she'd initially appeared. "I've shaped policies that welcome spirits and creatures of all kinds in the Space Forces, not just the human majority. I've strengthened the Space Forces by increasing its allocated budget, so that neighboring nations know they can't push us around. Everything I've worked for will go up in smoke if you give my identity away. Keep my secret, and I'll show you a better future for us all."

"All right," I said. "Your secret is safe with me."

And that was when the door opened.

FOUR
Sebin

I'd hoped to get to know Haneul better as Jee and I escorted her to the guest cabins, but she replied in words of one syllable, usually "Yes" or "No." As a result, I knew nothing more about her than I'd learned from Captain Chaewon's briefing: She was a cadet, and as a dragon she had the ability to control the weather around her, and she had some kind of connection to the bigwigs in the Dragon Council.

Well, that wasn't completely true. Haneul may not have been particularly communicative with her *words*, but she didn't have the same level of control over her *smell*. I don't mean her body odor, but her emotions. As a tiger, I could usually tell when people smelled unhappy.

It didn't take a tiger to discern it in this case, either. I could see the miasma of rain hovering over her, and the air around her smelled dankly of autumn storms and the wild sea.

Jee shot me a questioning look and pointed surreptitiously at the rain cloud. I shook my head. As an older cadet, Haneul was technically senior to us and we didn't want to offend her or make her lose face.

"We can help you—" I started.

"No," Haneul said, her face clouding over, almost literally—beads of rain or sweat or condensation formed on her brow and rolled down her cheeks, which looked seriously uncomfortable. She hurried into the cabin and would have slammed the door in our faces if it hadn't been an automated slider.

"Well, that went well," Jee said, frowning after her. "Do you think she didn't like us?"

I shook my head. "She didn't smell upset with *us*," I ventured, although I could have been wrong. "It's like she has a secret. Something from before she boarded the *Haetae*."

"That's not a good sign. Should we . . . Should we report it to someone?"

"Not yet." I could only imagine Ensign Hak's expression if I called her away from whatever mission-critical task she had in order to report that a fellow cadet had a case of the sniffles. She would ask me if I was sure it wasn't homesickness or something mundane that we could deal with on our own.

It would take six days from the pickup of Dragon Councilor Gwan and Cadet Haneul to get to our next stop. During the first four days, I scarcely saw Haneul, although by special dispensation the ship's computer tracked her location for me. Since Ensign Hak didn't mention anything, I assumed Haneul wasn't shirking her duties. When it came to these things, gossip moved even faster than the speed of light.

On the fifth day, Haneul showed up at the beginning of my first shift on the bridge. No sign of her personal rain cloud remained, and she had shed the awkward extra clothes in favor of a standard cadet uniform. She didn't smell unhappy, and

I wondered if she was getting along better with her mentor. I watched her closely as she saluted Captain Chaewon. Her expression gave away nothing.

The coveted bridge shift was intended for cadets (and higher-ranking crew, of course) who might someday hold command positions. After the ship sabotage incident, I'd been afraid that path would forever be closed to me. But Ensign Hak had told me that I was to begin joining the captain on the bridge, mostly to shadow the navigator and observe how things were done.

I couldn't help resenting the fact that my "secret" job of keeping an eye on Haneul had dimmed my ability to enjoy something I'd worked so hard for. Instead of being able to focus on the bridge crew, especially the captain herself, I had to concentrate on the cadet. Who had scored bridge shift only days after being transferred to the ship.

Rationally speaking, I shouldn't have resented her. After all, she was two years older than Jee and I were, sixteen to our fourteen. For all I knew, she'd already served bridge shift back on her old ship. Besides, I wouldn't be able to spy on her if we weren't together. It cheered me to think that Captain Chaewon had put the two of us in the same place at the same time so I wouldn't be deprived of my opportunity to learn.

My family had been strict, but one thing I'd learned from training sessions with my aunt was the importance of staying relaxed when possible. I found myself doing the breathing exercises she had so painstakingly taught me, because I kept glancing in Haneul's direction and tensing up. Halfway through the shift I had tight shoulders and a massive headache, not that I would have admitted it to anyone. I wasn't going to let a lousy headache keep me from doing my duty.

Infuriatingly, Haneul showed no sign of discomfort. She

was stationed not far from me, shadowing Weapons. I wouldn't have minded that position for myself, but realistically we weren't expecting to engage in battle. Not during a diplomatic mission. Needing to fire our guns would mean that we'd run into some crisis.

The shift ended without incident, and that troubled me. Haneul had played the part of a cadet flawlessly. I was a nitpicker and even I couldn't think of anything to criticize her for. If she was keeping something bottled up, I still had no idea what it was or what it meant for our mission.

And it didn't end there. Haneul didn't eat with the rest of us cadets, as Jee and I had found out, but took her meals with the dragon councilor. At mess later that day, I sat with Jee, Dak-Ho, and Yui.

Jee got along pretty well with the latter two cadets, who had joined the crew three months ago, not long after the hijacking. Dak-Ho had a taste for pranks and Yui often egged them on, which I didn't approve of. I couldn't remember ever taking my duty as lightly as those two seemed to, even when I'd been a very young cub.

"Don't look so glum, Sebin," Jee said. "It adds ten years to your face. You're going to have wrinkles."

I couldn't help but smile. "That would make me all of twenty-four," I said dryly. "I don't think people in their twenties usually have wrinkles."

"Unless they frown a lot," Dak-Ho chimed in. They put on an exaggerated scowl, then burst into giggles. Yui laughed, too. If it weren't for their faces—Dak-Ho's was all impish angles, while Yui had a classically elegant visage, belying her love of mischief—I would have thought they were twins. The two of them certainly acted that way sometimes.

"If anything's actually wrong with the dragon cadet," Jee said, "Ensign Hak will sort her out. Seriously, you worry too much."

"That's right," Dak-Ho said, producing a cookie out of thin air. "Hungry?"

I accepted the cookie, then squawked when it exploded into confetti. We spent the next several minutes cleaning it up. Dak-Ho and Yui giggled all the while, and I couldn't hide my exasperation.

I gave up trying to explain my concerns to the others. Especially since I couldn't admit that Captain Chaewon had entrusted me with a mission. Normally I would be honored that the captain considered me reliable, but lying to the other cadets, including my friend Jee, made me uncomfortable.

The day we made port, I wasn't on bridge shift when we docked. However, by luck or coincidence, I had a few minutes of recreation when we reached the space station, Ssangyong. I had bribed one of the senior crew members for a prime spot next to a viewport. I didn't approve of bribery, but (I told myself) it was pretty harmless to give the crew member a stash of choco pies I had assiduously saved up from a month's worth of lunches.

Starships traveled faster than light between the stars, which were separated by immense distances, using a network of Gates. A ship's main drive enabled it to open and pass through a Gate, each of which connected to several others.

My favorite part of life in space was the beauty and wonder of the Gate transition. Some people saw hallucinations and had to be medicated for the passage. This included a few members of the crew, as I'd found out. Those who were too badly affected were usually screened out of the Space Forces for safety reasons, but according to Ensign Hak, this only described a minute fraction of the population. For most people, meds made it possible for them to serve.

My breath caught as I witnessed the outward bloom of light, shifting between oceanic hues to a more mystical magenta and violet. I'd never seen anything like it elsewhere. Even the depictions on the holos didn't hold a candle to the real thing.

I waited as the glow faded and the starship maneuvered toward its berth on the station proper. At first walls of metal enfolded us, and then came the satisfying *thunk* of the ship docking.

My skin prickled. A person had come up behind me, and I hadn't heard them due to the *thunk*. I groaned inwardly. Why did someone have to ruin the moment?

I turned around. "Cadet Haneul," I said, attempting not to sound stiff, because of course it was her. Heat rushed to my face. I'd allowed my enjoyment of the docking maneuver to distract me from my duty. I should have known where she was at every moment.

"Cadet Sebin," Haneul said with a proper nod, at the exact angle I merited as her junior, and not one degree more or less.

I should appreciate her virtues, I told myself. "Did you need me, Cadet Haneul?"

She smiled, but it didn't reach her eyes. There was a lot of that going around. "I'm surprised to find you here."

Interesting. I gestured at the view, which now mostly consisted of painted marks and crates. "Any particular reason?" Maybe she was so jaded that the wonder of a space station didn't affect her anymore. If that was the case, I felt sorry for her. I couldn't imagine becoming so hardhearted that the joy of being on a starship withered away.

"You've been spying on me."

Uh-oh. I should have anticipated that a fellow cadet, especially one with an excellent service record, would have good observation skills. Too bad Captain Chaewon hadn't told me what to do if I got *caught* following her orders.

I didn't like lying, but I wasn't sure how else to handle the situation. My shoulders tensed, untensed. "I was worried about you," I said. Which wasn't the whole truth but came close enough that maybe she'd believe me.

Haneul blinked. "Worried?" She sounded skeptical—and offended.

I wished Jee were here. He was better at talking to people. "You must miss your old crew," I said awkwardly. "Forgive me, but it seems like you aren't here by your own choice. Does the dragon councilor treat you well?"

I'd definitely offended her with that one. She straightened and pulled her shoulders back, glaring at me. "I know my duty."

I could hear the subtext, though. The dragon elder might not mistreat her as such, but Haneul wasn't happy with this assignment. The only thing holding her upright was duty.

I was like that once, and it hadn't led anywhere good. "I'm not saying you don't—"

"I'm not interested in having random conversations with you, Cadet," Haneul said. "Just stay out of my way and I won't report you to Ensign Hak . . . or the dragon councilor."

This was a wrinkle I hadn't anticipated. Ensign Hak knew of my "mission," such as it was, although I preferred to handle the situation on my own rather than have her think that I needed bailing out. Either Haneul didn't feel the same way, or she was desperate.

What interested me most was that, though she realized I'd been spying on her, Haneul hadn't *already* gone to the dragon councilor, who had the standing to cause a huge fuss. That meant Haneul considered this either some kind of hazing ritual or a personal grudge, rather than something more sinister. *I* knew Captain Chaewon was exercising caution, but no one had informed Haneul, and that meant the councilor didn't know, either.

Still, the original mission was blown, and continuing to lie to Haneul wouldn't help matters. I inhaled deeply to steady myself. "Actually, Cadet Haneul, there's something you should know. Captain Chaewon was worried that someone might try to harm you, so she assigned me to keep an eye out."

Haneul blinked and started to stammer a response.

The PA system interrupted whatever Haneul might have said. "Cadet Haneul, Cadet Sebin, report to the bridge. This is Captain Chaewon. I repeat, Cadet Haneul, Cadet Sebin, report to the bridge."

Haneul and I looked at each other, then hurried to the bridge together.

Captain Chaewon hadn't said it was an emergency, so we didn't sprint. It was more like walking quickly while keeping to port so we didn't collide with other crew members. *She's not intervening*, I assured myself. The captain had better things to do than keep an eye on two lowly cadets.

Then I remembered that Haneul wasn't "just" a cadet, unlike me. She was tangled up in this diplomatic mission for reasons she hadn't divulged. The captain might have had the head of Security keeping an additional eye on Haneul, and me too just now. A creepy thought.

We arrived at the bridge, Haneul a half step ahead of me. Captain Chaewon didn't look at us, but we saluted anyway.

"There you are," Captain Chaewon said after turning from a holo image of Ensign Hak. The two of them must have been talking over the comm system. "Cadet Haneul, good of you to join us. Cadet Sebin, when did you last see Cadets Dak-Ho and Yui?"

I began to sweat. I wasn't technically in charge of those two, but as an older cadet I was supposed to set a good example for them. Something I hadn't been focusing on because I'd been preoccupied with Haneul.

The captain had asked a question, so I was obliged to answer. "I saw Cadet Yui just before recreation time, sir. She claimed to be headed back to her bunkroom, but now that I think of it, she was going in the opposite direction." I hadn't given that a second thought at the time because, face it, Yui had a history of changing her mind about what she wanted to do at the last second.

Ensign Hak spoke from her holo image. "Sir, they ditched their badges. I can't track them with the usual methods."

Oh no. I didn't think they'd meant to *desert*—even Dak-Ho wouldn't go that far—but I doubted either of them had thought through the implications of their latest prank.

"Chances are," Ensign Hak went on, "they decided this would be a great time to check out the space station." There was a brief pause, during which I could hear someone else snapping orders, then: "The officer of the deck confirms that they saw two cadets debark from the ship, apparently with orders to escort the Bearer of the Dragon Pearl."

"I gave no such orders," Captain Chaewon said with an exasperated sigh.

She must have caught a flicker of emotion on my face, because she glanced my way. "Don't worry, Cadet Sebin. I'm well aware of Dak-Ho and Yui's sense of mischief. But even if I don't intend to treat this as a genuine case of desertion, they will have to face a penalty for disrupting the mission."

"You'd be doing us all a favor if you did, sir," Ensign Hak muttered.

Captain Chaewon cleared her throat. "Regardless. Cadet Sebin, it is your task to find Dak-Ho and Yui and extricate them from any mischief they might be causing. We don't want the diplomatic mission to fail because a couple of youngsters chose the wrong time and place to play a prank."

"I bet they wanted to explore Station Ssangyong," Ensign Hak said. "Yui's been talking about it for days. I should have realized she and Dak-Ho would take the initiative in the worst way possible."

"That's exactly what I'm afraid of," the captain said dourly. "Forgive me, Cadet Haneul, but I'd like you to accompany Sebin. You can be their pretext for being on board Station Ssangyong. After all, as the apprentice to Dragon Councilor Gwan, you have some standing of your own. I know it's an unusual favor to ask. . . ."

Dragon Councilor Gwan had to be incredibly important for Captain Chaewon to ask a favor from a *cadet*. Ordinarily, the captain would be well within her rights simply to give an order and expect it to be carried out.

Haneul lifted her head. "I'd be happy to assist, sir. I don't need another cadet's aid, though."

"Nonsense," Captain Chaewon said, giving me a warning

look as I opened my mouth to object. "Sometimes two heads are better than one."

I wondered whether Haneul would argue, taking advantage of her elevated status, but she only nodded, mouth compressed. It made me think better of her, even though I didn't exactly like her.

"The key," Captain Chaewon added, "is to get the other two cadets out before they cause any disruption on the station."

"Yes, sir," Haneul and I said in unison.

"Dismissed."

Haneul and I headed toward the docking bay. I longed to shift into my tiger shape and break into a run, but I didn't dare. For all I knew, that would cause an incident in itself if the diplomats saw it. I'd heard that the Sun Clans had their own spirits, just as the Thousand Worlds had tiger spirits and fox spirits. But that didn't mean they approved of ours. For all I knew, the Sun Clans ambassador would welcome a fine tiger pelt as an addition to her collection of curios.

"I can do this without you," Haneul said under her breath.

"Are you good at tracking people?" I countered.

She winced, which I took as a no.

"I'm a tiger spirit. I know their scents." Dak-Ho and Yui were mostly human, not that it stopped the two of them from mastering tricks. Their ability to sidestep blame was nothing short of supernatural.

By then we'd reached the docking bay. The officer of the deck only gave our credentials a cursory check, which, I thought privately, was how this mess had started in the first place. But I couldn't say that to him.

The station itself was on high alert due to the presence

of all those dignitaries. *Their* screening procedures were more stringent, although they apologized multiple times to Haneul for inconveniencing "a revered apprentice of Dragon Councilor Gwan." I was starting to think that I needed to pay more attention to politics.

"How's that nose of yours doing now?" Haneul said after we'd cleared Security.

Weirdly, I liked irritable Haneul more than so-perfect-she-was-uptight Haneul, maybe because I preferred the honest expression of emotion. "One moment," I said, moving my head from side to side to catch the air currents. "That way."

The station was lavishly decorated, which I should have anticipated. I presumed it was to impress the guests from the Sun Clans with our power and prestige. Paper lanterns, more refined versions of masks from folk plays, and folding fans were prominently exhibited on the walls. Vases housed sprays of fragrant acacia and bright azaleas. Under other circumstances, I would have lingered to admire the displays.

Haneul kept pace with me as we followed the two cadets' scents deeper into this luxurious space palace.

Which would have been all very well, except we reached a dead-end corridor . . . and there was still no trace of either Dak-Ho or Yui.

"Oh no," I said, mad at myself for having been fooled by such an old trick. "I bet they doubled back—and headed to the party."

FIVE

Min

I was prepared for grumpy elders who wanted to drag me back to the pomp of the ceremony. Sure enough, that was what I got: an Important Person—I could tell by their flamboyant hairdo and glittering hairpins, their haughty expression—and their two out-of-breath guards. That last detail intrigued me, as did the whiff of panic. How much running had they been doing on a space station, of all places?

The guard spoke, not the Important Person. "My apologies for interrupting your meeting, Assistant Minister, but the Bearer of the Dragon Pearl is urgently needed."

My own bodyguard seemed disinterested. Still under the influence of Miho's Charm, I assumed. For the first time I missed Silhouette's disapproving sneer.

I wondered if Miho was going to blast the Important Person and their guards with more Charm, but instead she dimpled and said, "It's no trouble at all." She nodded at me, almost deferentially.

I would much rather have been quizzing Miho about her—*our*—fox heritage than bowing and scraping at a ceremony that involved endless recitations of poetry. But I also had a job to do. More to the point, if Seok found out I'd been shirking, he'd never let me out of his sight again.

"I don't like this," Jun said, more distinctly than usual. I was sure his chilly presence was the reason I kept running into inconvenient interruptions. But he was still my brother, and his more reasoned perspective on events had saved my hide in the past. "Think about it, Min. Seok is prepared for everything. He would have warned you if you had additional ceremonial duties. They must be improvising."

Jun was right. I gave him a tiny nod to indicate that I understood, as I didn't want to risk talking to him openly in front of these strangers or Miho. People got judgmental about ghosts because of the bad-luck thing. It didn't matter that Jun's death hadn't been his own fault.

"I'm ready," I said in appropriately formal language, addressing the Important Person rather than their guards.

The two guards ushered me back into the banquet hall. I avoided meeting Silhouette's gaze. Sooner or later Miho's Charm would wear off. Then my bodyguard would tell Seok that I wasn't behaving, and I'd get a lecture down the line, I just knew it.

Miho tagged along, and while the taciturn Important Person gave her the side-eye, they didn't stop her from accompanying us. It surprised me that the assistant minister, who'd used Charm so freely earlier, didn't smooth things over with her magic now. Perhaps she wasn't as powerful as I'd thought—or maybe she had other reasons.

Maybe she was worried about what I would do to her if she overused Charm. That was a funny thought.

The Sun Clans ambassador sat at the head table. She had shed her outer robe, and the one beneath it was even more splendid, with embroidered geometric motifs in gold-and-orange thread. The seat across from her was empty, while the rest were occupied by more Important People, including the minister of defense.

"Kind of you to join us, Bearer of the Dragon Pearl," Ambassador Tanaka said with a hint of reproof. "Your tea is getting cold."

She was guilt-tripping me, which was fair enough. She was the most important person on this space station, and I'd kept her waiting. Still, the "getting cold" part was nonsense and we both knew it.

"It's a good thing," I said with a sweet smile, "that the cups keep the tea heated at the perfect temperature."

We hadn't had anything like them back home on Jinju, just chipped stoneware for the adults and irregular cups, made from scrap metal, for the kids who were too young to be trusted with breakable objects. But one thing I'd learned in my time with Seok was that people who came from the wealthier worlds had access to luxuries I never could have imagined. Even luxuries as small as tea that didn't cool to a nasty tepidness.

I'd said the wrong thing, because Minister Baik looked faint, and the other Thousand Worlders had frozen as though I'd opened my mouth and burped directly into the ambassador's face. The only people who *didn't* look appalled were Miho, who kept her composure . . . and the ambassador herself.

"That'll teach me to be careless about my words," the ambassador remarked. "Because you are, of course, correct. The tea isn't the issue." As if to demonstrate, she took a sip of hers. "Please, have a seat."

I could feel Minister Baik staring a hole into my back. Heck, I could feel my handler, Seok, doing the same, and he wasn't even here. I didn't want to have to deal with the tremendous amount of paperwork involved if I started an international incident, so I sat, doing my best to look demure.

"My good friend Minister Baik has been remarkably close-mouthed about your relationship to the Dragon Pearl," the ambassador said, leaning forward.

I smelled her curiosity and also the feral sharpness of a predator. She might be human, but that didn't mean I could underestimate her. "You have questions?"

"Don't," Jun said at the same time, too late. "She might want something we can't give. Or that we *shouldn't* give."

Well, it was too late now. We were committed to answer.

At this point, Minister Baik interceded, to my relief. "You've probably heard about border tensions between our two realms," he said gravely to the ambassador. "Lately they center around the world of Jasujeong."

Jasujeong meant *amethyst*, although in my experience, the Thousand Worlds' planetary names didn't correlate neatly with their prosperity or geography. After all, the name of my home-world, Jinju, meant *pearl*, and mostly I remembered it for red dust and desiccated terrain.

The ambassador cleared her throat delicately. "You mean Artifact World Four."

I should have figured the historical enmity between the Thousand Worlds and the Sun Clans would extend even to the names of places. Fortunately, Seok had told me some of the backstory. Jasujeong, or Artifact World Four, or whatever you wanted to call it, was one of the early colonies in the initial diaspora from the lost homeworld that had been the origin of both nations. As with so many of the early colonies, something had gone wrong, and the colonists hadn't survived. Jasujeong occupied a strategic location between the two nations. Despite its unlucky history, both the Thousand Worlds and Sun Clans claimed it for themselves.

I cut in before the minister of defense and the ambassador could get into an argument over nomenclature. "If you're talking to *me* about that planet, it's because you want me to do something about it. Something permanent."

That was an understatement. The Dragon Pearl held the power of terraforming, doing in moments what ordinarily took years for trained dragon magicians. In the hands of a trained shaman, or its chosen wielder, the Pearl could transform an entire planet into a garden of lush forests and meadows, or a desolate wasteland. To the consternation of the Thousand Worlds' movers and shakers, the magical orb had chosen teenage me.

"Very blunt," the ambassador said. "But yes, that's essentially correct. We've been in talks—so many talks—about remaking Artifact World Four. Instead of a place of death, where skirmishes have taken place on its treacherous terrain, we want it to become a place of life. A place that both the Thousand Worlds and the Sun Clans can settle jointly, as a symbol of the new accord between our peoples."

Officially, Jasujeong/Artifact World Four occupied a neutral zone between the Thousand Worlds and the Sun Clans. Unofficially, special operations forces often clashed there, vying for control of the world due to its prime location. I hadn't heard about the skirmishes until recently, mainly because they were classified. It wasn't the sort of thing broadcast on the news holos.

I glanced at the minister of defense, who nodded encouragingly. "If my government is committed to this, I can do it," I said.

Gone were the days when I could gallivant through space doing as I pleased. I worked for the Ministry of Domestic Security now, as its most junior agent. Where I'd once been a free traveler, I was now a representative of the government. Sometimes I missed having more control over my own life.

But the Dragon Pearl was too powerful to be used on a whim, and even I saw the logic of that.

The ambassador closed her eyes for a moment, as though she hadn't been certain I would say yes. I caught a whiff of disapproval in the room and surreptitiously looked around me. Everyone was watching us, and not all of them looked happy.

I desperately needed a chance to talk this through with Jun, or Seok, or someone more familiar with the intricacies of the situation. Among other things, it was a terrible sign that the minister of defense, on my side, and the ambassador, speaking for the Sun Clans, couldn't even agree on what to call the dratted planet.

"I don't think this is such a good idea."

I narrowed my eyes at the woman who had spoken up, a white-haired shaman. Her outfit combined the old and new: a pantsuit, but one embellished with brightly colored knot-work talismans. Jun and I had reason to be wary of shamans because of what they could do to ghosts. I hoped this one was too preoccupied with the political discussion to examine me closely.

Minister Baik looked resigned. "Another objection, Shaman?"

"I don't believe we've been introduced," the Sun Clans ambassador interjected smoothly.

I couldn't tell whether that was true or not, but the shaman looked affronted. Maybe there had been introductions while Miho and I were talking about fox matters.

"I'm the head shaman of Cheonggeumseok," the woman said, neglecting to give her name. Even I knew that was a snub. "Given that the Dragon Pearl has chosen an ... unconventional Bearer, it should under no circumstances be allowed to leave the Thousand Worlds."

Ambassador Tanaka's eyes glinted slyly. "Surely you're not intimating that Jasujeong *isn't* one of the Thousand Worlds. Or are you conceding the Sun Clans' claim to that system?"

I schooled my expression to indicate bland interest rather than the admiration that washed through me. I respected the way she'd outmaneuvered the shaman. If only my classes included lessons on intrigue rather than just dreary histories.

"No one has asked the obvious question," I said, and all eyes were on me again. "Which is whether the Pearl itself *wants* to go."

"It may be a powerful object," said another dignitary, "but that doesn't mean it has opinions, any more than my shoes do."

A nervous smattering of laughter ran around the room. The fact was, we couldn't be certain that his shoes didn't have opinions. Most everyday objects were inert, but spiritual forces infused everything to an extent. For all I knew, the dignitary's shoes were haunted. I cocked an eyebrow at Jun: *Do they?* He rolled his eyes, then shook his head.

"The Bearer is quite right," the ambassador said, and I forgave her for sounding like she'd been about to say *youngster,* even if it was true. She nodded at me with more respect than she had earlier. "Among my people, there are shrines where you can leave broken needles in beds of tofu so you can thank them for their work."

I'd damaged my share of needles while mending, but it had never occurred to me to *thank* them. Maybe my stitchery would have improved if I had.

Reverently, I drew the Dragon Pearl from its silken pouch. It fit perfectly in my hand. Its colors shone in an iridescent swirl upon its pale surface, seemingly smooth but with a touch of grit. The undulant light that came from it brightened everything in the hall, from the gilt decorations on the walls to the embroidered motifs on so many people's clothes, from the ceremonial swords of the ambassador's guards to the hairpins that could double as daggers.

"You know the situation," I whispered to the Dragon Pearl. Its light swirled more rapidly in response. Whatever spirit inhabited it was listening. "Shall we go to Jasujeong?"

The Pearl darkened for a moment, turning the sullen colors of an incoming storm. I sucked in my breath, apprehensive. What would the consequences be if I wasn't able to "control" the Pearl? Would my own government try to take it away from me?

Then the pale cloud-light burst forth again, brighter than before. That was a yes, but a yes with a warning. Too bad it didn't speak in words because I didn't know *what* it wanted me to be careful about, other than the machinations of the politicians around me.

"So that's the power of the Pearl," the ambassador said, sounding shaken.

My bodyguard looked awed, and it was the first time I'd ever startled that emotion out of her. Most of the time her expression had only three modes: forbidding, exasperated, or scornful. Nice to know even she appreciated the wonder that was the Pearl!

Strictly speaking, the glow wasn't a big deal. Sure, the Pearl made for some great light shows, but you could do that with a bunch of lamps. I could rig up something even more impressive with some battery packs and holo units. The Pearl's glow only hinted at its true powers of transformation.

I glanced sideways at the minister of defense and Miho. The assistant minister's eyes were fixed avidly on the Pearl, which I still cupped in my outstretched hands. There was more than one person interested in its powers.

Still, I knew what the ambassador meant. The Dragon Pearl wasn't just a luminous piece of jewelry. Everyone had felt it: a barely tamed magic that held sway over earth, sea, wind, and fire. I'd tapped into that power once, on a world haunted by ghosts, to lay the unsleeping dead to rest. And now it looked like I was going to have to do it again.

"It's willing—" I said, or started to say, when all the lights went out.

I didn't scream, but others did.

My first priority was to secure the Dragon Pearl. Seok had assured me that this diplomatic party would have the best safeguards available in the Thousand Worlds and beyond, but I was skeptical. This attack—which I assumed it was—only demonstrated that there was no such thing as foolproof security.

I did what any sensible fox would do. I went to ground and let my bodyguard figure out her own plan of action. In my case, it meant shoving the Pearl back into its carrying pouch, fumbling it shut, scrambling for the next table over, and diving underneath. Someone almost tripped over me, but I managed to evade their flailing legs in time.

I hadn't spent much time in my fox shape thanks to my family's restrictions about using our powers. And I didn't dare take on that form even in the dark. But this was definitely a fox's-eye view of the action, so to speak. The Dragon Pearl's illumination leaked out of the pouch, which I had closed imperfectly. I could see, however dimly, all the rushing feet as people ran around like frightened chickens. Someone spilled a glass of rice wine nearby, and the smell assaulted my nostrils.

In all the tumult, I hadn't checked that my hiding spot was empty. Only Jun's vigilance saved me. "Someone's down here with you," he whispered into my ear. And then, in a very different voice: "It's *them*."

I sniffed again, wishing the rice wine stink wasn't so overpowering. What I smelled was a worrying bouquet of consternation and . . . embarrassment? And beneath all that, the primal musk of tiger.

"Min?" asked the person under the table with me, and then I was certain.

"Sebin? What are you doing down here?"

I heard rather than saw their grimace. "Failing to keep a couple of cadets from running amok at a party, apparently."

I'd known that *a* starship, a battle cruiser, had been assigned to convey the Thousand Worlds delegation to wherever it needed to go. But it had escaped my attention that the specific ship was the *Haetae*, where my kind-of friend Sebin was assigned. Served me right for zoning out during parts of Seok's briefing.

"I figured it was an attack," I admitted. Sure enough, I could hear stern voices ordering people to calm down and stop panicking. I could have told the guards that *that* never worked, but it had to have been standard procedure.

"I thought they'd hidden down here, but no, it's you." Sebin's voice sounded more growly and exasperated than ever. "I'll keep looking."

"Wait. I'll come with—" I started to say, but they had already left.

"I can either stay here where it's safe," I said to Jun, since I doubted anyone else was listening near where I crouched, "or I can help Sebin."

"Seok would want you to stay safe," Jun said. "But you're not going to, so you might as well make your move now. You could use Charm—carefully—to help calm the crowd."

Jun was a much nicer fox than I was. Or more responsible, at least. But I had a different concern. "That might alert Miho that we're foxes. Maybe we should find her and get *her* to do it."

I clambered out from beneath the table. I probably looked disheveled, but what with all the screaming and carrying-on, I wouldn't be the only one. The lights flickered, then came back on.

Where was Miho? My nose tickled, and I instinctively followed the direction of that uncomfortable, itchy feeling. *Lucky Jun*, I thought, since being insubstantial meant it was easy for him to navigate the crowd. I immediately felt awful; it couldn't be fun being a *ghost*.

As I began my search, Silhouette emerged from her own hidey-hole. I felt even worse when I caught sight of her expression. She took her job seriously, and I'd vanished. I gave her a thumbs-up and she looked startled, then nodded.

Jun and I located Miho hiding behind a chair. "Assistant Minister!" I hissed. "You can do something about this panic."

I could smell her reaction, a mix of annoyance and resignation. "You're right," she said. "If you insist."

I couldn't let this panic go on. "I'll owe you a favor," I said, wondering if I'd live to regret the promise.

That decided it. She stepped out from behind her cover and straightened up. "Honored guests!" she said in a voice that carried. "No need to worry. They were just testing one of the emergency systems."

A transparent lie—except Miho's power ensured that people would believe her and calm down.

My eyes watered at the outpouring of Charm that gusted from her, almost like a physical force. While her back was turned to me, I indulged in a sneeze. I wondered if I would ever be as powerful as she was and become a full-fledged nine-tail myself.

The shouts and yelps subsided. Even the security guards, who had flocked from their positions, turned toward us, their eyes glazed.

"Now, I believe a couple people have a confession to make," Miho went on.

I hadn't looked *behind* Miho earlier. I did now. Two cadets, both in Space Forces uniform, stared worshipfully at her. They had to be the pranksters that Sebin was looking for. How had she rounded them up so quickly?

And that wasn't all. Sebin accompanied them, gazing at Miho with that same entranced look, caught in the net of her Charm.

SIX

Sebin

I woke up, if you could call it that, in a holding cell on the station. The setup hadn't been designed to hold a tiger, which I could tell by testing the flimsy restraints, but no force was more powerful than my own honor. At least under normal circumstances.

The shreds of memory returning to me suggested that these were not normal circumstances.

I'd gone with Haneul to round up Cadets Dak-Ho and Yui and . . .

"They've come to," someone reported. I slowly recognized the voice.

Why was Haneul standing over me at a weird angle, while I was trussed up ineffectually in this chair?

My head lolled to one side. I sat up straight, spotted Captain Chaewon, and reflexively attempted to salute. Then growled when the restraints cut into my wrists. That was a mistake, I realized the moment the noise left my throat. The captain's mouth tightened as though I had disgraced myself.

I wished the jigsaw pieces would coalesce faster. I was still on Station Ssangyong, judging by the smell. It had an earthier tang than the metal-and-disinfectant reek of the starship. (Not that I would ever describe the *Haetae*'s smell to the captain that way, even if it had come to be the smell of home.)

"Cadet Sebin," the captain said, her voice flat. One degree from anger. "Explain yourself."

Haneul bit her lip. She stood behind the captain, and the cadet smelled intensely of frustration. I would have loved a chance to quiz her on how we'd gotten split up, because the last time I remembered seeing her, she'd been right behind me, watching my back as I checked under the table. Something must have happened to separate us, because there was a blank patch in my memory and then this.

Out of the corner of my eye, I saw Haneul mouth something. Too bad lipreading wasn't one of my skills, ancestral or otherwise. A headache pounded at my temples as I attempted to gather my wits.

The lights going out. Screams. Running into Min, of all people, under the table.

Fresh adrenaline flooded into my system. My jumbled memories finally made sense, or as much sense as they were going to. At least I had enough presence of mind—not that that was saying much—to force myself to sit still, rather than pulling against, and perhaps breaking, the restraints.

"Min," I croaked. "I ran into Min. And fox magic."

"Sir, I know Min," Haneul said. "She may be impulsive, but she—"

"Cadet Haneul," Captain Chaewon said, "I know the Bearer of the Dragon Pearl by reputation. Including her heritage."

Cynically, I wondered if Min had meant to keep her fox heritage a secret, because that ship had sailed.

"I'm not at one hundred percent," I said to Captain

Chaewon, as much as it galled me to admit weakness. "I have a hazy memory of searching for Dak-Ho and Yui with Haneul." More pieces returned to me as I spoke. "We followed their scent to a reception of some sort, and lost time persuading Security to let us in because we didn't have invitations."

"If I may, sir," Haneul said again.

I had to admire her persistence.

"No," Captain Chaewon said curtly. "I want to hear Sebin's account. Don't make me explain myself again, Cadet."

Haneul's face shuttered. It seemed that the captain was done deferring to Haneul on account of her high connections. I wondered what Haneul's previous captain had been like, and if the dragon had gotten used to special treatment.

I squeezed my eyes shut, which was probably a mistake, especially while the captain was watching. But my head hurt so much, as though someone had reached into my skull and squeezed my brain into a pulp. I needed a moment to regain my equilibrium.

"That's right," I said, opening my eyes again to the captain's unreadable expression. "The only reason we made it into the reception hall was that all the lights had gone out. I was too late to stop Dak-Ho and Yui from getting away with mischief."

Suddenly another thought occurred to me. "Dak-Ho and Yui—did they cause any more trouble?" And, just as important, because they were crew, the closest thing I had to family: "Are they all right?"

"You're very fortunate," Captain Chaewon said in a voice that implied anything but. "No one died in the chaos."

The headache was nothing to the gnawing anxiety in my stomach. I hadn't considered that the consequences could be worse than a little mayhem.

"You hadn't accounted for that, had you? The 'only reason' you got past Security was that Security was busy preventing what could have been an assassination attack."

"The junior cadets would never . . ." I whispered, but the idea shook me. The political fallout would have been catastrophic if any of the dignitaries had died.

The captain smiled grimly. "You're beginning to understand. Dak-Ho and Yui wouldn't have knowingly aided an assassination attempt, but there might well have been enemies of the Thousand Worlds ready to take advantage of any disruption."

I could see it now. As much trouble as I was in, there was no way that Captain Chaewon could go easy on the two junior cadets. Not after what they'd done.

Which wasn't to say that I was in zero trouble myself. I was sure I was in plenty, and I deserved it. She'd given me a straightforward mission, and I'd been outwitted by a pair of kids even younger than I was.

"Cadets Dak-Ho and Yui are in custody and will be dealt with accordingly," the captain confirmed.

I didn't ask what their punishment would be. I'd find out soon enough. That sort of thing didn't stay secret for long on any ship anyway. *Even the plumbing has ears*, as they say.

I squared my shoulders, which set off a whole new wave of pain in my wrists and temples, a one-two preview of punishment. But whatever the captain's sentence, I would accept it with as much dignity as I could muster.

"It does appear," Captain Chaewon said with a sideways glance at Haneul, "that there are some extenuating circumstances. The Bearer of the Dragon Pearl might hold us hostage to her whims, but she can't go around using her wicked fox powers on my crew. And it does appear that she used her . . . abilities to keep people from panicking."

I opened my mouth to speak, then closed it. What was there to say when I couldn't put my own memories of the past couple hours together in a way that made sense?

Min and I weren't best friends. In fact, we'd started out as enemies. But we'd learned to work together during the hijacking crisis. I'd thought we were allies.

I'd thought, too, that she wouldn't simply Charm me like I was nothing but an obstacle to whatever she wanted.

Something didn't add up. I was positive that Min wasn't the kind of person who used "wicked fox powers" for kicks. At least, I hoped that the Domestic Security Ministry, for which she worked, did a better job of screening its personnel than that.

All the same, if my headache and memory issues hadn't come from a run-in with a fox's Charm, what *had* caused them? Having no answer was almost worse than the one staring me in the face.

And of course, the fact that I was tied up suggested that the captain didn't entirely trust me. I cleared my throat. "Sir, I won't let it happen again."

As soon as I spoke, I realized it was an empty promise. Few countermeasures existed against a fox spirit's Charm, which was one of the reasons people feared them so much. I was no shaman or magician with access to the ancient magics. And I doubted that Captain Chaewon would be eager to add a Sapsali dog to our crew. For that matter, I wasn't positive that just any Sapsali would do—maybe only a shaman's dog had the ability to break a fox's mind-control powers.

Still, this satisfied Captain Chaewon. "You were thrashing about when we came upon you," she said by way of explanation. "As if you'd been ordered to resist capture."

I didn't remember that, but that didn't mean a whole lot right now. "Sorry, sir."

She nodded and released the restraints.

I rubbed my wrists as circulation rushed back into my hands, wriggling my fingers to make sure they all functioned. My aunt had taught me how to tie up someone so that no permanent damage was done, and I could appreciate the skill with which I'd been trussed. It hadn't occurred to me until much later that this was a weird thing to prioritize in a kid's upbringing.

"Your assistance is appreciated, Cadet Haneul," the captain said stiffly. "Please escort Cadet Sebin back to the *Haetae*. I have arrangements of my own to make."

The last person I wanted to escort me back to the ship was Haneul. But I wasn't being fair to her, I realized dimly. If anything, she'd been caught up in events just as much as I had.

We headed out of the room and back through the station's halls. This time the elaborate decorations stared at me accusingly. I wouldn't have been surprised if the masks came to life to rebuke me.

I did have one burning question, which I saved for when we were out of earshot of anyone I could see or hear or smell. "If Min Charmed me," I said to Haneul, "why didn't she do the same to you?"

She bit her lip, looking troubled. Vulnerable, for once, which might mean she was willing to tell me something of use. "Two reasons. One, we'd gotten separated. I must have been out of range."

Since her memory could hardly be worse than mine on recent events, I nodded. "And the other?"

"I know Min," she said in a rush. "We served together on the *Pale Lightning* once. It's a long story. Maybe she spared me because she didn't feel I was a threat to her."

I frowned as we approached the security checkpoint for the *Haetae*'s docking bay. "Did I growl at her? Threaten to turn into a tiger?"

"No, no! None of those things. I think . . . I think the captain was harder on you than she needed to be."

Huh. That statement made me warm to Haneul. She was doing her best, the same as me.

At that point we reached the checkpoint and the guards interrupted us. "Name and ID," said the taller one, a person with a nose that had been broken at least twice.

"Cadet Juhwang Sebin of the *Haetae*," I said, producing my ID for inspection.

The guard waved me through, and it was Haneul's turn.

"Cadet Haneul of the *Haetae*," Haneul said, showing her ID.

I expected them to wave her through as well, so it came as an unpleasant surprise when the guard ran her ID through a scanner and it beeped menacingly.

Haneul and I exchanged glances, united for once in our apprehension.

"Dragon Councilor Gwan requires your presence immediately," the guard said at last. "Your duty to them supersedes any other orders you have been given."

A flare of rebellion wafted from Haneul, but out loud she said only, "Understood, sir."

"I can make it back to my bunk alone," I started to say when the floor rushed up toward me.

Haneul caught hold of my arm and hauled me back upright. She was stronger than she looked. People didn't usually think of dragons in terms of their strength—they weren't primarily known for it like tigers or goblins—but in her true form, Haneul was probably several times bigger than even the largest tiger. Raindrops splattered against my forehead, so cold they almost burned.

"Sorry," Haneul muttered. The rain stopped abruptly, although the chilly humidity that hung around her didn't abate. "I'd better get you to sick bay. The dragon councilor can wait."

I had to say it. "I've been Charmed before," I said in an undertone as she helped me stagger toward the docked ship. "I don't remember it hitting me quite like this."

"Shh," Haneul said. "We can discuss this after you're better."

The officer of the deck recognized us both, so getting onto the *Haetae* proper was much easier. Still, I didn't want to get Haneul into further trouble. Bad enough that I'd botched my orders.

"Seriously, go on," I said. "I can make it to sick bay on my own."

I spoiled the effect by losing my balance.

Now Haneul smelled almost exclusively of worry. "I've never seen Charm do this," she said in a whisper. "Lean on me."

What could I do? I leaned on her, and together we hobbled to sick bay.

I woke up again, this time hooked up to a medical unit. "Water?" I croaked. My head felt much better. Clearer, as though an unknown veil had lifted.

"Objectively speaking," said the medic after bringing me a

cup of broth, "there's nothing wrong with you. All the readings come up blue."

I kept silent. It didn't seem discreet to say that I'd run afoul of fox magic—it was up to the captain to decide how to share that information. At the same time, I didn't like leaving the medic completely in the dark.

"I heard there was a big party on the station," the medic added, frowning suspiciously at me. "You didn't get into the punch or anything else you cadets aren't supposed to, did you?"

I'd certainly *smelled* plenty of rice wine at that party. It was only through luck that it hadn't gotten spilled on my clothes.

"Of course not," a voice interrupted. I smelled its owner before I saw her: Min. I couldn't detect the part of her that was fox, but that stood to reason. She was playing human, after all. "I was there. Sebin ran afoul of some magic business. A geomancer should go over the layout of the whole place again."

It sounded plausible, although I only knew the bare rudiments of pungsu jiri, or geomancy. My grandmother's estate had relied on careful arrangements of azalea and wisteria, willow and sycamore, to channel the forces of good fortune in favor of the Juhwang Tiger Clan. Of course, even geomancy couldn't save the family when misdeeds caught up with them. Something I'd found out the hard way.

Accompanying Min was a taller woman, perhaps in early middle age, with short hair and a red mouth. She had the kind of beauty that drew the eye like an unsheathed sword. It made me uneasy even though I had no objective reason to distrust her.

"Hello, Sebin," Min said, coming closer. "I thought I'd check in on you."

I bet Captain Chaewon didn't like having a fox wandering around loose on her starship.

The medic was unamused. "I'm sorry, who are you two and what are you doing in my sick bay?"

"Pardon me," the older woman cut in smoothly. "I'm Yang Miho, assistant to the minister of defense. I'm part of the diplomatic party that will be taking this fine vessel to the border world of Jasujeong. I thought I'd take a tour. . . ."

A twinge of headache returned as Miho steered the medic away from us and toward an office. I'd met her before. It must have been at that disastrous party. I hoped I hadn't offered her mortal insult and now she was snubbing me as a result. But then again, I wasn't a person worth the effort.

"Listen up," Min hissed as I stretched and rolled my shoulders, making sure all my limbs worked. "I need something from you. It's important."

"At least this time you're asking," I muttered.

She slitted her eyes at me. "Whatever you think is going on, Sebin, it's complicated. Much more complicated than anything you could imagine."

Granted, no one had ever lauded me for my flights of fancy. "Start talking," I said.

I hadn't meant it as a promise, but Min seemed to take it as one. "This mission is important, not just for the Sun Clans and the Thousand Worlds, but for me personally. There's a . . . family matter involved, I guess you could say. This has to succeed. I'll make things right with Captain Chaewon."

That was a whole lot of vague noises and nothing concrete I could put my paws on. "You're talking in riddles. Say it in words I can understand."

I smelled her uncertainty and . . . water? Salt water? "Please tell me you're not wandering around with the Dragon Pearl," I added. That had to be where the sea smell was coming from. "What if someone makes off with it?"

Min laughed. "And goes where? We're traveling into deep space. The Dragon Pearl will be safe *during* the journey, unless you think your fellow crew members can't be trusted."

She was trying to distract me, and it was working. The only reason to send the Dragon Pearl so close to enemy territory would be to use it. Presumably on Jasujeong, our destination. But that didn't explain her evasiveness about the "family matter."

Finally, the pieces clicked into place. I was convinced that *Min* wouldn't Charm me against my will. Not after everything we'd endured together. And only foxes possessed that power. Which meant . . . "*You* didn't Charm me," I said. "There's another fox, and you're covering for them."

SEVEN

Min

I panicked.

Sebin was a straight-arrow, law-and-order type of tiger. The very first thing they'd do if they discovered another fox had crept on board was inform the captain. That would cause diplomatic trouble, because Captain Chaewon would object to a second fox aboard her ship. We were already underway from Ssangyong Station and would have to turn back. The minister of defense was too ill to make a long space voyage and had sent his assistant, Miho, in his place. He'd said as much at the party. There'd be a scandal in the Thousand Worlds government that a fox had been in hiding among the high-ranking government officials all this time. I couldn't let Sebin cause this cascade of trouble.

The *Haetae* and the Sun Clans' cruiser *Hokusai* were accompanying each other to the world of Jasujeong. It would cause grumbling and discontent, possibly worse, if we had to rustle up a replacement assistant minister, a consideration that Sebin wasn't going to give me time to explain.

Once upon a time, the solution would have been simple—I

would have Charmed Sebin. It wouldn't have been hard, assuming I could do it before they overpowered me and knocked me out. Sebin had a tiger's reflexes, but I had a fox's, so that evened things out. Extra point to me because Sebin trusted me, so I'd have a moment's advantage over them.

But I'd learned that while Charming people left and right solved some problems, it created others. Charm had helped me track down my brother Jun, and at the same time it had almost cost me the friendship of Haneul and Sujin back on the battle cruiser *Pale Lightning*. I couldn't do that again.

I hesitated and knew I'd lost. I'd missed the opportunity.

"You were thinking about it," Sebin said, a hint of a growl in their voice.

They didn't have to spell out what *it* was. "I was," I said defensively, "but I didn't."

"I'm glad you didn't," Jun said quietly. He was more visible than usual as he looked at me, his eyes sad.

Shame burned my face. I was used to people looking down on me. Even my mother and aunties had always considered me a troublemaker who refused to settle down and play by the rules that had protected our family for so long.

But the one person who had always believed in me was Jun—and I'd almost let him down. Again.

Sebin narrowed their eyes at me.

"You're right," I said in defeat. "You should tell the captain."

Just as I said that, the assistant minister and the chief medic emerged from the latter's office. I could *feel* Miho's attention, as if a charged wire connected us, even though she wasn't doing anything so obvious as looking in my direction.

"Come on," I whispered to Sebin. "While they're occupied."

I didn't want to see the disappointment on Miho's face when she found out that I was breaking my promise to her.

Jun sighed gustily but didn't voice an objection.

"Why are you protecting the other fox?" Sebin asked me on our way to Captain Chaewon's office. The tiger cadet had wanted to tell Ensign Hak and let it be her problem, but I insisted that we go to the captain personally rather than trust an intermediary.

Jun and I looked at each other, hesitant. How much did I want to reveal?

Because there are so few of us foxes, I almost said. *Because we might become allies, if not friends.*

Sebin had never known a world where tigers had to crouch and scurry and hide. They had grown up secure in the knowledge that tiger spirits are accepted throughout the Thousand Worlds. I didn't think I could explain to Sebin what my connection to Miho meant to me, even if I didn't entirely trust her.

"Send the captain a message saying we're on our way and it's urgent we see her," I said. "I mean, it can't hurt to try."

Sebin's face didn't change, but we foxes have a good sense of smell. The whiff of discomfort rising from the cadet was a dead giveaway to anyone with a decent nose.

"The captain's already expecting you, isn't she?" I stifled another swell of panic. "She already knows?"

"It's about something else," Sebin said stiffly.

We paused in a corridor and waited for crew members to pass by before continuing our conversation. Other smells impinged on my awareness: the usual sharpness of disinfectant, hints of moisture and growing things filtering in from hydroponics or (I hoped not) poorly maintained ventilation shafts, and the occasional trace of sweat or rust or grease.

"Great!" I said, blithely ignoring Sebin's discomfort. "You might as well use that as a pretext to tell her what you're going to tell her."

"You'd rather I kept quiet."

I was silent for a moment, choosing my words carefully. Which wasn't something I was accustomed to doing. Usually, I just said the first thing that came to mind, relying on my quick wits. But this wasn't about outsmarting Sebin.

"You don't know what it's like," I said finally, "not being able to say who I am." Sure, I enjoyed tricking people—but I enjoyed it most when I did it because I *could*, not because I *had to*.

Going around in this older-girl guise, for example, was a little of both. Seok couldn't have openly permitted a fourteen-year-old to act as a Domestic Security agent, but my relationship with the Dragon Pearl had forced his hand. I liked the fact that people didn't know how young I really was.

At the same time, it sucked that being a fox had to be a gigantic secret, even if it was a gigantic secret that often worked in my favor.

"You're right and you're wrong," Sebin said with that attentive soberness I liked about them. "The captain is fair. And it's her ship, so it's her job to keep us all safe. She deserves to know."

"Worth a try," Jun urged.

I had my doubts about the captain's fairness, but I hadn't had the greatest experiences with ships' captains, not after my run-ins with Sebin's treacherous uncle. *He* was the one who'd gotten my brother killed. If I'd been feeling vindictive, I would have brought that up. Everyone had things they didn't talk about, though, and that one was Sebin's.

Technically, Sebin should soon report to Ensign Hak for their assignment. At the very least Sebin needed to let her know that they were fit for duty again. Or so they claimed. I had my doubts that they were ready, and the fact that Sebin had reacted so strongly to Miho's employment of Charm bothered me.

Sure, Charm could get people to do things they wouldn't otherwise have done. But I'd never heard of it having *physical* side effects. I suspected that it had to do with Miho's sheer power as a fully nine-tailed fox. No one in my family had warned me of such a thing, and by this point I'd blown my chance to ask Miho herself.

Sebin cleared their throat, then called the captain, using the phrasing I provided. The captain gave us permission to stop by.

There was a guard outside her door, a heavyset sergeant who looked like he would rather be arm-wrestling all takers. He told us to wait. I was tempted to sic Jun on him, but my brother was too nice to do something like that, even if we'd been willing to reveal his presence.

Sebin and I exchanged uncomfortable glances. I could smell their worry; I probably stank of it myself. Granted, I hadn't been aboard that many starships, but this was the first time I'd known a captain to set a guard in front of their own office. Especially when everyone aboard was supposedly friendly.

Did it have to do with the dragon councilor's safety? During the time when Sebin had been convalescing, I'd gotten a chance to survey the ship. The ship had three categories of notables, as I liked to think of them.

The first was, well, me, as Bearer of the Dragon Pearl.

The second intrigued me much more. Dragon Councilor Gwan served as a representative of the Thousand Worlds' dragons, presumably to keep me in check. I'd known for some time that the Dragon Council disapproved of me on principle. They didn't like having their monopoly on terraforming challenged. I couldn't find it in myself to feel sorry for them, given that their profiteering had resulted in worlds like Jinju languishing in poverty.

Normally I would have risked Jun's scowl and taken advantage of my sneakier abilities to do some listening in on the dragon councilor, despite their tendency to lurk in their cabin or show up for mealtimes at odd hours. But what complicated this was that Dragon Councilor Gwan had brought my old friend Haneul along as their apprentice.

Haneul and I had parted on more or less good terms back on the *Pale Lightning*. But on this mission, she'd been avoiding me with almost supernatural precision. I'd caught glimpses of her, and on the rare occasions I'd run into her, she'd been so busy catering to the dragon councilor's whimsical demands that we hadn't had a chance to talk. I'd gotten the impression that Haneul had decidedly ambivalent feelings about her new role. *Partly because of me?* I wondered.

The third group consisted of Assistant Minister Miho and her cronies. She'd brought a small contingent of secretaries and undersecretaries with her, the political kind. They smelled of intrigue and over-steeped tea, and I didn't trust any of them, even though I wanted to believe in Miho.

Normally, I would have strained my hearing to pick up any conversation within the captain's office. Sebin would have disapproved of that, though. But their opinion was moot. The guard wouldn't let me press my ear to the door unless I Charmed him, and neither Jun nor Sebin would have stood for that, which was the more important point.

The captain's voice finally came over the comms. "I know they've been waiting for some time, but tell them to come back tomorrow."

"Sorry, kids, you need to come back tomorrow," the guard repeated in a monotone. "Cadet Sebin, your supervising officer will let you know when."

I sagged in relief. Reprieve! But why had the captain invited us to stop by if she couldn't see us? She must have been interrupted by a more pressing matter.

Sebin's frustration was becoming more and more visible. Not a good sign for either of us.

"C'mon," I said, grabbing their arm.

They shook me off but came along, radiating reluctance.

"You can't be surprised," I said, willing them to understand. "Bad timing, that's all."

"I wonder if it's more than that."

"It does seem odd," Jun agreed.

"Do you both really think it's some kind of conspiracy?" I grimaced. "Anyway, it'll look odd if I walk you to your duty station, Sebin. I'll see you at mess or rec time, maybe?"

"Sounds good," Sebin said in a distinctly unenthusiastic voice.

We parted ways at the next intersection. I watched Sebin stalk off, my heart bitten by ambivalent feelings. On the one hand, cadets aboard a battle cruiser deal with all sorts of tasks that I didn't miss doing. Things like scrubbing toilets, chopping vegetables, or monitoring the plants in hydroponics. Then again, when I'd been a cadet—well, "cadet"—on the *Pale Lightning*, I'd belonged to a team.

"Psst," Jun said by way of warning.

As Bearer of the Dragon Pearl, I *still* had an escort. Who'd just now caught up with me.

I had to put up with having a bodyguard, a woman whose lean build belied her whipcord musculature and reflexes. Silhouette popped up, her face as smooth and blank as ever. "I can't protect you if you ditch me," she said.

"I can't take you everywhere I go," I protested. "People won't tell me things if they know someone else is listening in."

"I go where you go."

I frowned. But it would be too much trouble to lose her again. "Fine. Let's see if Haneul is willing to talk to me *this* time."

One good thing about Silhouette, who was, as far as I could tell, completely human, was that her tracking skills would have put any hound to shame. I couldn't swear that her sense of smell was worse than mine. It wasn't the kind of thing you could ask someone directly, even if she was your bodyguard.

We treed Haneul in one of the conference rooms, dancing attendance on Dragon Councilor Gwan. I'd first met Haneul as a fellow cadet on the *Pale Lightning*. Rather, she'd been the genuine article while I'd been an imposter, something she'd eventually forgiven me for.

Back then, I'd known Haneul as someone who would have gotten along really well with Sebin. Someone who cared about following the rules and doing things right. (I suspected I had given her headaches—not on purpose, of course.) Someone who took pride in her role even as one of the lowliest members of a battle cruiser's crew.

The conference room, ordinarily full of boring chairs around a boring table, had sprouted pots of flowering plants arranged to enhance the flow of good fortune according to the art of geomancy. I assumed this was a training exercise, because the *Haetae* itself, like all Space Forces ships, had already been designed with those principles in mind.

The dragon councilor, Gwan, looked like they belonged amid these plants. The embroidery on their green robes depicted the same flowers, most of which I couldn't name. Botany wasn't my strong point. As steaders on Jinju, my family hadn't had the luxury of growing something as frivolous as ornamental flowers. At least I could identify the azaleas and chrysanthemums as motifs so familiar throughout the Thousand Worlds that they'd even appeared on my family's old floor cushions.

"Bearer of the Dragon Pearl," the councilor said, politely enough. "Just the person I was looking for. You've been elusive. Come in, come in."

I wasn't fooled. I would never be friends with the people who had decided to leave my homeworld a ball of dust because our planetary government couldn't afford the extortionate terraforming fees. I'd hoped to get Haneul alone and had deliberately avoided the councilor. "The pleasure is mutual," I lied. "What did you want to talk about?"

Jun dimmed until I could scarcely see him or detect much beyond a faint chilly breeze. I wanted his support but had to concede to his common sense. Dragon Councilor Gwan was the type who would raise a stink if they discovered that I was harboring an unlucky ghost. I could consult with my brother afterward, once we were out of sight.

I came farther into the room, declining to sit. Silhouette, even more paranoid than I was, took up a position by the door. It swished shut behind us.

Haneul continued to fuss with one of the plants, refusing to meet my eyes. I couldn't tell whether the plant genuinely needed help or she was practicing close-range avoidance. What had I done to offend her?

I'd thought that we'd mended matters between us after I, well, impersonated her best friend. Kind of a big deal, and I couldn't blame her for holding a grudge. But when we'd last met, she'd shown no sign of that. What was going on?

"We're not friends," the councilor said, "but we do need to present a united front to the Sun Clanners." They spoke in that *Of course you'll do as I say* tone that I disliked so much when it was aimed at me. The Dragon Council had never liked it that the Pearl, with terraforming powers that dwarfed those of their own practitioners, had chosen me. I wasn't surprised that one of its members would assume the worst of me.

"United how?" I demanded. I bet they meant united on the Dragon Council's terms.

"The Sun Clans need to be aware that the Dragon Pearl is used at the will of the Thousand Worlds government," the councilor said with a patently fake smile. "Not at the whim of someone who hasn't yet reached their legal majority."

I'd been right. "Are you planning on taking the Pearl away from me?" I inquired. "Because I'm sure that wouldn't end well."

"Min, wait." Haneul finally spoke.

I looked at her, frowning. She was my friend. If she was talking to me again, I meant to hear her out. "Haneul."

"I know you're used to improvising," she said. "But I think the councilor has a point. We can't afford for the Sun Clans to sniff out any weaknesses in our delegation . . . or any divisions."

Haneul had a dragon's sense of smell, which meant she could tell I was upset. So there wasn't any point in my hiding it.

"Careful. You can't afford to—" Jun began, trying to save me from myself.

Too late. The words escaped me as my temper flared. "The Dragon Council is going to have to get used to the idea that they don't control everything," I snapped.

Haneul's eyes flashed. "You're being unfair, and you know it! The Dragon Council works for the benefit of the Thousand Worlds as a whole. It's not possible to terraform every world everywhere all at once."

"Well spoken," the dragon councilor said warmly. "You'll make an excellent successor when it comes time for me to retire."

Haneul flushed, and in the back of my mind I noted that she smelled ambivalent about this compliment. "Someone has to set priorities," she finished without looking at Gwan.

"You mean *rich people* get to set priorities," I shot back.

Haneul recoiled like I'd slapped her. "Is that how you think of me? 'Rich people'?"

That brought me up short. Haneul didn't know much about me. Not the real me. When I'd revealed my true identity as a fox spirit to her, we hadn't had time to exchange life histories. And after I'd left to pursue a career with the Ministry of Domestic Security, we'd fallen out of touch.

Haneul wasn't done. "Someone has to study the ecologies of planets and distribute those resources. People who know what they're doing. The Dragon Council can't just send terraforming teams to planets at random."

Gwan nodded approvingly, which only worsened my mood. Was Haneul so intent on cozying up to her new mentor that she didn't care about anything else?

"Fine," I said with a snarl. "If that's the way you feel about it."

I turned on my heel, but not before I saw the dragon councilor's slight smirk. Like they'd planned this whole confrontation. Were they that dead set on indoctrinating Haneul—and turning her against me?

But I didn't want to stick around for more of Haneul's platitudes. I stalked out, fuming, and not even Jun's anxious whispers could get me to return.

EIGHT

Sebin

Several days after I was released from sick bay, the captain summoned me and delivered some unexpected news.

"Once we reach Jasujeong," she said, "I'll be sending you down planetside with the diplomatic mission."

"Me?" I asked in astonishment, forgetting to speak with the correct formality level of cadet to captain. "Why would you send *me*?"

Captain Chaewon grimaced. "Aside from the occasional lapse—"

I winced, thinking of the disaster I'd failed to prevent at the party.

"—you've been a promising cadet. Of course, normally you would have been pulled off a mission like this one after that . . . incident."

That stung to hear, but it was right and proper. I nodded. I didn't want the captain to scent my shame. What was done was done, and I would have to work harder to redeem myself.

"However," the captain went on, "in a case like this, there are political considerations."

I blinked. Certainly politics *affected* the Space Forces, but that was a matter for captains and admirals, not a lowly cadet. Surely I'd misheard her?

"You didn't mishear me," she said, and her mouth pulled to the side in a sour smile. "Your uncle wasn't the only tiger captain in the Space Forces, you know. There are even tigers amid the flag officers."

I did know, although my ambitions had never leaped that high. I respected admirals in the same abstract way I respected the White Tiger of the West, as a creature someone like me would rarely meet. I *had* met the White Tiger once, but it was only in a vision.

"A certain Rear Admiral Hasun is concerned about blowback to the tiger clans due to ex-captain Hwan's actions. In order to mollify them, we have agreed that a tiger cadet will be a part of the delegation."

I understood now. The rear admiral was one of my relatives. But Hasun wasn't looking out for my welfare, and neither was the captain. "Let me guess," I said, although perhaps it would have been better to keep my mouth shut. "I'm a tiger, so I'm useful to you, and beyond that, I'm the tiger whose uncle turned renegade, so if I behave well, I redeem my kind. If I don't, you can always say that it's my *family* that's bad, not all tigers."

Also, cadets were more expendable than tiger officers with actual experience, but I wasn't going to say that part. Not to her.

Captain Chaewon shook her head ruefully. "You've seen your way to the hard truth. You can decline the mission, of course. If you're willing to deal with the consequences."

"No, sir," I said. I could guess the "consequences" she

alluded to. Offloaded from the ship and assigned to some backwater space station. I'd never become a captain if that happened. "I'll do it."

"Good to hear." And with that she dismissed me.

Halfway through our voyage, I couldn't wait for it to end.

Serving aboard a battle cruiser, I reminded myself, was the first step toward my dream of becoming a captain. Which meant that I should approach it with a cheerful attitude, rather than the dread that filled me every time I happened upon Min, or Haneul, or the dragon councilor.

"Cadet Sebin, are you paying attention?" Ensign Hak asked.

I straightened in my seat. "Sorry, sir."

She shook her head, and I resisted the urge to slump. I saw a private heart-to-heart in my future, the last thing I wanted. Why was it so hard to fly under the radar?

At least I didn't do anything else to provoke a warning the rest of the class. It concerned my favorite subject: strategy. I itched to graduate from two-dimensional tactics to the three-dimensional kind—starship battles took place in space, not on land, after all—but the ensign insisted that we tackle our curriculum in order.

Dak-Ho and Yui spent the entire class passing notes. If anyone had reprimanded them after the party-crashing fiasco, neither of them showed any sign of slowing down as a result. I tried not to judge them—that was the ensign's job—but it was hard.

My family would not have stood for this sort of constant misbehavior. I'd learned as a cub that I must always be obedient, disciplined, and ready for whatever emergency came my way. It wasn't the best preparation for life, as I'd learned the hard way. It was possible to be *too* obedient. But the opposite extreme wasn't so great, either.

I'd overheard discussions among the more senior members of the crew. Once upon a time, cadets who racked up too many demerits would have been drummed out of the service. Some of the older officers talked about the stricter standards that were now an artifact of the past. And I had definitely heard Dak-Ho's and Yui's names come up more than once in that context.

"Dak-Ho, Yui," Ensign Hak said at the end of class, after we'd wrapped up a brainstorming exercise on ways to defend a spaceport. I would have enjoyed a live exercise more, but it was a start. "I've revoked your recreation time today. You'll be scrubbing out the air filters."

Yui wilted, but Dak-Ho seemed unfazed. "Yes, sir!" They said this like scrubbing air filters was the assignment of their dreams.

I'd hoped to escape her attention, but when I got up to leave, Ensign Hak cleared her throat. "Stay a moment, Cadet Sebin. The rest of you, clear out."

My turn to wilt. I caught myself and stood at attention, hoping the ensign hadn't spotted my lapse in demeanor. I might not agree with the things my family had done, but that didn't mean I had to give up the valuable lessons they'd passed on to me.

Ensign Hak wasn't one to waste words. "What's going on between you and Min?"

I frowned. "The Bearer of the Dragon Pearl?"

"You don't usually call her that, do you?"

"It's her title."

"I know none of us got off on the right foot with her the last time we met," Hak said, "but she has an important job. More important than yours—or mine, for that matter."

I thought back to the last few times I'd run into Min. She'd smelled . . . worried? Furtive? And I'd caught a chilly wind around her, no doubt from that ghost brother who lurked near her at all times.

Hak shook her head, forehead creasing in concern. "Well, make sure you're at your best, Cadet Sebin."

"Of course, sir."

I headed to the rec room and ran into one of our guests: the assistant minister of defense, Yang Miho. She always had a friendly word for me, which I wouldn't expect from someone who held such an exalted position. Then again, maybe my experiences with the strict hierarchy in my family had given me overly narrow expectations of people in power.

Today a subtle fragrance of plums and lilies surrounded her. I was so unaccustomed to perfume in a starship context that I almost asked her about it. Dak-Ho had once forced Ensign Hak to admit there wasn't a Space Forces regulation about perfume, but common courtesy dictated that, since we were all breathing one another's air, we should avoid using fragrances as much as possible. Even Dak-Ho respected this unwritten rule because Yui was allergic to common perfume ingredients, and she was the one person whose welfare Dak-Ho cared about.

"How was class today, Cadet?" the assistant minister asked.

I couldn't tell if she was genuinely interested or just making conversation. She masked her mood better than most humans I'd encountered. But all of us had orders to treat the diplomatic guests with the same respect that we'd offer to an officer. More, to be honest. There were a lot of (say) ensigns and warrant officers, and only one of her.

"We were discussing ground tactics in the context of planetary warfare," I said. Tigers were often known as warriors, and my family had embraced that heritage. But the whole point of this mission was to dampen hostilities between the Thousand Worlds and the Sun Clans, not to reignite them. I was careful not to sound too eager to put these tactics into actual practice.

She made an intrigued humming noise. "Are you expecting to apply it?"

"It's just the standard curriculum, ma'am."

There might have been more to the conversation, but it slipped my mind after she said good-bye and I continued into the rec room.

I encountered Yui there. "Aren't you supposed to be working right now?" I asked suspiciously.

"I got out early," she said, sidling away from me and toward the Ping-Pong table, where three crew members were playing, two on one, in a recreational game.

Yui's excuse seemed unlikely. "Should I call and check?"

"Please don't," she said, widening her eyes at me.

I shook my head. "You know, the easiest way to avoid getting in trouble is . . . to not get in trouble in the first place."

"That's easier for some people than others."

I cocked my head at the uncharacteristic note of bitterness in her voice. "How so?" I asked, trying to sound curious rather than accusatory.

Maybe there was more behind Yui's shenanigans than I'd realized. I'd never asked myself *why* she and Dak-Ho felt compelled to get into every kind of trouble in the dictionary, and a few that weren't.

That had been shortsighted of me. I'd told myself that it was Ensign Hak's job to discipline them, and the captain's beyond that. I didn't have the authority to keep them in line.

But someday I *would* be that person. I would need to develop those skills. And in the meantime, I could do my part by helping cadets like Dak-Ho and Yui find their way to the discipline that came naturally to me.

"I don't often see you without Dak-Ho . . ." I ventured. That seemed like a safe place to start.

"We grew up together," she said. "Our parents knew each other."

I'd known that they came from the same station, but not that they'd been childhood friends. Come to think of it, I hadn't spent much time talking *to* either of them, as opposed to *at* them. "Dak-Ho must have looked after you a lot."

A faint smile lit her eyes, although her mouth curved downward. "Something like that. The two of us against the world, you know?"

My first instinct would have been to separate the two, to stop them from bouncing off each other into new and exciting heights of tomfoolery. But that was probably the wrong approach. And anyway, if it had been the right approach, Ensign Hak would already have tried it.

Before I could delve further into Yui's history with Dak-Ho, and how it might be influencing her toward too much recklessness, the rec room doors swished open again. I don't like surprises, so I turned to see who had just entered.

Min stood there in the fancier clothes she'd been wearing

ever since she boarded the *Haetae*. At first I'd thought she was putting on airs for this mission. When we'd originally met, she'd affected the humbler garb of a Domestic Security agent. I'd since rethought my assumption. She didn't look comfortable in her modern-day hanbok—all things considered, it was probably a requirement of her role as Bearer of the Dragon Pearl.

My eyes went immediately to the sturdy silken pouch that contained the Pearl, which was at odds with the rest of her outfit. I thought I detected a glimmer of light from within.

"Sebin," Min said, her voice flat. "How are you doing?"

I thought I heard the merest ghostly sigh, and the faintest breath of chilly air. That would be her brother, keeping a low profile.

I couldn't figure out why things had become so awkward between us. "My studies are going fine," I said. "It's life as usual for us cadets, you know."

I watched as Yui took advantage of the interruption to slip out of the rec room and go do something else. Hopefully nothing too disruptive. I ground my teeth. Just when I'd found an opening to talk . . .

Min smiled at me, but it did nothing to disguise the whiff of nerves that came from her. "Come have a snack with me?"

I wasn't hungry, but even I recognized a pretext for a conversation. "Sure."

I followed her out of the rec room. The first thing I noticed was that our route wouldn't lead us to the commissary. I didn't stop by it often, not on a cadet's stipend, but I'd made it my business to know the entire ship's layout.

"Is there a reason we're going this way?" I asked before we'd reached the elevator. I guessed we were really headed for the captain's office.

"Shh," Min said, her eyes darting around almost comically, as though she expected to be jumped. "Do you know how hard it is to lose my bodyguard?"

"Doesn't that negate the *point* of having a bodyguard?"

Min didn't answer, which was just like her. I had a vague memory of the bodyguard, vaguer than I liked. Ordinarily my mind was sharper than that. A woman, soberly dressed and slim, who moved like a predator despite her human ancestry. She went by an obviously fake name. Shadow? Night? Something like that.

"We don't have much time," Min went on, maddeningly opaque. "Can you walk faster?"

It was a ridiculous question. I was taller than she was. In an emergency, I could shift into my native tiger form and leap farther than any human. But this wasn't *that* urgent, or she would have said so.

I hastened my steps. We almost jogged the rest of the way there. "Could you at least say what this is about?"

"Shh."

We reached the elevator, which we had to share with two warrant officers, both men, who looked like they'd slept in their uniforms, judging by the wrinkles. I opened my mouth and Min glared daggers at me until I shut it again. I should have expected that she didn't want anyone to overhear our conversation.

The warrant officers got off the elevator before we did, neither paying us any heed. They didn't even seem to find Min's presence remarkable. Maybe ferrying important passengers was just another day for them.

We got off two levels up, confirming my suspicion that we were heading for the captain's office. "There'd better not be another delay," Min muttered as she preceded me, walking with a briskness that betrayed her anxiety.

"If this is so pressing," I ventured, "shouldn't we have phoned?"

"No time."

I could smell the lie. I was about to call her on it when we reached the captain's office.

"Tell Captain Chaewon it's urgent," Min ordered me. "And we both need to talk to her."

I balked. "I need a reason."

If Min had exuded any more frustration, she could have knocked out the entire bridge crew with it. "Haven't you noticed weird gaps in your memory? Especially when—" She hesitated.

A growl escaped me. "You can't keep me in the dark forever, Min. Not if you want me to help you with whatever this is."

"I think someone has tampered with your memory," Min said with a suspicious lack of detail.

"That's ridiculous. I'd know if that had happened."

"If it was your *memory*?" Min shook her head. "Fine, tell me the last time you spoke to the assistant minister of defense."

I scoffed. "Just before you showed up," I said. "She likes to make conversation."

"About what?"

"Class. I don't know, you'd think she would be preparing for her mission, but she seems to like poking around the ship. Maybe she's bored."

"'Bored . . .'" Min echoed, sounding unconvinced. "And there wasn't anything weird about the conversation?"

"Not unless you think homework is interesting."

This was exactly the right tone to take with her. *I* thought my tactics homework, which involved drawing up a defense plan for a bunker in the side of a hill, was interesting. But I doubted Min shared my passions, and I was right.

Min slumped. "Maybe I misread the situation," she said. She paced back and forth, unable to be still, and I wondered what was eating at her.

"*Think*, Min," I said. "If someone were running around messing with people's memories"—still a ridiculous prospect, since the only one who could do something like that was Min herself—"why would they focus on me? As opposed to the important people on the ship?"

The corners of her mouth twitched. "Yeah," she conceded. But her eyes were still creased with worry. "I guess I was imagining things."

I could tell she wasn't really convinced.

"Imagining what?" said a voice from behind us.

I whirled and snapped to. It was Captain Chaewon.

All that urgency and the captain hadn't even been in her office. I could have kicked myself. Min might have gotten careless, but I should have anticipated the possibility.

The captain looked warily at Min, as though gauging how much she could be trusted, then turned to me and said, "Did you have something to report, Cadet?"

We worked it out would sound stupid. I cursed myself for letting Min talk me into coming here in the first place. I had to say something—the *right* thing.

As ever, Min thought faster on her feet than I did. "Captain," she said, minimally respectful despite the difference in age, "I asked Sebin to show me the way here."

Captain Chaewon's lips compressed for a moment. "Of course."

"I wanted to ask if I could have access to maps of Jasujeong," Min went on.

I was 100 percent sure Min had just come up with that notion on the spot, but it wasn't a bad idea. In fact, I wondered why I hadn't thought of it myself. Other than the fact that they wouldn't be sending cadets down planetside.

The captain stiffened. It was subtle, and I almost didn't spot the reaction. "I'm sorry, Min," she said, politely enough. "Those are classified."

Classified meant we weren't going to get answers. I desperately wanted Min to accept the reply so I could haul her out of there.

Trust Min not to leave well enough alone. "As Bearer of the Dragon Pearl," she said sweetly, "I need all the information I can get on the planet. So I can prepare for whatever the government needs me to do for the mission's success."

Captain Chaewon shook her head. "Sorry. Is there something else I can help you with?"

"Who *is* allowed to look at those maps?"

Min must not have been using Charm or she would have gotten the information she wanted. That made me feel better. And guilty for doubting that she'd do the right thing when it came to her fox powers.

"That's classified, too," said the captain, to no one's surprise.

"Thank you anyway," Min said.

We left Captain Chaewon behind to enter her own office.

"That was a tremendous waste of time," I said sarcastically.

"That was the opposite of a waste," Min countered once

we'd reached the elevator. We had it all to ourselves this time. "I found out something important."

"What, that there's information you're not allowed to have?"

Min's face was serious. "I asked Captain Chaewon the same question when I first came aboard this ship, Sebin. I may not be the planner that you are, but I wanted to be prepared in case we crash-landed or something. And that time the captain *gave* me maps, Sebin. Maps that show nothing but a whole bunch of wilderness. Something's changed. Your memory isn't the only one that's being messed with. There's got to be something on that planet—something that the government is keeping secret. Maybe *both* governments. And I need to find out what it is before I do *anything* in the terraforming department."

NINE

Min

It figured that when I urgently needed to talk to Assistant Minister of Defense Yang Miho, she made herself hard to locate. So I did the next best thing, after a quick consultation with Jun. I slowed down long enough for Silhouette to catch up to me.

About half an hour into my dawdling around the mess hall and commissary, it occurred to me that Silhouette was making herself hard to find, too. That bothered me. I'd done my best to keep out of her sight because I hated feeling like I was being followed by a babysitter. But having a bodyguard who *chose* to spend time elsewhere was, as Sebin had pointed out, kind of useless.

"Where do you think she's gone off to?" I asked Jun, fretting.

"Maybe she has other orders," Jun said. "Who knows, it might be paperwork."

Ridiculous, but plausible. I put the matter out of my mind.

I'd paced half the length of the ship—good exercise, even if all the crew members gave me annoyed looks—when I finally ran Miho to ground. This would have been good if I hadn't first encountered Haneul.

We'd never cleared the air between us after that last argument. I still felt bad about it. After all, she and I had been through hard times together.

On the other hand, finding out that she *agreed* with the corrupt Dragon Council stung. And seeing Miho and Haneul laughing and talking easily over tea *really* stung.

"Min! Care to join us?" Miho asked as I pranced into the conference room that they'd taken over.

I couldn't believe my eyes. They weren't just having tea—this was a *fancy* tea, complete with both of them dressed up in embroidery and glitter.

Jun had faded to a mere suggestion of shadows. This way he could sneakily observe people while I talked to them in case I missed something. Still, I was good at reading his expressions. He looked impressed, too.

"Sure," I said faintly as I contemplated the elegant stoneware teapot, the cups glazed with cherry blossom patterns, the tiny, delicate, sweet-smelling almond cookies. I had to admit I was hungry.

Haneul's gaze slid toward me, but she didn't say a word of greeting.

Well, if you're going to be that way about it . . . I took a seat next to Miho, kitty-corner from my friend. Maybe *former* friend, the way things were going. "I didn't know the ship had tea this nice."

"Taste it first," Miho said dryly. "It's jasmine."

I did. A little like green tea, with a hint of floral sweetness. I hadn't had anything resembling this before, not that that was saying much. No one in my family was a tea connoisseur.

"The Sun Clans ambassador sent it over at the beginning

of our journey," Miho said, "as a gift. I suppose she thinks we can be bribed."

That didn't sound promising. I reached for one of the cookies, on the grounds that food was made to be eaten.

Haneul glowered at me.

I considered confronting her, but if she wasn't going to use her words, why should I? Instead, I popped the whole cookie in my mouth and munched. It was crisp, lightly caramelized at the edges, and absolutely delicious. I swallowed, suppressing the urge to sigh in pleasure. "They must have great bakers in the Sun Clans," I said.

"They've been scanned for toxins, of course," Miho added as an afterthought.

My hand froze on the way to its second cookie. It hadn't occurred to me that Miho would consider me a threat. But, as Seok had warned me, some people would be glad to get rid of me so they could snatch the Pearl. And the fact that I knew Miho's true identity probably didn't help.

She laughed, but not unkindly. "I wouldn't serve you poison, Min! Not when you're the Bearer of the Dragon Pearl. Arguably the most important person on the ship who's not the captain."

I snatched the cookie and chomped on it.

Haneul didn't look like Miho's words sat well with her.

Once I would have preened over the compliment, but right now it bothered me, too. "Everyone's interested in what the Pearl can do for them." I hadn't meant it to come out in such a grumpy tone.

"It does represent a lot of power," Miho said.

I hesitated. Was that an opening? A threat?

And more to the point, how could I ask *her* the questions I wanted answers to when Haneul was sitting in the room?

Aha! I had it. I needed to find a way to offend Haneul so badly that she would storm off in a huff, leaving me an opportunity to talk to Miho in private. Given the frosty atmosphere between the two of us, that shouldn't be too difficult.

"Certain people on this ship don't think the Pearl should be in my hands," I said. "Which is too bad for them, because it's not their decision."

Just as I'd hoped, Haneul sucked in her breath like I'd slapped her.

"The Dragon Council provides a valuable service," Miho noted coolly.

I hadn't planned for her intervention in the discussion. "My homeworld—" I began to say.

Haneul cut me off. A gray cloud formed over her head, and the air was heavy with a hint of lightning. I would get zapped if I did something out of line, like snatching up a third cookie. It beat eating military rations, though, and if the Sun Clans wanted to provide us with delicious snacks, who was I to refuse them?

"Every planet is someone's homeworld," Haneul said. She met my eyes, and I was taken aback by the earnestness in them. Like she'd made up her mind to convince me. "Someone has to be first in line, and someone has to be last. And someone has to put everyone in priority order."

To my dismay, Miho was nodding. "There's a lot of truth to that," she said. "Some planets come with more resources than others, and those resources benefit everyone in the Thousand Worlds. Especially since dragon magic can only improve a world so much. If a planet has metals and minerals that can be used to build more starships for the Space Forces, of course the Dragon Council will prioritize it over a desert world with little to offer."

Miho's ready agreement made me mad. How could she speak so casually about condemning whole planets and their settlers to hardscrabble existences?

"You must come from a steader background," Miho went on. She caught my eye as though willing me to hear her out. "It's a hard life, and people fall through the cracks."

"It's one thing to say that," I snapped, "and another to live it." Had Miho ever known anything but luxury? It sure didn't seem like it.

"The Sun Clans claim, and the minister of defense believes, that this peace treaty will benefit us both," Miho said. "If we don't have to build as many ships, the Dragon Council will be able to shift its priorities."

"The Dragon Council only cares about lining its own pockets," I said coldly.

I'd gone into this squabble meaning to shoo Haneul out, not to debate in earnest. But as the words left my mouth, I found that they'd become real. I believed what I'd said.

It was funny to think of myself as someone who would get in a spitting match with one of my friends over a planet I'd barely spent any time on in the past year. A planet I'd once been desperate to leave behind forever, so I could serve with my brother Jun.

There were lots of things I didn't like about home. The haze of dust in the air despite the filters, and the fact that we had to wear special masks whenever we left one of the protective domes. Always having to fix the dishwasher and the generator and everything else that tended to break all at once because I had the cleverest hands and was the best with machines. Sharing a crowded bedroom with my cousins.

Shipboard food got dreary—tea aside—but at least it was plentiful. Even when I'd been a fake cadet aboard the *Pale Lightning*, I'd never had to worry that dinner would be scanty or go to bed with my stomach empty and growling. My mother and aunties had been scrupulously fair about dividing up food on the occasions we had to go short, taking care that the very youngest and the sick had enough to eat, but I remembered resenting the fact that I couldn't eat my fill, or that my dinner sometimes consisted of half a ration bar that had expired two years ago.

Haneul was looking at me with those betrayed eyes, as though I'd turned into a stranger. Maybe that wasn't wrong. She didn't know me, and I didn't know her. Not the way we'd thought we had.

"If that's the way you feel," Haneul said at last, "we don't have a lot to say to each other." She looked down at her plate, empty even of crumbs, as though she wished she could hold it up to hide her face.

Haneul rose and bowed politely to Miho. She'd always had beautiful manners. I would have envied her the deportment and etiquette classes, except, to be honest, I wouldn't have enjoyed them. Besides, Mom had drilled me on how to be polite. I wasn't going to let fancy upper-class manners intimidate me.

"Thank you for the tea, Assistant Minister," Haneul said in a low voice, with only a trace of strain. "I hope the mission goes well."

"Don't we all," Miho remarked with an answering nod.

Haneul walked out so softly I couldn't have told she was upset if not for the lingering static charge in the air and the sea-storm humidity. The next cookie I nabbed zapped me. I took that as a sign of her displeasure, although it wasn't enough to deter me from eating it.

After Haneul was gone, Miho leaned back in her chair and regarded me cynically. "So what is it you wanted to ask me that you couldn't risk your friend overhearing?"

I wasn't sure which alarmed me more, the fact that she'd seen through my ploy, or that she knew I had a history with Haneul.

As though she'd divined my thoughts, Miho said, "Haneul mentioned in passing that she'd met you aboard the *Pale Lightning.*"

I hoped Haneul hadn't mentioned that I was a fox . . . but if she had, Miho would have confronted me about it. "You're very persuasive," I said. It wasn't a compliment.

Miho shrugged. "Most people like to talk, if you give them the right incentive. Half the trick to using . . . certain techniques, let's say, is knowing when *not* to use them."

I frowned, wishing I could believe her. After all, hadn't she made a display of her Charm back at the party instead of using non-magical methods of persuasion and trickery? I was positive that Miho spent Charm freely, not least when attempting to intimidate her adversaries.

I didn't want to waste more time on paranoia, especially since I had no way of forcing Miho to answer my questions. And when it came to regular persuasion, two could play that game.

"There's something on Jasujeong that no one has told me

about," I said. Intuition told me the direct approach would be best. "Want to fill me in, or do I have to sneak around the ship spying on my own people?"

Miho's visage could have been a porcelain mask. "That's classified," she said at last.

"That's what the captain said. But I'm not messing with the planet until I have that information."

Miho shook her head ruefully. "If only I'd known . . ."

"Known what?" My heart thumped painfully. Had she finally figured out my true identity?

"That the Bearer is a magician. Of course, it makes sense. I'd wondered why the Pearl would attach itself to someone so young. We could have coordinated our efforts. . . . But never mind."

This only increased my determination not to use my fox powers around Miho. She'd confirmed that she was keeping secrets from me, ones that affected my mission. Safer to keep playing magician. "There's no reason," I suggested, "that we can't coordinate now."

"There are regulations about these things. I can't randomly divulge top-secret information."

I rolled my eyes. "Sometimes I think people make up rules and regulations because they have nothing better to do."

"You're not necessarily wrong," Miho murmured, "but some of the rules do have a purpose. And I can't exactly call home for authorization." All interstellar communication had to go by starship courier through the Gates, and we weren't in a position to go back home without completing our mission.

"Aren't you the highest-ranking person on this ship?" I demanded. After all, she was a *government official.*

I hadn't meant the question literally, but Miho answered as if I had. "Technically, that's Captain Chaewon," she said. "She's subject to Space Forces HQ and Ministry of Defense oversight, but when it comes to the implementation of any orders, she's the absolute authority."

I kicked myself internally, hoping that Miho couldn't scent my dismay. In my earlier inventory of the forces I had to contend with, from the Dragon Council to the government, I'd forgotten the Space Forces.

"Honestly, Miho," I said, permitting myself the insulting familiarity of using her personal name despite the difference in our ages, "how long do you think you can keep the secret from me? Are you going to make me close my eyes and stick my fingers in my ears the whole time we're on Jasujeong? Or is it an *invisible* secret?"

She regarded me for a long moment, then nodded slowly. "I had instructions to whisk you off-planet right after you did the deed," she said. "But now I see that wouldn't have worked."

Instructions from whom? I wanted to ask, except it was probably the minister of defense. Instead, I nodded, hoping it wasn't obvious that I was holding my breath in anticipation of her answer.

"Have you ever wondered why Jasujeong never *stayed* settled?"

I shrugged. "Too much conflict?"

Miho's mouth twisted. "That's never stopped steaders before." Before I could bristle, she added, "Steaders from either the Sun Clans or the Thousand Worlds, or even the realms beyond, like the Jeweled Worlds. Desperate people will always find a way to scratch out a living no matter how hostile the environment."

"Hostile . . ." I echoed. "Is the atmosphere poisonous?"

I'd only used the Dragon Pearl's terraforming magic once before, on the Fourth Colony. It was a deadly world, but not because of any fault in its environment—it had, in fact, once been a celebrated colony. But, thanks to the colonists' failure to honor the smallpox gods, everyone had been wiped out by disease. Future visitors had perished at the hands of vengeful ghosts. My job had been to provide the dead a proper funeral site and lay them to rest.

Seok had told me only that Jasujeong was a dangerous planet, even if it could sustain life. I wished now that I had grilled him for details while I had the chance. Would I have to, say, change a poisonous chlorine atmosphere into a breathable one? Dragon magicians spent years studying biochemistry, geology, meteorology, and other disciplines to make sure that the worlds they transformed were truly hospitable. All I had to rely on was the Pearl's magic—I hoped that would be enough. I'd heard horror stories about botched worlds.

Miho hesitated again, then nodded firmly, as though she'd come to a decision. "There's an ancient ship on Jasujeong, the *Sejong-Daewang*. Named after the king who invented the Hangeul alphabet. Old technology . . . *lost* technology. A dreadnought with superweapon capabilities that nobody has anymore. Whoever controls it will irrevocably shift the balance of power."

I narrowed my eyes at her. "So all that stuff about Jasujeong being in a strategic location is hot air?"

"It *is* strategic," she conceded. "It sits on top of a major Gate nexus. That alone would be enough to have the Thousand Worlds and Sun Clans vying over it. But the dreadnought is the real prize, and what makes Jasujeong unique."

I digested this. I didn't like having something this important kept from me when it came to a mission I was supposed to be an integral part of. Had Seok known and purposely left me in the dark, or had he been ignorant as well?

I was getting distracted by a side issue. Whatever Seok had or hadn't known, he wasn't aboard the *Haetae*. I had to make the most of the situation.

"Then my job," I guessed, "is to show up and destroy the *Sejong-Daewang* so *no one* can have it?"

"The minister of defense believes the ship has much to offer us as a historical artifact," Miho said. "Lost technologies that can help us build better ships, bigger cities. But the Sun Clans ambassador feels differently. If it were up to her, the ship would be cindered to prevent anyone from tipping the balance of power."

As she spoke, I made two piles of almond cookies, one for the Sun Clans and another for the Thousand Worlds. I laid a spoon in between, to represent Jasujeong and its dreadnought.

Miho's quirked lips suggested that she'd figured out why I was playing with my food.

"This isn't the kind of thing that the Thousand Worlds government is going to let *me* decide," I said, " 'Bearer of the Dragon Pearl' or not." The Thousand Worlds government didn't have an especially high opinion of me as a person, let alone as a fox spirit. Making me a Domestic Security agent had been a last-resort stopgap as far as they were concerned.

"No, it's not."

"How were they planning to stop me from destroying the ship?" All evidence suggested that they didn't trust my better nature.

"Well," Miho said with a touch of wry humor, "they weren't planning on telling you about it."

I picked up one of the Thousand Worlds cookies (or so I had labeled them in my head) and pulverized it. Crumbs dusted the table. Something didn't add up. "It would be very easy," I said, "for me to accidentally vaporize a ship I didn't know was there!"

"The minister of defense is hoping to have removed it before we get there. Without, I might add, the Sun Clans ambassador realizing what happened."

"Sounds like a great way to start a peace treaty," I said sarcastically.

"Regardless, the *Sejong-Daewang* won't be a factor by the time we arrive. So you see, there's no need for you to worry about it."

Miho smiled impersonally at me, and I knew I was dismissed. I took one last cookie for the road and headed out.

Only after I'd left the room did I realize that Miho had never said how *she* felt about preserving the ship.

TEN

Sebin

We reached Asa-Achim, the station that orbited Jasujeong, in the middle of the night, ship's time.

I stole a glimpse of the station during our approach. It was a vast cylindrical structure with an outer shell and an inner one. The outer shell rotated to simulate gravity, a design that a number of older stations and bases used. Modern stations relied on artificial-gravity generators instead.

I was awake to see it because Ensign Hak had told us the ship's ETA ahead of time. Besides, I was used to keeping odd hours thanks to the rigorous training regimen of my childhood. My friend Jee always looked horrified when I told him about being roused by my parents in the middle of the night to run evacuation drills. At the time I had known that my life might someday depend on my preparedness.

So I was at the airlock with Ensign Hak, in the dress version of my cadet's uniform, wide-awake despite a tiny complaining voice in the back of my head that observed I'd only gotten half my allotment of sleep. I remembered what Captain Chaewon had said about the honor of tigers everywhere riding on this. I couldn't afford any more screwups.

I was hardly the first to arrive. Captain Chaewon stood to the side like a dignified statue. She wouldn't be accompanying us to the station, but she was seeing us off.

Next to the captain stood Dragon Councilor Gwan, their apprentice Haneul, Assistant Minister of Defense Yang Miho, and Min, in that order.

Haneul looked as tense as I felt. I overheard Gwan murmuring to her, "Remember, your behavior reflects on *me*." No wonder Haneul was stressed all the time. Min, on the other hand, yawned openly, unfazed by the gravity of the mission.

A voice came over the intercom. "Station Asa-Achim gives you permission to board."

The hatch opened and the ramp extended into the station. At first all I saw was a surfeit of light, tinted golden like the sunlight on the planet where I'd grown up. Nothing like the sterile white light aboard the *Haetae*, which I had gotten used to over time.

One by one we trooped out into the station's docking bay. I tried not to stiffen at the assault of unfamiliar smells. Sweat, grease, dirt, rust—those I knew. But mingled with these were curiously gardenlike fragrances, as of flowers and nearly ripe fruits.

For that matter, the docking bay itself troubled me. The proportions seemed wrong, as though the place was too wide, the ceiling slightly too low. The decorations included installations of the flowers I had smelled, perfuming the air and leaving a snowdrift of pink-white petals everywhere.

"Move forward," Ensign Hak hissed at me, and I was jolted out of my trance. "Good-bye and good luck!"

I could tell from the slight hesitation that she had almost said *Good hunting*, as though this were a military mission. I hoped that wasn't a bad omen.

As I began moving obediently, the realization hit me. This station—or this part of it, anyway—hadn't been built by people from the Thousand Worlds. The architects must have come from the Sun Clans. I only had the faintest clue what Sun Clans architecture looked like, but it was the only explanation that made sense. This was a jointly held station.

I caught sight of the Sun Clans ambassador at the head of the welcoming party with her entourage. She couldn't have been anyone else. Her layers of robes were embroidered with the same five-petaled blossoms that grew, incongruously, in the docking bay. Accompanying her was a sturdy person in a practical gray uniform that I didn't recognize as either Sun Clans or Thousand Worlds. *Pirate?* I wondered, but that seemed even more unlikely.

"I'm Ajin," said the person in gray, "currently administrator of this station. I welcome you all aboard. Follow me."

Ajin had a dry voice almost devoid of emotion. But they smelled honest, if first impressions were good for anything, and I instinctively liked them. Maybe it was Ajin's military bearing.

Of course, my uncle had also had a military bearing, and I had liked him from the moment I first met him, and *that* hadn't turned out well.

As we walked, Min dawdled until we were side by side, taking advantage of the group's disorganization.

"Hello?" I said in an undertone, wondering what she wanted. I liked Min, but trouble followed her wherever she went. Then again, the same could be said of me, despite my best efforts.

"I've been trying to find you! Where have you been?"

Busy with my duties, because I have things to do, unlike some *people.* But I stopped myself from saying that. As occupied as I'd been on the ship with classes and routine maintenance tasks, I was hardly essential personnel on a mission like this, and I knew it. I consoled myself that standing around and smiling politely at people would at least be easy, if boring.

"You need to—"

At that point, I became aware that the diplomat to my left was shooting us curious glances.

"Is there something wrong with the accommodations?" the diplomat asked.

"Nothing wrong," Min said quickly. "Just catching up with a friend, that's all. Sebin—"

I couldn't very well quicken my step and walk ahead of her, given that she was much more important than I was. Instead, I mumbled an "Excuse me" and dropped back to bring up the rear. The smell of her frustration wafted back to me, but she resumed her walk.

The halls of the station gave me the same sense of alienness, and it was difficult to lower my guard. I realized with alarm that someone was piping in music, and the sounds, too, were alien. My family hadn't been particularly musical, but the Matriarch had sometimes allowed us to listen to recordings of solo singers accompanied by the gayageum, a traditional plucked zither, and occasionally also the piri, a traditional wooden flute. This music featured some kind of Sun Clanner stringed instrument, which someone had mentioned was called a biwa, but beyond that I knew nothing useful. Pretty, in a melancholy sort of way.

With a start I realized that Ajin had been speaking, although I had been too distracted by the disconcerting sights and sounds and smells to pay attention to the chatter up front.

"You might be interested in the music," Ajin was saying.

"The performer is one of those rare people of both Thousand Worlds and Sun Clans heritage, and she has made it her life's mission to learn instruments from both sides and perform in a multiplicity of styles."

All too soon we arrived at a banquet hall. This reminded me of the reception that Haneul and I had crashed back on Station Ssangyong, and yet it, too, was alien. Trees in large pots had been arranged around the hall's perimeter, featuring more of those five-petaled pink flowers.

The decor didn't resemble anything I'd seen in the Thousand Worlds. The five traditional colors that we favored were black, red, blue, green, and yellow. Here, everything from the wallpaper to the tablecloths was in gentle pastels—pinks and lavenders and soft sea greens. The very colors discomfited me.

The music was louder here, although not so loud that it made it difficult to understand conversation. It came from speakers arranged around the hall. With my keen hearing, I could pinpoint the location of each and every one.

More than anything else, though, the smells overwhelmed me. Unfamiliar fruits and vegetables, meats in strange sauces, and . . . that wasn't raw fish, was it? At least the rice was familiar. Mingled with them were Thousand Worlds dishes, from sautéed bracken fiddleheads to mandu dumplings, and, of course, gimchi.

The only incongruous thing were the guards, dressed in utilitarian gray uniforms similar to Administrator Ajin's. They circulated in a pattern that I recognized was meant to maximize coverage of the area, rather than being as random as it might look at first glance. One of them, perhaps trying for festive cheer, had a spray of blossoms tucked behind his ear.

"After a long journey," Ajin said, gesturing expansively at the banquet laid out for us, "the least we can do is offer you the hospitality of the station."

It was the middle of the night, so I was hardly hungry. I couldn't imagine that anyone else was, either. Well, maybe the Sun Clans delegation was. I had no idea how their timekeeping worked.

"We're honored," the Sun Clans ambassador said with a radiant smile. "To be honest, I'm famished."

Whether or not she was telling the truth, we understood the cue. I trailed after Min, feeling superfluous. I would much rather have joined the gray-uniformed guards circulating through the hall than be cadet-shaped eye candy. But Captain Chaewon had made my role clear, and I was determined not to disappoint her.

While Min struck up a conversation with some Sun Clans guard, who looked just as uncomfortable as I felt, I made a show of picking up a plate and dishing some food onto it. I told myself that none of it would be poisoned, which was probably true. Besides, my family had taught me that tiger spirits were immune to most toxins. I knew it was unlikely anyone was watching *me* all that closely, but I made a point of picking up things I didn't recognize to show I wasn't afraid.

You didn't prepare me for this, I thought at my long-ago family. Only now did it occur to me that neither my grandmother, the Matriarch, nor my parents, nor my aunt Sooni, had ever specified exactly *who* our enemies were. I'd simply gone along because I hadn't known any better.

Well, I thought glumly, *it's not like I'm going to see any action on this mission.* I looked around at the milling guests and guards. To be honest, I expected the hardest part of my job would be concealing my boredom with the song and dance of negotiations and people talking everything to death. None of my training was going to do me any good here. If I was lucky, there might be a firing range or a rec room where I could keep in fighting shape, assuming *that* wouldn't jeopardize the peace talks.

It turned out that the real problem with the mystery food wasn't its taste. I tried one of the rolls of vinegar rice, raw fish, and seaweed with a dab of some green spicy substance and discovered I liked it very much, to the point where I wondered if the recipe was a state secret. (But really, if the fish was *raw*, how much of a secret could its preparation be?)

No—the real issue was that I had no idea *how* to eat some of the tantalizing foodstuffs. At least the utensils were the same spoon and chopsticks that we used in the Thousand Worlds. I had heard that some nations used different ones, but I found such a thing difficult to picture. Imagination isn't my strong point. The Sun Clans had dumplings similar to our mandu, which someone let slip were called gyoza.

Some of the other delicacies, however, stumped me. Was I supposed to eat the slippery seaweed salad with rice, or by itself? Was it okay to use the green spicy paste on other foods, or was that strictly for use with the raw fish? Was sucking down the delicious noodles okay, and should I drink the broth directly from the soup bowl?

After fifteen minutes, I realized that no one was paying attention to my manners. Or if they were, mine weren't notably worse than those of the other people in the delegation. Min, for instance, happily slurped her noodles, so I decided to fol- low her lead.

I was starting to relax and pay attention to the conversation rather than the food and the awkwardness of being among strangers. I'd had to get over my insular background before—I'd been raised on the Matriarch's estate, and the only visitors she allowed were family—when I joined the Space Forces, but in fact, I had only traded one family for another, that of the *Haetae* and its crew. I hadn't actually spent much time around anyone else.

I'd lost track of Min again. Thankfully, she wasn't hard to locate. After scanning the room, I spotted her over by the gyoza. She moved around a lot. Apparently, she had more of an appetite than I did. Then again, I imagined that the Bearer of the Dragon Pearl could keep her own schedule. Stay up all night (ship's time) playing video games and wake up at noon. Maybe she hadn't gotten a proper dinner the way I had.

Other than Haneul, who was following the dragon councilor like a faithful if resentful shadow over on the other side of the banquet hall, Min was the only person close to my age. I was so focused on her, and so confounded by the elegant but alien surroundings, that I almost jumped out of my skin when the Sun Clans ambassador floated up next to me.

"We haven't been introduced, Cadet," she said in very good Hangeul. Certainly much better than my nonexistent Nihongo, the major language of the Sun Clans. "I imagine you know who I am."

I was instantly wary. "Of course, Ambassador."

"You're the tiger cadet, aren't you?"

It discomfited me that she knew that about me, even though every single person on this diplomatic mission would have been vetted three times over. She probably had a dossier on all of us. I wondered what mine said.

"That's correct, Ambassador," I said at my politest.

"What do *you* think of the peace mission?"

She was certainly direct. I would have appreciated the quality in anyone else, anytime else, but right now I felt put on the spot. "It will be good for both our nations." A rote response, and I doubted it convinced her.

The ambassador began to say something when she was interrupted by the blare of alarms. The soothing music—I'd already developed a taste for it—and the gentle, sunlike light were replaced by flashing red lights like a bloody tide.

"What—" I began to say, realizing I had no idea where the exits were, or what the evacuation protocols were for this station. No one had briefed me on them.

I couldn't tell whether the Ambassador had blanched, or whether that was a trick of the light.

Before either of us could get out another word, a tremendous concussive explosion thundered from outside the banquet hall. More sirens went off. A shock wave passed through the hall and swept the dishes with their delicacies off the tables.

I shifted into my tiger form and knocked the ambassador down, no doubt a diplomatic gaffe in itself, although I only intended to protect her from any flying shrapnel. She made a muffled sound of protest, quickly stifled. Perhaps she realized what I was trying to do.

Above the shrieks and tumult, I heard Ajin's bellow: "Everyone follow the path lights to the escape pods! The station is no longer secure. I repeat, the station is no longer secure."

We're under attack, I thought, stunned. I had a moment to wonder why the explosion hadn't taken out the banquet hall itself—surely the most decisive way to snuff out the peace talks. But there was no time to think, or to investigate.

I shifted back into human form and rolled off the ambassador.

"Go," she cried. "My people will escort me." Indeed, two Sun Clans guards, their eyes wild, were already advancing toward her.

I saw the lighted paths that Administrator Ajin had referred to, presumably leading to the escape pods. I hesitated, glancing back at the chaos. People were shouting, gesticulating, fighting. I had no idea what was going on.

Then Min and her bodyguard caught up to me. "Come on, Sebin!" she hissed, grabbing my arm.

Another explosion thundered. That decided the matter. I wouldn't be of any use if I stayed here. I would follow the administrator's orders. "This way!" the bodyguard shouted. Together, she, Min, and I sprinted toward the pods.

ELEVEN

Min

Silhouette led us to the escape pods. She and Sebin and I reached one just ahead of Haneul. I knew the moment she showed up because her personal rain cloud drenched me from top to bottom. My toes squished wetly in my shoes.

"Where's the dragon councilor?" I demanded.

I followed Haneul's gaze back over my shoulder. Her eyes were red, but that might have been the flashing lights. "They told me to get out of the way."

Despite the chaos around us, despite the earsplitting noise, I could hear the hurt in her voice. Smell it, too, combined with the reek of fear.

All of us had keen vision, made less helpful by the on-off glare of the red lights. Sebin spotted the dragon councilor first. "They're following path lights in the other direction," Sebin reported. "They'll be fine. Come on, we've got to get out of here!"

Sebin fumbled at the controls. *They must really be shaken*, I thought.

"I wish I could help," Jun murmured to me, sounding crestfallen.

I hoped the bad luck he carried with him wouldn't affect our escape, but it would have been cruel to say that out loud.

"Here, let me," Silhouette snapped. She quickly got it open. "Get in."

I nodded at Sebin, who hesitated, then stepped aside.

The door sprang open. We almost trampled each other in our haste to clamber inside. Even Jun floated *through* me, a chilly and unpleasant sensation. There were six seats, and I had a fleeting moment of relief that it wasn't unlucky four, *four* for *death*.

Silhouette lingered outside.

"Come on," I urged her, panic seizing me at the thought of being trapped on this station. "We're not leaving without you." I regretted all my earlier pettiness toward her and thought about gasping out an apology, but the words stuck in my throat.

Silhouette's mouth twisted in a rueful smile. "With only three of you, the air will last longer."

I lunged for her, hoping to drag her in anyway, but she slammed the button and the hatch closed in my face.

"Silhouette!" I screamed, but it was too late.

The pod launched.

Silhouette must have overridden the controls from the station. For my part, I was flung back against the wall of the pod. The others had possessed enough sense to buckle up, but I hadn't had the opportunity.

My world narrowed to the pod and its seats, and the two cadets' faces—Haneul's pale, Sebin's stoic.

What about the peace mission? I wondered ruefully.

None of us, myself included, could complete the peace mission if we were blown to smithereens.

The acceleration eased off, and I spidered my way to the

nearest seat, next to my controls, and strapped myself in. I held back my tears. Maybe Silhouette had already found an escape pod of her own. I had to believe that.

A chill breathed against my cheek. "She'll be fine," Jun said. "Silhouette's a survivor."

I choked back a sob of gratitude.

The pod vibrated furiously, then accelerated again with a suddenness that made me swallow a scream. I wasn't the only one. Sebin emitted an un-tigerlike squeak and Haneul bit her lip so hard I was sure she was bleeding.

The only one who didn't react was Jun. For a second, I was afraid he would float out the side and be left behind, but fortunately he had more control of his location than that. Besides, he was connected to me, so wherever I went, he did, too.

Silhouette . . .

Better not to think about her, and instead figure out how we were going to survive this. I couldn't afford to fall apart, not now, no matter how much I regretted leaving her behind. Later, I promised myself, I would find out if she had survived.

On a more mundane note, I wasn't looking forward to spending the rest of this interlude in my drenched clothes. Thousand Worlds equipment would have been hardened against foibles like a dragon spirit's personal weather system, but whoever had designed *this* escape pod hadn't allowed for that possibility. Already I was beginning to shiver in the miserable damp. The chill that accompanied Jun didn't help, either.

"Where are we going?" Haneul thought to ask.

We all looked out the single viewport, although the view was dismal. The shielded glass was tinted dark, like sunglasses. For a moment all we could see were the stars like scattered jewels and the several moons of Jasujeong floating close by. The pod was tumbling slowly, causing the view to shift in a way that made my stomach roil. The curse of being planet-born and expecting a fixed *up* and *down*.

I considered using the pod's thrusters to neutralize the spin, but we only had so much fuel and I wanted to save it in case we needed it later. Needless to say, I wasn't so cruel as to mention this to the other two. They had enough on their minds as it was.

"We could get into the sleeper units," Haneul said reluctantly. She gestured to the casket-shaped units in the back of the pod. "In hibernation we'd use less oxygen."

"We'd also be helpless to correct our course or avoid other trouble," Sebin said. "Best to save that for a last resort."

"With any luck," I said, striving to control the quaver in my voice, "we'll be flung into orbit until—"

Then the tumbling brought the station into view. A gasp escaped me before I could stop it.

Earlier, Asa-Achim had been a serene, imposing pair of cylindrical shells, many times larger than either the *Haetae* or the Sun Clanners' *Hokusai*. It had seemed impossible that anything could threaten something of its bulk.

Now, half the station was a flaming wreck, its shell shattered as though a monster of flame and spite had hatched out of it. I tried to visualize the layout of the station, superimpose it on the spinning exterior. I couldn't manage it, not with my nausea.

"Oh no," Jun said thinly.

"That's what we escaped," Sebin said in a dry near-whisper.

Had Silhouette gotten away in time? What about everyone else on the station?

"Look at those holes," Haneul said, also quietly despite the fact that there was no one else to hear us, and only vacuum outside the pod. "It's venting atmosphere. I don't—I don't know if anyone in those sections is going to be able to breathe. Assuming they weren't expelled by the decompression, too."

Before we had much opportunity to reflect on that depressing and all-too-real scenario, the station exploded. Fire and light rushed out like a furious tide. Metal shards sped past us, almost too fast to be seen.

"The station!" Sebin exclaimed, almost a curse, into the silence.

That was the other thing: The lack of sound in vacuum made the sheer level of devastation seem unreal. Even in the holo dramas I'd once watched of brave captains fighting off pirates in ship-to-ship battles, they'd included sound effects so that every explosion was suitably punctuated by thunder and percussion.

It wasn't entirely silent inside the pod, of course. I could hear the slight whine of the electronics and the thrumming of the life-support machinery we'd be depending on until someone rescued us. But those were such small sounds, just a whisper, in comparison.

Maddeningly, the escape pod continued its inexorable rotation, so the station sank out of our sight like a conflagrant sunset.

"I can't believe that just happened," Haneul said. Her hair was dripping. The only reason I hadn't noticed *my* hair was dripping was that it was already soaked through.

In fact, we were *all* drenched. The life-support filters whirred as they kicked up a notch to deal with all the moisture.

I didn't bother asking Haneul to tone it down. She wasn't stupid—I could tell she was doing her best from the chagrin on her face as she pushed errant, kelp-slick strands of hair back behind her ear.

We were so torn between the escape pod's increasingly uncomfortable interior and the horror of what we'd just witnessed that it took a moment for all of us, even experienced Haneul and Jun, and militant Sebin, to realize we had landed in another kind of trouble altogether.

A loud, bell-like signal replaced the previously unnatural quiet. I was stumped for a moment. Earlier, we'd known that the red lights and blaring meant Bad News. But alarms were standardized across the Thousand Worlds, more or less. Oh, there were occasionally differences due to obsolete equipment, but I knew the general trends.

"Oh no," Haneul said, "what does *that* mean?"

"I wish they'd briefed us on safety protocols *before* offering food that I couldn't eat anyway," Jun said grimly.

This entire escape pod, despite its helpful bilingual labels in both Hangeul and Nihongo, didn't follow Thousand Worlder conventions. I took a shaky breath and dug through the control panel's menus, praying to the celestial dragons and the ancestor foxes that the water wouldn't knock it out of commission.

"Uh, Min?" It was Sebin.

"Not now," I growled, too tense to be polite. I muttered a curse under my breath as the words came up in bright red. At least both cultures agreed that red meant *bad news*.

"No, really, I think you should see this—"

Haneul's eyes met mine. "Proximity alert," we said at the same time.

"That's what I meant," Sebin said, aggravated. *"Look out the viewport."*

I did. My heart clenched painfully when a jagged shard whizzed right by us. It had missed us by—a couple meters? Less than that? Without a way to measure distances in the black void of space, I couldn't be sure.

"Whew," I said.

But the proximity alert didn't stop blaring.

This time, I could tell for sure that both Haneul and Sebin had paled. Jun, of course, was always pale.

"Min," Sebin said, and swallowed dryly. I could see their Adam's apple bobbing in an uncharacteristic display of nerves. "Min, the station's explosion flung debris in all directions. That probably wasn't the last of the—"

The proximity alert let out one more shriek. And then something hit us.

None of us could see what it was. I hoped it was a piece of the station, as opposed to a body. I didn't think I could bear it if I had to look at corpses.

The control panel's message changed. Now it said ORBITAL DECAY.

"That's not good," Haneul said feelingly.

Sebin frowned. "More trouble?"

I punched in some commands, bringing up a diagram. "More trouble," I confirmed. "Because the planet is contested territory and also apparently super unfriendly, we don't want to land on it if we can help it. We're *supposed* to stay in orbit until friendly forces pick us up."

I tried not to think about the fact that both the *Haetae* and the Sun Clans' *Hokusai* had been docked on the station and we had no idea whether either ship had survived. What if they had gone down with the station, instead of being able to evacuate in time?

The diagram showed the orbit we were *supposed* to be in, indicated with a tranquil green circle. Our new orbit—or more accurately, crash trajectory—appeared as a stark red curve heading inexorably down toward the planet of Jasujeong.

"We've been knocked off course," I added, "but we have some thrusters. It might be possible to maneuver back into orbit."

Haneul looked at Sebin. Whatever animosity had existed between them previously, it was gone now. "Do it," she said. "Meanwhile, we should all suit up in case—in case of hull puncture."

I wished she hadn't brought the possibility up and jinxed us, but Haneul was right. Even if we survived a collision, or a puncture, the vacuum outside could kill us. And that was something entirely preventable.

Besides, if anyone had jinxed us, it was Jun. This was a precarious situation to begin with, and Jun's bad luck hadn't helped. From his chagrined silence, I knew he realized this, too.

In silence, Sebin and Haneul retrieved the suits from the compartments, helpfully marked in both languages. I noted the compartment closest to me but didn't put mine on yet. I had no time to lose if I was going to counteract the escape pod's torturous descent.

"Come on," I crooned under my breath. I liked to imagine that talking to machines encouraged them to behave. This wasn't the first time I'd worked with unfamiliar equipment. How hard could it be?

Pretty hard, it turned out. The issue wasn't the interface, despite my initial misgivings. While it wasn't the same as a Thousand Worlds design, the menu options were easily visible and put in a logical order. Adjusting to the system was less difficult than I had anticipated.

Give me options, I thought at the pod's small onboard computer.

It was trying. The problem was, we didn't have much time, and—oh no.

By then, Sebin and Haneul had both suited up. It had taken them a long time, given their experience as cadets, I assumed because there were some inexplicable differences between Sun Clanner equipment and ours. I hadn't really been paying attention, preoccupied as I was by the pod's control system.

"Something *else* is wrong," Jun said quietly. "I can tell from your face."

I hadn't been making any attempt to smooth over my expression. Besides, Jun had always been able to tell how I felt. I jabbed at the control panel again, futilely. "I have a choice," I said, "and it comes down to math."

Sebin made a face. Haneul nodded as if she had expected as much.

"I can use what remains of our fuel to get us into a higher orbit," I said, "but we don't have enough to achieve a *stable* orbit. At best it's just going to delay the inevitable. And that won't leave us any margin for evasive maneuvers if there's more shrapnel, or if there are pirates or other hostiles."

"There's another option," Sebin said, studying my face intently. "But it isn't any good, either."

Jun winced. He was radiating guilt so strongly I wondered if the others were picking up on it.

"I can save our fuel," I said, "and soften our landing. That'll also allow us to—"

The proximity alert stopped tolling. I didn't have any time to breathe a sigh of relief, though, because a completely different alert, one that sounded unbearably shrill, replaced it.

HULL BREACH, the display said now.

We foxes are nimble, but I had forgotten how fast Sebin could move when they were motivated. They all but tore open the second-nearest compartment and shoved a suit at me. "Put it on!" Sebin shouted.

If I'd been in fox form, my ears would have flattened against the back of my skull. I didn't like being yelled at. But this was not the time to argue. I unharnessed myself, then began pulling on the suit and its boots.

"Don't fight it," Sebin advised me, although I was tempted to do just that. This wasn't like any Thousand Worlds suit I had ever donned—an experience that was becoming a theme. "Just wrap it around yourself and let it do its thing."

I didn't like the idea of cocooning myself in a suit I hadn't had a chance to check, assuming there *was* a way to check it. Thousand Worlds spacesuits looked like, well, spacesuits, made of tough metal-weave fabric and hardened, articulated joints plus a helmet with a faceplate that filtered out radiation and an accompanying air tank.

The Sun Clans suit, on the other hand, resembled nothing so much as a blanket. A sheer pink blanket with tasteful . . . was that *embroidery*? And yet it flowed to conform to the shape of my body, even forming a hood over my head.

My instinct was to shift into my fox shape and claw it off rather than allow myself to be smothered. For a moment I almost did.

"Don't!" Jun said sharply. "You'll be fine."

Sebin and Haneul were clad in suits that looked similar to the ones I knew, and neither of them had been strangled or turned into blanket monsters. And besides, if I didn't trust them here and now, who *could* I trust?

So I forced myself to hold still. The blanket-thing came up over my head. To my surprise, it formed a panel in the front through which I could see clearly. In a matter of moments, despite the stink of seawater and sweat and my own dread, it had transformed itself wholly into a suit.

"Look," I said shakily, making exaggerated mouth movements so that the other two could read my lips. Who knew how long our supply of air would last now that we had a breach. The readouts had assured us of a month's air originally, but the gauge now showed the supply rapidly running out. The puncture must be a bad one. If the projection was correct, we had hours at best. "Waiting it out in the pod is no longer an option. We're going to have to crash-land."

Haneul's eyes went wide, although she had to have known that this was coming. She gulped, then pulled herself together. "There must be supplies in this pod," she said. "Min, you'll have to guide our touchdown and hope for a soft landing. Sebin, you and I will have to brace for the landing. Afterward, we'll scavenge what we can."

"Sounds like a plan," I said, and returned my attention to the control panel. Funny how something that looked like the world's most boring video game controlled our fates.

Seriously, while the interface was easy for anyone with the slightest bit of technical training to figure out, it lacked the pizzazz of a good video game. Not that there had been many of *those* during my childhood. Jun had taught me how to play traditional board games like baduk and yutnori, and my cousins and I had grown up playing make-believe and tag on the rare occasion when we'd had respite from chores. One of the neighbors had let us borrow a game console on holidays, but that had only lasted a couple years before it broke down.

And here I was again, with a broken-down escape pod. Story of my life.

"Hang on," I said. Sebin and Haneul were already braced for maneuvers, such as they were. Both of them looked much calmer than I felt. I couldn't decide whether I preferred the nerves or the nausea.

I wrestled the pod around so the main thrusters faced the planet and caused us to decelerate. They made a dull roaring sound, and I was relieved to see our rate of descent slow to something survivable.

"Got it!" I crowed. Objectively speaking, there wasn't that much to celebrate. But now we had a chance, at least.

With what remained of the fuel, I pointed the escape pod toward the joint military base on Jasujeong, thanking all the ancestral foxes that I'd paid attention to *that* portion of Seok's briefing. I hoped my aim was good.

As we plummeted to the surface, I caught a glimpse of another red-glowing falling star—an escape pod just like ours. Who was in it, and would we land anywhere near them?

TWELVE

Sebin

I woke up on another planet.

Which was a shame because I'd been having such excellent dreams. At least, they started as excellent dreams. I was a tiger (why had I not taken on my tiger form for so long?), lying on my side in a sunbeam back at the Matriarch's estate.

It was a great sunbeam, as sunbeams went. In the dream I could feel the caress of wind in my fur, which needed grooming—tigers are just as fussy about cleanliness as house cats, if not more so—and the fragrance of flowers tickled my nostrils. I felt warm and cozy, as though I were wrapped in a blanket. No self-respecting tiger would admit to wanting a blanket, though. Especially when I had a fine coat of orange-and-black striped fur.

Lazily, I pried open one of my eyes, at which point I noticed that there was something weird about the sunbeam. The Matriarch's estate had been located on a beautifully terraformed planet, complete with white-gold sunshine and well-behaved weather, so that it never rained on the days she wanted to take a walk in the garden or hunt some deer.

The sunbeam here, on the other hand, had a green-purple hue, like that of vegetation gone putrid. I could almost *smell* the rot, a sickly sweetness that made my nose wrinkle. I couldn't imagine why the Matriarch would have allowed her cosseted property, with its flowers and tall grasses, to reach such a state.

Also, I heard dripping water. The sound of droplets hitting a hard surface, rather than the friendly earth.

"Sebin! Wake up!" a voice was saying. A voice I should have recognized.

Someone else spoke, softer but no less worried. "Do you think they have a concussion?"

"I'm not concussed," I protested, eyes still mostly closed. I wondered why everything smelled of water and sweat, sap and charred metal.

My eyes flew open at the sound of my own voice . . . and at the smell of blood, which I had managed not to notice before. Quite a feat, considering a tiger's predatory nature. Blood didn't automatically make me hungry—I wasn't a *beast*—but normally I noticed it before anything else in the environment.

I struggled to sit up. I wasn't a tiger, but in my human form. A rip in my spacesuit explained the odors coming in from the environment, which ordinarily should have been filtered out.

Panic gripped me. "Dak-Ho? Yui?" I was supposed to be watching over the younger cadets, wasn't I?

"Stay down," Haneul said as she fiddled with my suit. I recognized her voice now, even though her face was a blur. "Dak-Ho and Yui must be safe with the rest of the *Haetae*'s crew. They'll be all right." Her voice quavered slightly.

"We can't hole up in here forever," Min argued. Hers was the first voice I'd heard when I drifted back toward wakefulness.

"Did we land safely?" I asked. Memories of our crash landing slowly returned to me. I was worried about the state of my vision, but slowly the two others' faces came into focus, and then a third, transparent one, belonging to Min's ghostly brother, Jun. Min and Haneul retained their spacesuits, while Jun didn't need one. I hoped my improved sight meant that I didn't have a concussion, because that would suck. Last I checked, this escape pod didn't have any kind of medical unit for people with injuries.

I looked at the others, reminding myself that the goal was for all of us to survive, and a little injury on my part was no big deal. Min had bruises along the side of her face, visible even through her suit's visor. Haneul, like me, had suffered a suit breach, and while she'd sealed it using a substance I didn't recognize, I could still smell dried blood. At least Jun was immune to physical damage.

"We're shaken up but otherwise fine," Haneul reassured me. "I'd hate to waste the heavy-duty stuff in the medical kit for a bunch of bruises. None of us is qualified to carry out field surgery anyway."

I could tell she was putting on a brave face for our benefit. As a tiger, I could scent her stress and fear, as distinct as a fingerprint.

"How bad is it?" I asked.

Min hacked up a laugh. "What do you think?" She gestured around.

We hadn't left the shelter of the escape pod, such as it was, but the force of the landing must have knocked me out. I couldn't remember what had happened in those last moments, just the growing heat of our descent as the pod built up friction with the planet's atmosphere, and then bracing for impact. The impact itself—well, maybe it was better that I didn't recall it.

The pod's computer systems must have shorted out, because there was no light except what came through the cracks in the pod's walls. *That* had a murky quality, as though filtered through particulates or fog of some sort.

"Air's breathable, at least," Min continued briskly. "The gravity's surprisingly close to Thousand Worlds standard, maybe a bit lighter. Those were the last things I was able to verify before the computers and sensor suite went down. We can ditch our suits if you want. It would probably be a good idea, since the climate is so hot."

This made sense, and the three of us who were living gladly shed our suits. I didn't want to survive a crash landing only to be felled by heatstroke.

"This is all my fault," Jun said, chagrined, his long hair waving in the opposite direction of the wind that filtered into the pod. "I attract bad luck. If only you'd gotten one of the shamans at the party to exorcise—"

"Don't," Min snapped. She stank suddenly of acrid desperation, so thick that I could almost taste it on the back of my tongue. "I'm not giving up on you."

"Well, there's no shaman here," Haneul added, her gaze darting between Min and her ghostly brother as though she wished she could physically step between them. "Besides, we might need your help to survive."

"I'll do my best," Jun promised.

"First things first," I said. "*Where* did we land?"

Min pointed behind me to a panel that she and Haneul must have wrenched free after the pod landed. One of its edges was jagged, and I winced, thinking of the force that had caused it to break. "We found this," Min said.

It wasn't, I realized upon closer inspection, just a panel. Somebody had scratched a crude map of Jasujeong into it. There was a big symbol on one location, like the X on a treasure map.

"That's a good idea," I said grudgingly. "But the fact remains that we're stranded on this planet. I don't suppose this pod comes with a way to send a distress signal?"

Min's face fell, which told me the answer was going to be unpleasant. "Well . . . yes and no."

I didn't understand this. Either we had a working distress signal or we didn't. I hoisted myself up, trying to get oriented.

"If only we'd thought to use the pod's comm system while we were still in orbit," Jun lamented. "We might have gotten a message out."

"We're out of power," Min said. "But the survival kit"—Haneul held it up—"contains a distress beacon. It also has all the non-medical stuff, like screwdrivers and ration bars and batteries. There are two problems with using the beacon."

Better than *four* problems, but I didn't say that out loud. *Think positive.*

"One," Min said, "we have a limited supply of batteries. Two . . ." She hesitated, then gave herself a little shake, as though telling herself, *Chin up.* "The distress beacon broadcasts in the clear. Anyone in the area will be able to hear us."

We all looked at one another. "In other words," I said, voicing what my companions were reluctant to state outright, "we'd be telling whoever blew the station up exactly how to finish the job."

Haneul drooped. "I can't believe anyone would do something so horrible."

Min hesitated, then patted Haneul's shoulder awkwardly. "I know we haven't been on the best of terms lately—"

"It's not you." Color rose to Haneul's cheeks as words spilled out of her in a rush. "I'm being trained to succeed Dragon Councilor Gwan. At first I thought it would be nice to be important, just like having the Dragon Pearl makes *you* important. But Gwan only cares about political games and prestige, and I'd rather go back to being a cadet in the Space Forces. My parents will be disappointed . . . if I live to tell them."

Min's breath huffed out. "Working under Gwan must have been tough."

"Yes." Haneul looked at her, eyes softening. "But it doesn't matter anymore. What's important now is *us*—working together."

Min nodded, and the tension between the two eased for the first time since they'd both come aboard the *Haetae*.

"We don't even know if the dragon councilor—" I started.

"Maybe everyone managed to escape," Jun said. "We did get some warning before the final explosion. . . ."

"Maybe," Min echoed, not sounding entirely convinced. She scrubbed at her eyes. "I kind of liked Ambassador Tanaka, even if she was on the other side. Her *and* her almond cookies."

"Well, what's done is done," I said, although I didn't want to believe it either. "And the enemy could still be out there."

Part of me wanted to be a cub again, curl up and look for that elusive sunbeam, and let someone else take care of our dilemma. But that wasn't an option. Thanks to bad luck and circumstance, we four had ended up on the same escape pod, without a senior officer or Min's heroic bodyguard. From here on out, survival was up to us.

I thought furiously. It wasn't exactly comfortable in this smashed-up pod with its cracks and stench and the incessant sound of dripping water, but getting shot at or—

A spine-chilling howl reverberated through the air. It made the walls of the pod, mangled as they were, vibrate in sympathy.

"What was *that?*" Min asked in a threadbare whisper.

"Jasujeong is classified Yellow Three," I said just as quietly. "Technically habitable by Thousand Worlders . . . but with natural hazards like poisonous plants and wild animals. I bet that was one of them."

"I'm a dragon and you're a tiger," Haneul said, her voice firming. "I don't think we have a lot to fear."

"That's easy for you to say," Min objected. "Foxes are prey as well as predators."

"So pretend to be a tiger," Haneul said. "This is your chance to put your shape-shifting powers to good use."

"I'll scout and see what's out there," Jun said. Before anyone could object, he vanished in a swirl of chilly air that stung my eyes and nose.

Min stared glumly after him. "He did that because he's feeling guilty."

"It's not a bad idea," I said reassuringly. "He's faster than we are, and I don't think anything on this planet can harm a ghost."

"What kinds of predators do you think live on this planet, anyway?" Min asked. "If I'd realized that we were going to be stranded down here, I would have done more research. . . ."

"I think the time for research is past," I muttered. "Let's make sure we've gathered all the supplies in this pod."

I helped double-check. Not much had survived beyond a first-aid kit containing things like painkillers, antibiotics, and bandages, which Haneul claimed, and the survival kit, which Min hung on to. She also had the makeshift map under her arm.

"Let me see that," I said. "If something happens and we get separated, or worse, we'll need to have this memorized so the survivors can carry on."

Haneul frowned at me. I could smell her disapproval of my pessimism.

In the distance I heard the eerie howling again. The sound made me uncomfortable, but not because I feared monsters. It was the uncertainty. I had no idea what to expect on Jasujeong.

"Sebin's right," Min said. "We could get separated. Someone might get injured. We might even"—she gulped—"lose the map. There's no telling what could go wrong. Especially since . . . since we're traveling with a ghost. We have to be prepared for every possibility."

Sobered by her words, we crowded around the makeshift map. No matter how ambivalent my feelings were toward my family, whom I would never see again, I thanked them once more for teaching me rigor and discipline, giving me the ability to memorize things like this on short notice. Sometimes I was afraid that my family's crimes would rub off on me, especially at times like this; but surely it was harmless to use the skills I had so painstakingly learned to help us all survive.

"This is all very well," I said, "but *where* are we going? Literally to 'heaven marks the spot'?" I looked at the character for *heaven* drawn on the map with a grease pencil, which resembled nothing so much as a tent with two platforms on top.

"It's a pun," Min said, regaining a smidgen of her usual cheer. "According to some intel I got my hands on, that's the site of an ancient starship. Both the Sun Clans and Thousand Worlds were squabbling over it, but that's not the part that matters to us. If we can get to the ship—assuming it's still there—maybe we can use it to leave this planet."

"Ancient as in how ancient?" I demanded. "There's no guarantee it still works."

Haneul's expression had gone still and sober. "The Dragon Council believes the ship is fully operational."

I looked from Haneul to Min. "And Domestic Security thinks so, too?"

Min's somber face told me everything I needed to know. *"Everyone,"* she said carefully, "agrees that the ship is operational. There are people who wish it wasn't. Probably the people who bombed the station."

"Then they're going to be expecting us to head toward the ship. Every survivor will be going there," I said.

"We don't have any better option," Haneul said.

"All we have to do," Min added, "is get there first." Her face lit up with impish glee. "Once Jun gets back, maybe one of you could give me a ride? I'll be loaded down with all this stuff, and I can't shift into a really large form. I'll slow you down otherwise." After a moment, she added, "I'm sure Jun will be here shortly."

The howl came again.

"We better get moving soon," I said.

I waited until we had all exited the smoldering remnants of the escape pod to flow into my tiger shape. Good thing we'd shucked our suits, or shape-shifting wouldn't have been viable. Most of my senses were heightened in this form. Here, danger only enhanced the effect.

I was hit as though by a wall of fetid air containing the smells of uncanny plants with their thirsty blossoms, alien pollen, smoke, wet earth, and strange, secretive fungus. I could almost see heat radiating not just from the wrecked pod, but from our surroundings: trees with hidden, hungry hearts, and the trails of predators that even a tiger might fear.

I had become used to cultivated gardens not only on my once-upon-a-time homeworld, but on the civilized planets controlled by the Thousand Worlds. As a cadet, I'd spent most of my time aboard the *Haetae*, visiting hydroponics whenever I thirsted for a glimpse of greenery. Even on the couple of shore leaves I'd enjoyed, I'd stuck to the port cities and their carefully landscaped parks.

Jasujeong, on the other hand, looked as though it had never been tamed. If this world had ever known the touch of a landscape architect or a geomancer, it didn't show, at least not where we were standing. Trees towered over us, hung with a drapery of vines and mosses. Fallen logs sported brilliant carpets of mushrooms and molds. In the gaps where light filtered through the canopy, tall ferns and swaying flowers reached skyward.

Anyone attempting to walk a straight line through this wilderness would either need a blowtorch or the bulldozer strength of an elephant. I wondered if the entire planet was covered in this jungle. Surely not—surely it had different climate zones.

At least, I consoled myself, we hadn't landed in a desert or arctic waste. Water wouldn't be a problem—quite the opposite.

The howling resumed. I couldn't help myself. I let loose a mighty roar, fit to shake the stars out of the sky.

For my trouble, I was blasted in the face by rain so icy cold it almost made my tongue stick to my teeth. My roar ended in a much less impressive whimper.

Haneul objected to my display. "Do you *want* to signal to everyone that there's a tiger spirit ready to be hunted?" she snapped.

"I'm not sure who's the hunter and who's being hunted," Min muttered.

"Let's get out of here while the going is good," Haneul said. "We don't know how much daylight we have left, and I don't want to find out what lurks out here once the sun goes down."

"We have to wait a little longer," Min insisted. "Jun hasn't returned from his scouting mission yet. We can't abandon him."

Was I imagining the dark smudges beneath her eyes? I doubted I looked much better. We were all stressed and anxious.

The pod sparked and rumbled ominously, and we all startled.

"We can't wait forever," I said. "I'm afraid the pod is going to blow. And let's face it, Jun should be able to track us after he makes it back to the landing site. It's not like we'll be able to hide our path in a jungle this dense."

I took one last look at the pod, which resembled nothing so much as a smashed, scorched tulip with smoke and sparks leaking out of the far end. Hard to believe it had brought us safely down to the planet's surface. The rest was up to us.

"All right," Min said reluctantly. "C'mon, Sebin, kneel so I can ride you."

I grumbled deep in my throat. I wasn't sure how I felt about being *ridden* like a pony. But Min was right. This was the fastest way.

I crouched and felt Min clamber up onto my back, then

her solid weight atop me. This was one thing my family hadn't prepared me for. I couldn't imagine anyone being so bold as to suggest riding the Matriarch!

Haneul had taken her serpentine dragon form, vaster than her human one. A star sapphire shone in her forehead like a jeweled lantern, and antlers sprang from her head. I heard the crunch of the unfortunate vegetation she had destroyed during her transformation. I couldn't tell exactly how long she was—at least twelve meters, with her sinuous tail vanishing into the undergrowth. Her blue scales glimmered iridescently in the fading light.

We headed north according to Min's guidance. As we took off into the jungle, we were startled by the roar of an immense explosion behind us. I glanced back, nose wrinkling against the blast wave of heat and the acrid smoke.

The pod had exploded. There would be no returning to it.

THIRTEEN

Min

If I was honest with myself, the only reason riding a tiger wasn't a dream come true was that I'd spent my childhood dreaming of *becoming* a tiger (or a dragon, or a unicorn). The practical reason I hadn't changed into an all-terrain tiger to travel on Jasujeong was that I would be a smaller one than Sebin, and I didn't want to hold up the group. The selfish one was that being a mini tiger would be *embarrassing.*

I had the good sense not to express any of this to Sebin. I could smell their disgruntlement—hard to escape it when I was perched on their back trying not to fall off. The one consolation was that Sebin couldn't sprint at top speed, as much as I wished for a tiger joyride. Haneul, with her long, ribbony body, seemed to have an easier time snaking through the underbrush despite her shorter limbs. The jungle, choked with thick, leafy trees, logs, brush, and hanging vines, contained so many obstacles that we might as well have been navigating through a living labyrinth.

For the first hour—half hour?—I allowed exhilaration to sweep me away and distract me from the horrors of what had happened recently, and even my worry about whether Jun would catch up to us soon. I was an explorer on a new planet, riding on tigerback. I might be the first one to see some of these vistas!

For a so-called planet of death, Jasujeong was full of *life*, so much that the air seemed stuffed to bursting with it. Most plants had leaves of deep purple-green. Flowers nodded like bells from the trees and vines, many of them immense, and immensely fragrant. Some of the plants were fruiting, although the bright, lurid colors, pinks and purples and oranges, made me wonder how horribly we'd die if we ate the produce.

We also caught sight of animals—furtive glimpses. At least, I *thought* they were animals. For all I knew they were robots or ghosts. Dark fluttering shapes as of wings, and snaky movements among the vines. And of course, there was the howling, which we'd left behind us—for now.

But soon the reality of the situation crashed down around me. I'd expected Jun to rejoin us a short distance from the escape pod—he never strayed far from me—and it hadn't happened.

"Slow down," I told Sebin, although they weren't exactly galloping through the undergrowth. "Something's happened. Jun should have caught up to us by now."

Sebin growled under their breath.

Haneul's head snaked back. Her eyes were large and luminous, and the star sapphire in her forehead gleamed with an intense blue light that contrasted with the murky sunlight. "We have to get to safety as soon as possible."

You don't understand, I wanted to say. *He's my* brother. Even if he was a ghost. What if he had fallen victim to his own aura of bad luck?

Then I remembered that, in all the time we'd spent on the *Pale Lightning*, Haneul had never spoken much about her own family. For all I knew, she had siblings of her own.

"We're going to have to stop at some point to sleep or eat," I argued.

Sebin growled again. I remembered that tigers had their own language, and unlike foxes or dragons, had to take human shape to make themselves understood to us.

"I agree," Haneul said. "We don't have to stop right this minute"—never mind that we had, in fact, paused in our flight north so we could talk more easily—"but we should start looking for a campsite for the night. How fast do ghosts move, anyway?"

I was starting to feel frightened. I didn't want to admit it, though I was sure both Haneul and Sebin could smell it on me. I was scared that the tie between Jun and myself had snapped forever, after everything I'd done to be reunited with him.

Once upon a time, I'd run away from home to clear my brother's name. Disguised myself as a cadet and gotten into trouble—and out of it, too. I hadn't dreamed then that my brother had died before I even set out.

But I'd found his ghost, and for a while I'd thought that would be enough. We could explore the Thousand Worlds together, visiting every one of them. We were still sister and brother, two fox spirits with something to show the world.

I hadn't accounted for our getting separated on one of the first worlds we visited. Or for that visit to be caused by a crash landing because someone had attacked a space station.

I was in over my head. That, at least, should have been familiar territory. And I'd always been able to think my way out of trouble before.

But before, I'd always been secure in the knowledge that everything I was doing was for my brother. For family.

And now I'd left him behind.

"Cheer up, Min," Haneul said consolingly, her muzzle nudging my shoulder.

I chose not to mention that—little-known fact—dragons in their actual dragon form have fish breath like whoa. And this despite the fact that she couldn't have eaten *that* much of the fancy raw-fish stuff—sashimi, it was called—at the reception. I didn't want to hurt her feelings, not when she was trying to lift my spirits.

"You're right," I said, drooping, then remembering I was on a tiger's back—Sebin's back—and I didn't want to slide off. I clutched at their fur to steady myself, ignoring Sebin's huff of disgruntlement.

We continued in a dismal . . . It wasn't silence. The jungle was *quiet*, which probably had to do with our passage, but it wasn't *silent*. Insects chirred and screeched, and the wind made a rustling, percussive music among the leaves and branches, as of bones knocking against one another.

Most troublingly, I thought I heard the howls from earlier, faint but ever-present. What if whatever it was caught up to us once we camped for the night?

And the smells! So many smells. If I could have sated myself on scents alone, this would have been a good planet for it. The honey-sweetness of pollen and fruit perfumed the air, and even the odor of rotting meat that wafted from deeper in the jungle was not entirely unpleasing. Foxes delight in carrion, after all.

"The sun is low in the sky," Haneul said after a while. "I think this is as good a place as any to make camp for the night."

Sebin made an affirmative growl.

I had to agree with them both. We had come across a miraculous clearing, bathed in the dimming slantwise light of Jasujeong's ruddy sun. Feathery ferns and mosses underfoot meant that we wouldn't have to sleep too roughly, and there was even a limpid pool fed by a trickling brook.

First things first. I sniffed for any scent of fox magic, or the chilly wind that accompanied ghost presences. Nothing. "Jun?" I called into the jungle. "Are you there?"

"He'll find us," Haneul reassured me again, but she was starting to sound doubtful.

I shimmered into my fox shape, just in case that made me easier to track. Foxes have a natural affinity for one another, and on top of that, Jun was specifically haunting *me*. You'd think that would make it easy for him to jaunt his way over.

I tried to think of something that could hurt a ghost, other than a shaman. Surely Jun hadn't run into someone able to exorcise him, not after we'd crash-landed. If only I'd insisted that he stay close to us. If only I'd gone with him so that we could have faced whatever threat it was together. If only, if only, if only.

But it had been a long day's travel, and I needed food and a place to pee.

Sebin flowed back into their human shape. "We should take turns keeping watch," they said, "unless there's dragon magic that can do that for us."

Haneul shook her head regretfully. "That'd be a shaman's work, or a magician's. I can control the weather where I am, but warding isn't something I've been trained in."

I thought of how Miho had mistaken me for a magician. Too bad I didn't have *that* on my résumé.

"I'll stand guard while you two eat," Sebin said, although they sounded wistful about it.

Haneul bent to sniff the pool of water. It glowed softly for a moment as she chanted over it, her breath raising ripples. "This is safe to drink," she confirmed.

"Let's refill our water supply while we can," said Sebin. "Just in case."

"Water supply, heck," I said, splashing into the pool after making sure the Dragon Pearl's pouch was securely fastened. "I need to get clean."

As much as I wanted to luxuriate in the water, it was bracingly cold, a shocking sweetness after the long tiger ride to get here.

"Oh!" Haneul said as she washed herself next to me. "Allow me."

For a second, I wasn't sure what she was referring to. Then the water became pleasantly warm.

"I didn't know you could do that," I said, astonished.

Haneul smiled shyly. "I learned it recently. I don't need warmth as badly as mammals do, but even a dragon likes to be cozy once in a while. And there's only the one pool, so why not share?"

"Thank you," I said, glad we were no longer at odds.

I kept my bath quick, mostly scrubbing out the odors of sweat and soot, and then drank from the brook upstream. That water remained cold and caused my teeth to chatter.

"Do we risk trying the local fruit?" I asked, sniffing longingly at the luscious globes of red and magenta and orange.

"Better not," came Sebin's voice as they paced around the clearing. "Not unless we run out of rations. It's an alien planet. I'm immune to most poisons, but you two shouldn't risk it."

I had an idea. "Yes, the planet's alien," I agreed, "but we have a solution for that."

I cradled the pouch that had never left my possession, even while I was cleaning up. I could feel the warm, eager pulsing of the Dragon Pearl within. "We have with us the one magical artifact that can carry out fast terraforming." I hesitated, then eyed Haneul. "Just to create a source of food to help us survive, that's all. Nothing more, nothing frivolous. That is, if you think it's okay. . . ."

Haneul nodded slowly, and I could tell she was pleased that I'd asked her, even though I generally didn't think much of rules and regulations. "Considering the situation we're in," she said, "I think even the Dragon Council would allow it."

"Thank you," I said softly, meaning it. I knew how hard it was for Haneul to deviate from protocol or acknowledge that the Pearl had ended up in the hands of someone who wasn't a dragon. It meant a lot that she was willing to bend on this matter.

Haneul's face brightened. "We could have edible fruit, maybe?" She added shyly, "If the Dragon Pearl is taking requests, I really like tangerines. . . ."

Of course a dragon would remember that this was all about the Pearl's will more than mine. As the Bearer of the Dragon Pearl, I could influence it to a certain degree. But I never forgot that the Pearl had a strange intelligence of its own, even if it wasn't expressed in words or smells. It had chosen me for its own reasons, and at the time I hadn't questioned it.

Now, though, I wondered. It could have chosen a dragon like Haneul, or a shaman like the one who had originally lost it so many years ago, or a captain like Hwan. Someday I hoped I'd find out what it wanted of me.

Meanwhile, it was time to find out what the Pearl thought of Haneul's request.

Sebin smelled interested. "We'll get to see it at work? Really?"

"How can you keep watch effectively if you're distracted?" Haneul teased.

Sebin stiffened in indignation. "I'm paying attention! If anything comes after us, I'll hear it first."

That reminded me that I should get down to business while we still had a trickle of daylight, even though the Pearl provided its own seafoam-colored illumination. Carefully, I drew it from its silken pouch, marveling anew at the smoothness of its surface, the way its light dappled the entire clearing.

In the Dragon Pearl's glow, Haneul's hair wasn't just blue-tinted, it was completely blue, like a tropical sea. The smells of salt and kelp and fresh breezes suffused the air, in contrast to the warm, pungent humidity of the jungle. I could have sworn I heard the cries of seagulls, and terns, and the roar of waves.

I closed my eyes, although I could still see the radiance of the Pearl beating against my eyelids. I let myself drift into communion with the orb, imagining this clearing transformed into a glen full of fruit we could safely eat. I'd never seen a tangerine tree, just the fruit at banquets, so I concentrated on the tangerines themselves and their refreshing scent.

For a moment I heard nothing but the ocean-roar in my ears, white noise blotting out awareness of anything but the smooth warmth of the Dragon Pearl in my hands. Then I opened my eyes—and almost dropped it. Only my quick reflexes saved me from doing so.

The entire glen had transformed. In place of the alien plants with their fleshy purple-green leaves, there were tangerine trees heavy with fruit. I breathed in the delicious citrus fragrance.

"The terraforming affected a perfect circle," Sebin reported a few moments later, having traversed the boundary of the grove. They sounded shaken. "I'd always heard of the Pearl being used on entire worlds, not . . . not small areas."

"That's because, under normal circumstances, you wouldn't use the Pearl for selfish reasons," said Haneul. "But this is an emergency."

Maybe the Pearl had obliged us because it didn't want to get stuck on this planet with our bones, I thought.

Haneul looked around at the trees in wonder. She stepped right up to one of the tangerines and inhaled deeply. "It smells real."

"Let's eat what we can and pick some to carry with us tomorrow morning," I suggested, elated by the miracle I had created—er, that the Pearl had allowed me to create.

They weren't just tangerines. They were perfectly ripe, perfectly fresh, perfectly delicious, both tart and sweet. I even managed to peel them without squirting myself in the eye, which proved their magical origin.

"Maybe you're right about the Pearl," I said to Haneul, anxious for things to be fully resolved between us. "It is a lot of power for one person to hold."

Haneul was also feeling conciliatory. "It must have picked you for a reason, though. I'm sure the Dragon Council will figure out a way to work with you. They just need time to get used to the idea."

If Dragon Councilor Gwan was any indication, I doubted it would come that easily. But it was a nice sentiment. More important, Haneul and I were friends again.

I gestured to our other comrade. "You should eat, too,

Sebin," I said. "I'll take over watch." Reluctantly, I put the Pearl back in its pouch for safety's sake, as loath as I was to give up its light. Besides, all three of us could navigate by smell, and Sebin at least could probably see pretty well in the dark.

Sebin's face lit up. "Magical tangerines!"

"Mmmf mmf mmmf," Haneul agreed. I'd always known her to have prim, proper manners in the past, but apparently those fell by the wayside when it came to her favorite food.

While Sebin made a beeline for the pool, I took up their patrol of the glen's circumference. This gave me the opportunity to examine the boundary between the terraformed area and the rest of the jungle more closely. When Sebin had said the area of effect was perfectly circular, I'd had to take their word for it. I guessed it was more or less a circle, but it wasn't like I had an exact sense of the geometry involved.

More interestingly, the transition from the brand-new tangerine grove to the jungle was not abrupt the way I had expected it to be. There was a gradual change from the kinds of plants that I had become used to in the Thousand Worlds to the alien ones, as though they planned on coexisting harmoniously. I rather liked the thought, although I hoped I would be off-planet before I saw what happened to the grove in the long term.

None of us had a particularly accurate sense of time on this world, and we didn't have any other way of keeping track of the hours. I strained my eyes for any sign of Jun and was disappointed over and over again.

I kept watch until I felt my attention wandering. Then I woke Haneul. "Your turn," I said.

I relaxed into my natural fox form and curled up amid the

ferns and mosses. It would be more comfortable to sleep this way, and besides, I liked to think my senses were more acute when I was a fox. Not that I didn't trust Haneul, but just in case.

I had scarcely slept at all (so I thought) when I heard a dragon's roar, not unlike the roar of the sea. I snapped awake and shifted back into human form, clutching the pouch against my side to make sure I hadn't lost it. "Who's out there?" I whispered.

Haneul roared again, and then I heard what must have alarmed her: the howling from before. There must have been a whole pack of the creatures, whatever they were. I shivered at the cacophony, trying to count the number of distinct voices. Either way, we were definitely outnumbered.

By now Sebin was awake, too—who was I kidding. Sebin, with their single-minded focus on combat-readiness, had probably roused before I had. Unlike me, they maintained tiger form, which made sense if we were going to have to fight.

I didn't *want* to fight, but it didn't sound like we were going to have a choice. After all, not to be prejudicial, but who was going to howl in friendship?

My eyes had adjusted to the darkness, and what little light was available from the local stars and moons. I saw hulking shapes in the jungle proper, advancing toward us. Whether they had fur or scales or chitinous armor, I couldn't tell. I thought I glimpsed a gleam as of fangs, and the fangs were not small.

One of the creatures came forward so I could see it more clearly. That didn't really help. If pressed, I would have described it as a cross between a vulture and a wolf. "Stay back!" I yelled shakily, as if a mere human was going to intimidate it if a tiger and a dragon hadn't done the job.

More of the vulture-wolves advanced. I stepped backward, maintaining my distance. I didn't want one of them pouncing on me.

There came a light from beyond them, like an electric lantern. I squinted, startled.

To our astonishment, the vulture-wolves parted to either side, revealing a regal figure in their midst.

It was Miho.

FOURTEEN

Sebin

I growled despite the familiar smell that wafted from the slight figure. She was flanked by vulture-wolf creatures. Nothing about this situation made sense. Normally I would have been glad that we weren't the only survivors of the space station disaster, but what was Yang Miho doing with an escort of monsters?

Some people think of tigers *as monsters*, a voice in the back of my head reminded me.

I don't go around growling at people, I thought, except I was in the middle of growling at Miho, so that was a lie.

"Come forward slowly," Min said from behind me.

I tensed, ready to pounce at the slightest indication of an attack. Min might be clever, but it was up to Haneul and me, with our greater size, to deal with physical threats.

"Min, it's all right," came a hollow voice.

Min's jaw dropped. "Jun? Is that you?"

Jun approached first, translucent and glowing faintly in the way of ghosts. For once his long, disheveled hair didn't look out of place, maybe because everyone was looking rumpled in the wake of the disaster. (Unlike the rest of us, Jun didn't smell. In both senses of the word.) "I came upon Miho's tracks and went to fetch her," he said. "I thought we'd have a better chance of survival if we were all together."

I turned back into my human shape just in time to see Min's expression—she looked as if she couldn't decide whether she wanted to hug Jun (impossible) or throttle him (fortunately also impossible).

"You *idiot!*" Min scolded him. "I thought you'd gone to the afterlife for good." Tears sparkled in her eyes.

Jun had the grace to look embarrassed. "I didn't mean to make you worry." He gestured as though he was going to put his arms around her shoulders; then he let them drop. I could feel the cold aura of his presence from where I stood.

Miho entered the clearing. One of the vulture-wolves whined softly, and she stroked its head absentmindedly.

Even travel worn as she was, Miho's presence filled the newly created tangerine grove. She was sheathed in a Thousand Worlds spacesuit, marked by dust and dirt and bruised purple-green streaks, and yet she made it look like a queen's outfit. The only thing missing was a crown.

"Who are your 'friends'?" Min asked. She was looking at Miho as if she didn't know what to think. I noticed that Haneul, too, hadn't left her dragon shape, just in case.

"They're creatures native to this world," Miho said. "The initial survey called them Gwaemul Number Twenty-Seven, unhelpfully enough."

Gwaemul simply meant *monster.* "Let me guess," I said. "Everything got tagged with a number and that was it."

Miho shrugged. "I can't speak for the survey team. They're

long dead, anyway." She sounded genuinely regretful, as if death were something to be cheated, or as if she'd known the people involved. But of course, that was impossible.

"How did you . . . ?" I asked, frowning. It was hard to think clearly, and I wasn't sure why. Sleep deprivation and the stress of the past day, I told myself. A good tiger should be able to go long hours on little rest, but I had to admit that my time aboard the *Haetae* had made me soft.

"I was fortunate enough to reach one of the escape pods in time." She whistled sharply. The vulture-wolves—the whole pack of Gwaemul #27—flung their heads back and howled one more time. Then they slunk away into the night, disappearing as if they'd never existed.

I opened my mouth to ask for more details, and whether anyone else had also survived. Then the questions slid out of my mind like water out of uncupped hands. It wasn't important—if she wanted me to know, I would know.

Haneul finally seemed to relax as well. There was a whisper of water as she took on her own human shape, the last of us to do so. "Do you want some tangerines?" she asked. "You must be tired." She plucked one from the nearest tree and offered it to Miho.

Miho sat and peeled and sectioned the tangerine with almost surgical neatness, as if she were enacting *divide and conquer* on the unfortunate fruit. She removed her spacesuit's helmet and ate the segments one by one. As she did so, she looked not at Min but at the pouch that Min bore. I thought it was good of her to acknowledge the real source of the power that had made the grove possible.

"I have many questions," Miho said. "But it's been a long

night for me, and I assume for the rest of you, too. They can wait until morning."

"I'll stand watch for the rest of the night," I said. I didn't feel sleepy in the slightest.

Soon the grove was filled with the sleep-song of wind whispering through leaves, the steady breathing of the others, and . . . Haneul's snore.

Finding the now-transformed glen had been stroke of fortune enough. But now we'd met up with another survivor. I doubted she had a way to signal for help or she would have done so already. But we could travel together, and there was strength in numbers.

Eventually morning came. I was still awake and alert, and grateful that my shipboard service hadn't weakened me as much as I'd feared. We might have gotten lucky with the apparently docile pack of Gwaemul #27 that Miho had befriended, but I didn't expect such luck to continue.

We refilled our canteens and bundled as many of the tangerines as we could reasonably carry for snacking along the way. As we did so, Miho quizzed us about our plans.

Min showed her the map. "That's our best hope of getting off-planet," she said. "Getting to the ancient starship and using it to call for rescue."

Miho's expression was inscrutable. "There are a lot of uneasy legends about the dreadnought *Sejong-Daewang*," she said. "Getting there will be the easy part. Persuading the ship's guardians to cooperate . . ."

"Guardians?" I asked.

"Ghosts," Miho said.

Haneul looked perturbed. "Ghosts that old must have left something great and terrible undone in order to linger so long."

My eyes went to Min and Jun. Min scowled as if she could feel the weight of my regard. "Ghosts aren't always bad," she said defensively.

"Those ghosts have kept people from retrieving the ancient ship for decades," Miho said soberly. "We're fairly sure they're the ship's crew, tied to its final resting place. But that's a problem we can deal with later." She regarded Jun speculatively. "They'll be more favorably inclined toward one of their own kind, which is good."

We agreed that Min would continue to ride me (sigh). At least I had the consolation that Haneul wasn't going to escape steed duty anymore, because Miho was going to ride *her.* Haneul didn't seem as annoyed about this as I had expected, accepting the task with surprising grace.

"Just don't tell my parents that I carried a human on my back," Haneul said with a laugh. "Even if that human was an assistant minister! My moms would throw a fit."

Then we set off again, and for a while, at least, there was no more conversation. I would have envied the others the ability to talk, but the smells and textures of the jungle engrossed me.

There was a gradual transition from the plants with their purple-green leaves to younger growth. As we traveled, the trees became shorter, the canopy less dense. There were fewer molds and mushrooms in the soupy dampness of the fragrant air, sprightlier plants and shrubs in the undergrowth, flowers swaying in the wind of our passage.

The part of me that was a tiger, and that longed for sunbeams and starry nights and long hunts, thought that this was not such a bad planet. That part of me could have been content to prowl the jungle and its outskirts forever, while the human part drifted in lazy sleep.

But Min's weight on my back, slight as it was, reminded me that I couldn't go rogue and vanish into the jungle. If nothing else, we had to survive so we could report what had happened to the station and investigate the cause of its destruction. Perhaps even salvage the peace talks, if that was still possible.

The wild beauty of the foliage all around us was so seductive that I eventually let my guard down. It happened little by little, so I wasn't even aware of it.

Not until the ambush.

My senses were alert to the trees and the serpentine vines, to the drifting golden haze of pollen and the gleaming wetness of dew as it dried. But as a tiger, I was an earthbound creature. I had allowed myself to forget that dangers could come from above, as well.

Out of nowhere a raptor swooped down, followed by another, and another, talons extended. Jun screamed a warning. I jumped to the side barely in time, with Min crouching low on my back.

The raptors had a wingspan a good three meters long, along with their wicked beaks and barbed talons. They had oddly patterned feathers, plumage in colors so brilliant that it felt like an assault upon my eyes. I couldn't risk either Min or myself getting raked by those talons. Who knew if they were venomous, or if they harbored some alien disease?

Haneul reared to her full height. Dazzled for a moment, I thought she touched the bellies of the clouds themselves, which were gray-winged and threatening, like kin to the raptors.

Perhaps that wasn't as far-fetched as I would have otherwise thought. What kinds of magics brewed on this world?

Winds swirled and gusted around Haneul's gleaming blue form with its scales and sinuous coils. It was then that it struck me, like a fist to the sternum, that while I had seen a dragon in her native shape, a sister to sea and storm, I had never experienced the full force of a dragon's power, her mastery of wind and water magic.

The clouds gathered like eager dogs in response to her roar. Sheet lightning flashed and illuminated their undersides, and gleamed palely in the whites of Miho's eyes and her spacesuit. Rain pelted us. I was almost instantly drenched, my fur soaked all the way down to skin.

The raptors screamed. Perhaps they recognized the sudden storm as unnatural weather, perhaps not. They redoubled their efforts for one last attack, clawing at Haneul's flanks and avoiding her antlered head and snapping teeth.

In the Juhwang Clan I'd been taught that dragons were benevolent, preferring peace to violence. But even a dragon's patience had limits, and no one could blame Haneul for defending herself. I eased Min off my back. Then I gathered myself and leaped, lashing out with my powerful forepaws to drive off a raptor that was harrying Haneul from behind.

I knocked the raptor out of the air. It fell to the ground, stunned, wings fluttering uselessly. I roared my triumph.

The other two raptors, deciding enough was enough, wheeled out of reach and fled, leaving the third behind.

I struck the downed raptor with my paw again, ensuring that it wouldn't cause us any further trouble.

The rain eased off. I was a sodden mass of fur and I probably smelled of wet cat, or maybe wet socks. I wrinkled my nose. While tigers can swim, we also like getting dry quickly afterward.

Min, too, was dripping. "Haneul!" she cried. "Are you all right?"

"This is one time being a ghost isn't so useful," Jun said ruefully. "I don't think animals are as easily intimidated by the undead as sentient people."

I'd never thought of that before. Maybe somewhere in the Thousand Worlds some shaman was running tests on a willing ghost. (I hoped a willing one, anyway, rather than the alternative.)

I shook off the flight of fancy. Haneul collapsed back into human form with an undignified squelch, leaving Miho in a fallen heap next to her. I hurried to Haneul's side.

My sense of smell should have told me what was wrong: blood. And a strange, acrid undertone that I didn't recognize. Up close, I could see that the raptors' talons had torn through Haneul's sides, leaving livid gashes.

"I've got the medical kit," Miho said. "Let me take a look."

"It's nothing," Haneul objected. "Just put some antiseptic and a bandage on it, and I'll be as good as new."

The wound did not look like "nothing." I'd had the requisite Juhwang Tiger Clan training in first aid and field medicine. (*Don't try surgery yet*, Aunt Sooni had told me once upon a time. *You're not ready for that.*)

Over Haneul's objections, we hauled her up onto my back—this was forever going to be That Planet Where I Was a Tiger Steed in my memoirs—and trekked a little farther, out of the seeping damp. Miho said that cleaning wounds was all very well, but a sodden bandage wouldn't do Haneul any good.

Like the Dragon Pearl's magic the night before, Haneul's

storm had been localized. That said, water traveled its own paths, and we had to detour uphill to escape the rivulets of water and the clinging mud.

"Come down from Sebin and sit," Miho told Haneul, so authoritatively that Haneul obeyed without further argument. With deft hands Miho peeled back the ragged cloth and cleaned the wounds with an antiseptic pad from the kit. Haneul made faint noises of protest, and I whined low in my throat in sympathy with her distress.

Then came the bandages, and Haneul made more of those faint noises. The acrid smell had now been joined with the stinging odor of the antiseptic.

"You sure you feel all right?" Min asked, her anxiety palpable. If it had been any stronger it would have overwhelmed, well, the dismal smell of wet fur. I hoped the sun would dry me soon. I would have liked to nap in a sunbeam until it did, but we didn't have the time for that.

Haneul smiled weakly. "I'll manage, promise."

"There are painkiller patches," Miho said, "but . . ."

Haneul shook her head vigorously. "No, save those for an emergency. I've been hurt worse stubbing my toe."

Nobody called her on the lie.

Having treated Haneul, we proceeded at a slower pace. Haneul stayed in human form, presumably so she could retain the benefit of the bandages, and stoically refused my offer of a ride.

We didn't have bandages that would have been big enough for her wounds when she shifted into her dragon form. I could tell that whoever had put together this first aid kit hadn't been thinking of shape-shifters' needs. Someday I wanted to talk to a Sun Clanner about the magics that were common in their worlds and unknown among ours. But before I could do that, I had to get off this planet.

I walked rather than loped, in keeping with Haneul's labored movements. Min walked too, perhaps in solidarity with Miho, while Jun drifted at Min's side. For a moment I fancied that Miho and Min were related in some way, an aunt and her niece, perhaps. Was this the "family matter" Min had mentioned? No, surely Min would have mentioned that she had an aunt who was an *assistant minister*. And Min's prickly demeanor didn't suggest a familial relationship.

As we continued our uncertain journey, I didn't make the mistake of neglecting the sky a second time. I understood now that it was my enemy, just like the ground underfoot with its secret kingdoms of insects and grubs and stealthy fungal roots. Everything about this planet stood in the way of our returning home to sanity and people who spoke our language.

I was so alert, I felt stretched beyond the boundaries of my skin. Perhaps this was how a starship's sensor suite felt, or an alarm bell, or an open eye. Maybe alertness would swallow everything else so that nothing was left but perception and reaction to perception.

I was determined not to let the others down again. If I'd caught sight of the raptors earlier, maybe Haneul would have been able to drive them off before their strike. (Flashback to a memory of the Matriarch saying, in her cold dry voice, *Did you know that the peregrine falcon dives at three hundred and twenty kilometers per hour? A tiger is fast, but not that fast.*) Perhaps the raptors were as fast as peregrines; I'd had no way of measuring. But it felt as though I ought to have been able to prevent Haneul's injury. And it stung all the more that no one, not even Haneul herself, had rebuked me.

As we continued through the lowlands and toward the heavy, heady smells of swamp and the distant song of insects, I listened with half an ear to Miho and Min talking. For her part, Haneul seemed little inclined to speak, her head bowed as though its weight troubled her. Jun and his cold wind swirled in front of us all as he scouted ahead.

"My mother would be horrified by this latest adventure," Min said, looking sidelong at Miho as though she expected this perfectly ordinary declaration to mean something special. "Did your family approve of you going into politics?"

I bristled, wondering if Min was needling me subtly about my own family. There were tigers in politics, mostly in the Ministry of Defense. The Matriarch had spoken of them from time to time, but I hadn't been much interested as a cub. Not when I had a career in the Space Forces to look forward to. In retrospect, that had been shortsighted of me.

I hadn't expected the road to becoming captain of a ship to involve so much trudging over a planet's surface, was all.

"My family is no more," Miho said with a simplicity that made me shiver even as a tiger. "They were meddlers, but they didn't believe in what I do. It's moot, anyway. The Sun Clans killed them in the battle of—"

Which battle it was we didn't find out, because just then Haneul cried out hoarsely and collapsed.

FIFTEEN

Min

"Oh no!" I heard myself exclaim after Haneul collapsed, heedless of whoever might be listening. Face it, our group was anything but stealthy. Sebin might have been prowling quietly through the grasses and underbrush, and Jun's movements were always silent, but while I walked softly as a matter of habit, I'd been talking to Miho in a normal tone of voice. And Haneul herself, of course, had been too ill to make any effort at subtlety, her footsteps labored . . . until now.

Miho was already at Haneul's side, a hand pressed to the dragon spirit's forehead with her fingers spread in an odd pattern. I resented Miho for being faster than I was, then questioned my pettiness at a time when my focus should have been Haneul's well-being.

"She's got a fever," Miho said curtly, then began rummaging in the medical kit.

How could Miho tell through her suit? I couldn't help putting the back of my hand to Haneul's forehead, which was damp with sweat and unpleasantly hot. I'd been about to ask Miho if she was sure without a thermometer, even though I'd grown up with Mom and the aunties "taking our temperature" by hand. (We'd owned one instant-read thermometer, but it was broken beyond even my ability to repair.) A thermometer would only have confirmed what my sense of touch told me.

"Infection?" Sebin asked in a voice that suggested they dreaded the answer.

"Worse," Miho said grimly. "She doesn't smell like infection. This is some kind of alien poison."

Sebin and I looked at each other aghast. "You have medical training . . ." I began.

"For things like combat injuries," Sebin said grimly. "Not toxins."

"You weren't trained to deal with the possibility of being poisoned?" I regretted my peevish tone as soon as the words left my mouth.

Sebin growled in the back of their throat, then answered civilly enough: "The Matriarch *claimed* that tiger spirits are immune to most poisons. But she also claimed that her special hot baths made her immune to the common cold, and she still got those, so I don't know what to believe."

"It's an *alien* poison anyway," Miho interrupted. She smoothed the hair back from Haneul's brow as the dragon cadet, her eyes squeezed shut, groaned softly. "It's a pity we don't have a shaman or a medic with us."

"You know how to use the kit?" I asked, hoping against hope that it had a cure for Haneul.

Miho went through its contents. "Antibiotics. Bandages. Painkillers." All of which we'd already known about. "No antitoxins."

I drooped. "Unless one of us is secretly a shaman . . ."

Sebin shook their head. "Haneul said she isn't."

Miho sighed. "I always knew that someday I'd regret picking politics over medicine."

That interested me. "You could have been a doctor?"

"There are types of family magic that involve healing," Miho said, looking at me.

By "family magic" she had to mean fox magic. *My* family hadn't told me about any healing powers, but they'd been so secretive about foxy abilities that it wouldn't have surprised me if they'd held back the information.

"But I'm not knowledgeable about any of them, unfortunately. That died out with my sister."

"Tell us about her," I urged as I contemplated our options for carrying Haneul with us. "Maybe you'll remember something that will be useful."

"She's gone," Miho said shortly, and a melancholy scent drifted from her. "There's not much to tell."

So much for that.

"There's one more thing in the kit," Miho said. She pulled out a small package that looked like a folding umbrella. It came with the now-ubiquitous instructions in both Hangeul and Nihongo, and curiously, a couple other languages that I didn't recognize. At another time I would have wondered how many nations there were out in the wide galaxy that I'd never heard of, let alone their languages. Miho might know, but this was a bad time to ask her.

"Stand back," Miho warned us.

It was a good thing she did, because both Sebin and I had crowded closer out of curiosity. It was also a good thing Miho had pointed the contraption *away* from Haneul.

The package, which turned out *not* to be an umbrella, expanded . . . into a stretcher of medicinal-smelling canvas and locking poles. My eyes widened as I watched the clever way it unfolded. I admired the ingenuity of whatever engineer had come up with this, and I wondered if I could improve on the design someday.

"Too bad it doesn't lift itself," Sebin said, but even they looked impressed.

"It actually does have a levitation mode," Miho said, showing us the relevant section of the instructions. "But it runs off an unspecified power source." She sniffed the air, as though she could *smell* energy. For all I knew that was another fox spirit thing, like the way we always sneezed when we used our magic around each other.

That was the other problem: Miho had been using Charm subtly but constantly, to ease the others' reactions to her. My nose itched and I had to keep suppressing the urge to sneeze. Earlier I hadn't wanted to pick a fight with her in front of the others, knowing that Miho would be tempted to Charm them even more strongly to hide the conflict. On the other hand, if I kept letting her do this, what kind of friend was I to the cadets?

I looked down at Haneul, her skin pallid and marred by rivulets of sweat. At the moment, Miho's magic wasn't doing anything to her one way or the other. Which left Sebin, Jun, and me. I was unaffected, which I suspected had more to do with natural fox immunity than Miho's goodwill. It was probably the same story for Jun. Sebin, on the other hand, would cease to be cooperative once they realized that they'd been ensorcelled and *I had let it happen.*

No. I couldn't break Sebin free of Miho's magic. Not yet. *It's for Haneul's sake,* I told myself.

So why did I feel so guilty?

Miho was watching me. I bet she had traced every coil and barb of my thoughts. I hadn't been making any effort to keep my countenance blank.

"We have to bring Haneul with us," I said. The alternative—leaving her behind so we could progress faster—was unthinkable.

But I saw from the expression on Miho's face that she was thinking it.

"Of course," she said, but it was after a split second's pause, and I knew. I knew. "We'll take turns carrying the stretcher."

"That makes sense," I said. "Sebin and I will go first."

I looked at Jun then. Agony was written across his features, although not the physical kind. He wanted to do something useful, and he couldn't.

"It's all right," I whispered to him, and he smiled weakly in thanks.

Sebin helped Miho load Haneul's limp, trembling form onto the stretcher. Sebin and I then took up our positions, the tiger cadet in the front bearing the brunt of the weight, myself in the back. Miho brought up the rear, while Jun floated alongside me.

I was soon huffing and puffing from the unaccustomed exertion. That left Jun free to speak to me. "I never imagined it would be like this," he said softly, so softly I imagined no one else could hear him. "That I'd see other worlds, and that people would get hurt in the course of events and I'd be unable to help."

I felt wretched, although that couldn't have been his intent. After all, I'd failed to save him from his fate. I wondered, for the first time, if he would have gone peacefully to the afterlife if he hadn't had an overeager younger sister traipsing after him in a quest to clear his name. He'd *said* his mission was to see every one of the Thousand Worlds, but what if part of it now was just a desire to keep an eye on me, like the dutiful older brother he was?

"You can scout," I said stubbornly. "You're immune to anything that this planet can do to us. Even if . . . even if something happens to Sebin and Haneul and Miho and me, you'll endure."

Jun gave me a sad look. "I'm not sure whether that's a blessing or a curse."

That only made me feel more miserable, so I dropped into a dismal silence. Thankfully, Jun didn't continue that conversation. He could tell it wasn't helping anyone's mood.

It was hard to think of anything that *would* have helped our mood, to be honest, other than a miraculous rescue. Here we were, trapped on a planet where the critters liked to attack us, unless they were being Charmed by Miho. Oh, I'd made my own brief attempt to Charm the diving falcon-things that had attacked Haneul, to no avail. Maybe I needed more tails before I could become powerful enough to affect aliens. I'd thought—hoped—that Miho had been too distracted by the conflict to notice, and thankfully, she hadn't sneezed. Come to think of it, I hadn't sneezed during that entire fight, either, which meant that Miho had decided not to intervene for whatever reason.

We trudged upward on a deceptively slight rise leading to the crest of a hill haired with brambles and trees and more of those vibrantly colored fruits that still tempted me despite the Dragon Pearl's ability to provide for us.

I wasn't thinking much about the landscape, except in the bleary, blurry way of steps taken. Mostly my world was full of other sensations: The abominable ache in my shoulders and upper back from the unaccustomed exertion. The way my feet sank slightly into the sodden earth, making each step that much more difficult. The hot, sticky trickle of sweat down my face and back from the quixotic heat of the alien sun. The smells—not only the aforementioned sweat, but also the nose-tickling fragrance of pollen and crushed leaves, the stink of exhaustion, and . . . water?

"Min!"

The alarm in Sebin's voice jolted me out of my reverie. I was brought up short by the fact that Sebin had halted abruptly in front of me. I staggered, almost dropped my end of the stretcher, and was shamed into hanging on for dear life at the sound of Haneul's agonized moan.

"Sorry," I whispered, and then I looked up.

We'd come to water. I'd been so distracted by the work of carrying Haneul that I hadn't stopped to think about *where* the smell of water was coming from. Well, I could see it now.

A river.

"We might as well set Haneul down," Sebin said, so we did. Sebin stood so that their shadow fell over Haneul's face, sparing her from being overheated by the sun. I appreciated their thoughtfulness. Doing that wouldn't have occurred to me.

No longer burdened, if only for the moment, I shaded my eyes with my hand and looked at that glittering expanse of water. That wasn't some tiny trickling brook. I could see the foam that the rushing current threw against rocks. You could die in that white water. I started to shake, queasy all the way down to the pit of my stomach. I would rather have turned back than face that.

Sebin and I looked at each other. They rolled their shoulders uncomfortably, then said, "I don't suppose the Dragon Pearl would make us a bridge?"

"I don't know . . ." I said. "That's a lot of river."

This wasn't just hypocrisy on my part. After all, the Pearl and I had terraformed an entire planet once. But that had been to create a proper resting place for the ghosts of the Fourth Colony. And sure, we'd terraformed that tangerine grove so we'd have something safe to eat. But that had been a matter of survival. I was afraid of asking the Pearl to accommodate us once too often.

I pulled the orb out of its pouch and closed my eyes against the shimmering pressure of its radiance. *A bridge?* I wondered, wishing I'd had an opportunity to study engineering formally.

Back when I'd terraformed the Fourth Colony at the behest of the restless dead, I hadn't had any specific results in mind. When my handler, Seok, had debriefed me afterward, he'd looked at me, just *looked* at me, when I'd explained how it had worked.

"I let my mind drift, and when the Pearl's spirit made contact, I just went with the flow."

"Do you have any idea," he had asked in that tight, perfectly controlled voice that meant he was trying very hard not to shout or throw things, "what could have gone wrong if your control had slipped for one moment?"

I hadn't attempted to explain to Seok that one didn't *control* the Dragon Pearl. (I had a private theory that the Pearl had *chosen* to get lost out of sheer aggravation after Shaman Hae had made off with it during a power trip of her own many years ago. The Pearl had *opinions*.) Instead, I'd smiled, nodded, and filled out all the forms he'd insisted on (Seok was a great believer in paperwork, not one of his more endearing qualities), and neither of us had ever brought up the subject again.

Still, as much as I chafed at Seok's tedious insistence on things like getting authorization from the powers that be, there were times when I had to concede that he had a point. And this was one of those times. I was good at improvising, but sometimes it was better to go in with a plan.

And this was the problem, although I hesitated to call it one in front of Jun and Miho and Sebin. We were all pretty worn down already—except maybe my brother, who didn't tire the way mortals did. I hated the thought of discouraging everyone further by admitting that I had no idea what a bridge should look like.

"Min?" Sebin asked. They were going to force me to come clean, I just knew it. "What's the matter?"

"We need a bridge," I said.

"Yes," Miho said. She was looking at me with that thoughtful expression that I was increasingly coming to dread. She had lots of thoughts, all right, that much was clear. But I couldn't tell what they were, which made me nervous.

"The Pearl doesn't do engineering as such, as far as I can tell," I said. "I've seen it raise forests from nothing, and mountains as well. Not so much with buildings and skyscrapers and temples and so on."

"That shouldn't be a problem," Sebin said with what I recognized as desperate cheer. "You just need a natural bridge. Some sort of rock formation going up and over the river."

"You created the tangerine grove," Miho said. "Are you an expert in tangerines?"

"No," I admitted. "But I've eaten them, so I knew something about them."

I'd never seen a bridge over a river except on the holo shows and the news. Not once in person. Why would I have? My home planet was as dry as unexcavated bone. In theory there were ravines and canyons elsewhere on Jinju, but as a steader I hadn't exactly had time to go on camping trips, nor had the rest of my family.

I'd been on other worlds since then, but between training on a space station and gallivanting on *spaceships*, I hadn't exactly had a chance to get used to the sheer variety of topographical formations that showed up on different planets. Or time to explore the natural features around the cities I'd visited, either.

"Right," I said, more steadily than I felt. "I'll ask for a bridge."

The Dragon Pearl's light was muted, perhaps in response to my nerves. I wasn't sure whether that should worry me or not. I breathed in and out, in and out, forcing myself to focus not on the terrifying rush of water but instead on the solution to our dilemma: a bridge of solid rock.

That was the issue, wasn't it? The water. I knew what water was, remembered how we'd struggled to conserve it back home, and on the ships I'd served on as well. I was used to thinking of water as something scarce. Something contained.

Even during the time I'd known Haneul, I'd trusted her to keep control of her own personal rain cloud. (She wasn't very good at it, but it was the principle of the thing. She did her best.)

Water wasn't supposed to be something that rushed and roared beneath you, ready to sweep you away.

"Min?" It was Sebin again. They had come up to my side.

I looked at them and realized from their spring-loaded

stance that they were ready to catch me if I fainted. That only had the effect of making me more nervous. What if I fell off the face of the world and into the horrible splashing waters below?

"This is the only way we can get Haneul across the river," Miho said. "Unless, of course, you're willing to leave her behind with Sebin while you and I swim across."

When I didn't answer, Miho figured out the real source of my fear. "You can't swim."

"I come from a planet that's made of rocks and dust all over," I almost yelled at her. "Of course I can't swim!"

Someone had once told me that all Space Forces cadets were required to pass a swim test, in case a situation like this ever came up. Since my own service in the Space Forces had been slightly (okay, very) irregular, I'd skipped right past that requirement.

Miho stood before me. I hadn't realized she'd come so close. She reached out and tipped up my chin with her fingers, the lightest of touches. "Look into my eyes, Min," she said. "Let me help you deal with your fear."

This was a terrible idea, but so was leaving Haneul behind, even with Sebin or me to guard her. Besides, Miho's voice was so soft, so soothing. Something about her reminded me of a city fox I had met once. I tried to figure out what that was, and then the thought dissolved like honey on the tongue, and just as sweetly.

My nose itched, and I bit back a sneeze. I shouldn't sneeze all over Miho. It would be rude.

Fear of the river and its waters no longer gripped me. I looked down at the vast expanse of white-laced blue and smiled. "A bridge," I said aloud.

The Pearl dimmed further.

Miho said something under her breath that I didn't understand, and probably didn't want to. "It's no good," she said. "You have to master your fear yourself."

And then my panic came rushing back just as surely as the river itself. *She Charmed you and you let her,* whispered a voice in the back of my head. I told it to shut up so I could concentrate on what needed to be done.

For Haneul, I told the Pearl. *So we can get her to the ship, and from the ship into orbit, and then call for help.*

The Pearl blazed up then, although my knees were knocking from how badly they shook.

The earth rumbled. For a moment I was terrified that I'd set off a quake and we'd be swallowed up by the ground instead of perishing by water. Then gray-and-brown stone burst out of the river's banks on either side, growing into a rough-hewn arch, wide enough for one person at a time.

We had our bridge.

SIXTEEN

Sebin

I watched in awe as Min raised a bridge from the bones of the earth. Rock rose with a rumbling sound from either bank and met in the middle like two hands clasping. The ground shook, and I almost lost my balance. Dirt fell into the river, only to be swept away by the splashing waters.

"You did it, Min!" I said, and then I noticed her shaken expression. I wondered why she wasn't prouder of her achievement—well, the Dragon Pearl's achievement.

"Yes," she said, sounding anything but happy.

"At least you won't have to swim now," I said, attempting to cheer her up.

She smiled wanly. "Right. All I have to do is not fall over the side."

The smell of her dread finally made an impression on me. I hadn't realized just how much she feared falling into the river. She had never seen one before. If her homeworld had no rivers at all, no wonder she clung so tightly to the Dragon Pearl and everything it promised.

"We'll make it across together," I said. "All of us. Miho, if you and I take the stretcher, Min can focus on crossing."

"No, it's fine," Min protested. "Carrying the stretcher will distract me from . . . from the river."

Miho and I exchanged worried glances. It would be disastrous if Min lost her nerve during the crossing. On the other hand, if she was right and helping with Haneul steadied her, we had to let her try.

Reluctantly, I nodded. Miho did too after a moment. "But let us know if you need help," the assistant minister added sternly.

"Haneul," I heard Min murmuring to her friend. I could scarcely hear her over the noise of the river. "We're going to be crossing the river. It'll—it'll be all right."

I admired her for taking time to reassure a sick friend even when she was so manifestly terrified herself. I hoped I would do the same if I were ever in a similar situation. My family had talked a good game about how tigers should never show fear, but that didn't mean we never *felt* it.

When we checked on her, Haneul wasn't any better, but she wasn't worse, either. I hoped the crossing wouldn't trouble her. She was out of it, muttering nonsense rhymes about stars and ley lines in her delirium. I doubted she would have noticed if we'd stumbled upon an ice cream parlor in the middle of the wilderness.

I would have welcomed ice cream right then. Not that I wasn't grateful for the tangerines that Min and the Dragon Pearl had produced, but I regretted more than ever that I hadn't gotten a chance to try the desserts at the banquet. The stress must have been getting to me if I was daydreaming about food.

When Min and I picked up the stretcher once more, my stomach rumbled. Fortunately, the roar of the river concealed it.

Miho went first without being asked. That was very trusting

of her. It was one thing to eat magically produced fruit, and another thing entirely to trust your life to a magically produced *bridge*.

I couldn't sniff her fear, or lack of it. The wind coming off the water must have wiped that away. It was a refreshing change from the earth and crushed leaves and sweat that I'd been smelling for the past couple days. Fresh river water, not dragon-summoned rain or mud.

My shoulders ached, not so much with Haneul's weight—she wasn't all that large in her human form—but from hunching over to take the stretcher's burden. As irksome as it had been to serve as Min's steed, carrying the stretcher forced me into an unnatural posture. At least in my tiger form I had still been able to lope more or less freely.

Still, the important thing was crossing safely so we could reach the dreadnought. What we'd do once we got there was a problem for another day. I hadn't asked what the plan was, mainly because I had a strong sense that nobody knew, and nobody wanted to admit that fact, either. Best not to draw attention to the problem until we absolutely had to.

(I liked being prepared, but there was a time and place. Morale mattered, too. Sometimes more, as now.)

Water spray hit me in the face as we proceeded, even though we were some distance above the river proper. The bridge seemed solid beneath my feet, but I couldn't help remaining alert to any tremor or vibration that indicated it was about to fail.

Just as well, too. We were about halfway across when I felt it: the telltale shaking that meant the stone under us was giving way.

I had never experienced an earthquake. I knew they existed,

in the sense that the Matriarch had occasionally conde-scended to tell stories about the damage they'd done in the faraway lands where our ancestors had lived and fought and died. I had assumed that they belonged in the same category as horse-drawn carriages and palanquins, things that didn't exist anymore in a well-ordered civilization.

Except no one had told Jasujeong that it was civilized, or that its rock formations needed to stay in place for our benefit. I had assumed that Min would have conveyed this little instruc-tion to the Dragon Pearl, but apparently not. Maybe she had less control over the orb than I'd previously supposed.

All of which was moot, because we had to get across with our burden *now*, and that wasn't possible.

"Min!" Miho screamed. Jun, of course, was already on the other side, having floated across in an economical ghostly fash-ion that was not available to the rest of us flesh-and-blood beings. I didn't need a tiger's keen vision to read the panic on his face.

Min dropped her end of the stretcher and sprinted, her face white and terrified, leaving me alone with Haneul. I had to abandon the stretcher and hastily snatch up the dragon spirit. "Sorry," I mouthed to her, feeling guilty and hoping she was so out of it that my rough handling wasn't hurting her worse. The bridge crumbled away before I could move forward, and I transformed into my tiger shape as we fell.

It seemed like we fell for a long time. Everything went white. I thought of many things in that small eternity: the whiteness of stars, the whiteness of bone, the whiteness of the White Tiger who had visited me not so long ago, in another faraway story.

The whiteness of death, above all, although I would never say so.

Then we landed, and the water hit me like a blow, even though in reality we had only fallen three or four meters. *Only* is a fine word when you're sitting in the rec room discussing make-believe scenarios. It's another matter when you're living the situation.

I was more comfortable in my native shape, but more importantly, as a tiger I was not just stronger, I was better at swimming. Especially in rapidly moving water like this. I almost lost my grip on Haneul during the shift, which would have been disastrous. But before the current could carry her away, I snatched up her shirt in my jaws.

I was in luck, up to a point. The fabric didn't tear. But my mouth was filled with the foul taste of sweat and sickness, contrasting with the sweetness and mineral tang of the river water.

More importantly, I was swimming. The waters closed over my head. For a moment I panicked; then I regained control of myself and fought my way to the surface, bringing Haneul with me. I prayed she was still breathing. No way to check, not while I was a tiger.

I couldn't see the remnants of the bridge, although I thought I sustained a bruise in the side where a chunk of rock hit me. Thankfully my thick hide had prevented any worse damage, and I didn't think I had any broken bones. But the water was cold and deep and swift, and it was all I could do to swim crosswise to the current, toward the riverbank.

The shore might have been kilometers away. I had a hard time seeing it except in snatched glimpses, surrounded as I was by splashing water. I'd formerly had a high opinion of my swimming. I had not, however, previously tried to swim with my mouth full of half-conscious dragon, even a dragon in her human shape.

As I soon discovered, the only thing worse than swimming across a raging river with your mouth full of a semiconscious person's shirt was doing the exact same thing except with your mouth full of a *completely* conscious person's shirt.

In retrospect, I should have anticipated that the shock of the cold water and the noise would have roused even someone in a poison-induced delirium. Haneul didn't know (I assumed) that she was safe in my jaws. Disoriented by the situation, she yelled and lashed out with her arms and legs.

I grunted involuntarily and managed to inhale water. *That* nearly caused a coughing fit. I lost several precious moments flailing as I tried to swim, cough, and not-cough simultaneously.

That became moot when the shirt in my jaws became attached not to a panicked girl but a panicked girl *dragon*. Between one moment and the next I was bowled aside by Haneul in her dragon form, twelve meters long—long enough to have served as a bridge herself if she had been in her right mind, which she wasn't.

Haneul slapped me aside with a force like that of an unleashed thunderbolt. Intellectually, I knew she didn't mean to harm me. But instinct didn't care about intellect, especially when I'd been hurt.

I went under. Banged against a rock. I was lucky I didn't hit my head, because then I would have been in real danger of drowning. I didn't think Miho or Min had the ability to save me, not without risking themselves.

Especially when the river was suddenly full of angry, confused dragon.

My problem was no longer getting Haneul across. I assumed she could manage that herself whenever she wanted to. Mostly

I came to this conclusion because the river had stopped in its tracks.

I hadn't ever stopped to ponder how powerful Haneul's magic was. I'd assumed that the thunderstorm she'd summoned against the venomous bird-creatures was the extent of it. It hadn't occurred to me that she might have been holding back then, consciously or unconsciously.

Definitely consciously, I thought as I dodged a length of dragon-coil. To either side of us, the river waters seethed, frustrated by the unnatural magical barrier that had turned a section of it into a "lake" churned only by Haneul herself.

I heard shouting, but the words were impossible to discern over the splashing and roaring. Haneul's bellowing reminded me of thunder, of the collapse of the ill-fated stone bridge. It dwarfed even a tiger's roar, not that I had time for any such nonsense while I was striking out for the opposite shore.

I got a better glimpse of the bank and redoubled my efforts. I could finally understand the words and I recognized the voice. It was Min's.

"Haneul, it's us!" Min was shouting at the top of her lungs. Astonishing that I could hear her over my own flailing. I would have endeavored to swim more quietly, except I was preoccupied with the trivial matter of my personal survival.

In answer, Haneul bellowed again. This time I thought I heard words in the roar, rather like poetry in the language of cloud and rain, if the poem went something like *I WILL THUMP YOU.* If Haneul was in a thumping mood, I planned to be out of the river and well away from the splash radius of someone who could stop an entire river in its tracks before anything bad happened to me or the others.

"We're your friends, remember?"

I didn't think *We're your friends* was going to be persuasive to a giant angry dragon. Especially when Haneul roared back, "YOU TRIED TO DROWN ME!"

"WE WERE CROSSING THE RIVER!" Min hollered.

At this point, my fur was so drenched that I doubted I would ever be dry again unless you launched me into the local sun and left me to barbecue there for a few decades. Maybe I would serve as emergency rations for whoever found me.

Finally, I hauled myself up onto the far bank. I almost didn't believe it was real. I would have liked to fall onto my side and pant for breath like I'd been starved of air for the past century.

I glimpsed Min and Miho standing well back from the bank, both intact, and I thanked the White Tiger they were safe.

On the other hand, Haneul was still throwing her serpentine coils about, and I didn't want to be caught here if she lost her temper further and unleashed all that pent-up water in a localized flood.

I shifted back into human form so I could talk and rushed to Min's side. "Min," I said urgently, not caring whether Haneul overheard me because I figured that was a lost cause. "Shouldn't we get to higher ground?"

Min looked at me like I'd spoken in thorns. "We can't just leave her in the river," she said, thankfully in a more normal tone of voice—I was busy trying to shake the water out of my ears. "She has to come *with* us."

When she put it like that, I felt like a jerk. "You're right," I said through the taste of river water. "What can I do?"

"Miho," Min said, "I don't like it, but maybe *you* could persuade her. Use your . . . skills. Just enough to calm her down so we can get her out of the river."

It came to me then. Miho was a fox. A fox who'd employed her Charm—on me. And Min had known. A snarl started up in the back of my throat.

I forced myself to take deep breaths. I could confront Miho later. Right then, dealing with Haneul was more urgent.

I never thought our progress would be impeded because of a berserk dragon, or that the solution would be trickery. But I had to ask myself rationally, what was so bad about using Charm for a benign purpose like this one? After all, some people had a calming, authoritative presence even when magic wasn't involved. Surely this wasn't so different, especially since Min was doing it to help Haneul.

Surely.

Miho stepped forward. Somehow her suit was perfectly dry, a minor miracle of its own given the circumstances. A spiteful part of me was glad that at least her hair was as messy as mine felt. (I didn't want to know how many hours of grooming it would take me to fix my fur.)

"Let me help you with this," Miho said.

"Wait a second," I said as my misgivings redoubled in force. Unfortunately, my new clarity only lasted for a moment. I had just a moment to realize that Miho was Charming me, and not for the first time.

Then my worries washed away again. Min was frowning, but I wasn't sure why. Miho had offered her support, wasn't that wonderful? I was so glad we had someone as helpful as Miho on our side.

"You shouldn't have," Min said in a low voice.

"It's the best way to help Haneul," Miho said in that smooth voice of hers. "That's all. It's not so much different than using it"—there was the subtlest emphasis on *it*—"directly on Haneul herself, you know. Just a little nudging, for our safety." Also that emphasis on *our*.

I wondered vaguely about the subtext of the conversation, but then a jagged stroke of lightning slashed across the sky directly above Haneul. "Whatever you're doing," I said, "you might as well make it fast."

"Yes, of course," Min said, sounding sad for no reason I could discern.

Min and Miho stood side by side, and I was struck anew by how much they looked alike, although they weren't related. Miho's features were more finely sculpted, and she held herself regally, while Min couldn't disguise the scrappiness at her core. But there was a kinship between them, and it made me long to go back to the *Haetae*, where I had crew and friends, my makeshift family.

Miho's voice rose in a chant. I recognized a few words here and there in an archaic form of Korean, the ancestor of the language we speak in the Thousand Worlds, and that was only because the Matriarch had ordered all of us to learn some of the old texts by heart. Linguistics wasn't my strong point, so all I knew was that the chant had something to do with *peace* and *friendship* and . . . *toothbrushes?* I had probably misunderstood that last word.

Haneul's head, large enough to chomp the three of us for a midafternoon snack, swayed back and forth on her long, snaky neck. Little by little her head lowered until it was resting on the mud of the riverbank, her eyes heavy-lidded. She made a sound that was half exhalation, half snore.

And then she was human again, lying curled up on the shore.

SEVENTEEN

Min

The river surged, no longer held in check by the force of Haneul's magic. I groaned at the thought of having to flee for higher ground, but the current stayed confined to its bed. Silently, I thanked Haneul for coming back to her senses. The water's relatively good behavior had to be her doing.

I tensed anyway, ready to help move her despite my exhaustion. However, Miho beat me to Haneul's side. That made sense. Unlike Sebin, Miho hadn't just completed a perilous swim while defending herself against an enraged dragon. Unlike Jun, she was made of flesh and blood. Unlike me . . . well, I'd simply been slow to react. Still, Miho had taken care of Haneul earlier, so she'd probably be more helpful than I would have been. I was better with machines than people.

"If only I had managed to calm her down," Sebin said ruefully.

Miho looked at them strangely. "Don't be ridiculous, Sebin. You were ferrying Haneul across the river in the first place. You did your best."

"'Ferrying' isn't the word I'd use," Sebin said, and grimaced as though they'd tasted something foul.

Miho pressed her hands to Haneul's temples. Haneul seemed to flinch at her touch, but I must have imagined it. Miho might be a trickster, but surely she wouldn't hurt my friend for no reason. For a second I thought Haneul might rally, but then the dragon cadet sighed and lay back on the riverbank, paler than ever.

"The transformation must have exhausted her," Miho said, frowning slightly.

"We lost the stretcher," Jun said glumly, looking downstream.

"I screwed up," Sebin said. "I had to drop it in order to carry Haneul."

"It's not your fault," I said. "We all had other things to worry about." Who knew where the stretcher would end up? Maybe, a thousand years from now, some explorer or archaeologist would come across it washed up on some floodplain and devise a theory of an "ancient civilization" of inventors to explain its origin.

"We'll have to carry her the hard way," Sebin said.

"I'd hoped she was starting to recover, but . . ." I looked sadly at my sick friend. "I guess not."

Jun watched me with dark eyes. "We'll get help for her," he said. "She'll be fine eventually."

I eyed him hopefully. "Is that a prophecy?"

Jun's laugh was strained. "If only. That's not one of my powers. It's just an ordinary wish."

In silence, Sebin shifted into their tiger form. Miho and I draped Haneul across their back, securing her with some cord from the survival kit. Sebin promised to use their smoothest gait so she wouldn't fall off. With that, we set off.

The minutes blurred into hours, the hours into days. We'd spent two weeks on the planet and were nearing the starship, according to the map. Haneul's condition didn't improve. Every so often she would stir, and I could *smell* my own desperation. I was grateful that Sebin didn't mention it. But each time we checked her over, Miho gave the unhappy verdict: It was only an interlude, and Haneul's condition remained unchanged. "She's powerful to have made it this far," she added once.

Curiously, the only times Haneul revived was when we stopped to eat. Our abandoned campsites would mark our progress for anyone tracking us, because we weren't making any effort to hide our trail and we were leaving a series of tangerine-grove waypoints. We'd worried about the Pearl's reliability after the bridge incident, but that had—I suspected—been due to my fear rather than a fault of the Pearl's magic. You'd think we'd be getting sick of them, but the tangerines remained as delicious and filling as ever.

"I didn't realize Haneul loved tangerines so much that she'd rouse from the dead for them," Jun said, clearly trying to lighten the mood. Haneul only ate sections that Sebin and I would peel and feed to her, bit by bit, taking turns. Neither of us considered asking Miho to do it.

We traveled from the lowlands into marshes, which were the most exhausting of all. I grew used to having my shoes soaked through. Sebin walked with curious mincing steps, presumably so as not to drop Haneul from her perch on their back, as we wound our way between the tall grasses.

Small buzzing insects tormented us with their bites, and I longed to shift into my fox form so my fur could protect me from the worst of the welts. But I didn't want to give away my true identity to Miho even now. I could endure the bites a little longer. My fox instincts warned me that I shouldn't trust her completely, despite the fact that we were traveling together.

My world narrowed not only to the marsh, but to my immediate surroundings. The leaves that tickled against my nose and made me itch painfully whenever they brushed against my bug bites. The wet sloshing of mud. I bathed every time we found a suitable source of water for the Pearl to transform, but that didn't do much to erase the wear and tear of travel.

The smells of water and rotting logs pervaded the air, as well as the eerie cries of the birdlike creatures that hissed menacing songs at us. The bugs seemed to bother Sebin and me but leave Miho alone, and I wished I knew what her magic was and if I could someday get her to teach it to me. But mostly I was too sunk in my own misery to think much.

So absorbed was I in the problem of walking steadily without being distracted by the glare of sunlight in my eyes or the stinging bugs dive-bombing my vulnerable eyes, ears, and nose that I crashed into Miho and Sebin when they came to a dead stop. Luckily, thanks to the cords still holding her in place, Haneul didn't fall off Sebin's back. In fact, she didn't so much as twitch a muscle.

"We found it," Miho breathed. A complex smell rose from her, discernible even over the stink of swamp water and sweat. Triumph and . . . desperation?

I craned my neck to see beyond her.

I hadn't recognized it before because it was so immense.

I'd mistaken it for a mountain in the distance, sheened over by a shimmering layer of fog. Marsh gases and light reflecting off the water sometimes created strange illusions.

But this was no illusion. I had dreamed of serving aboard a starship all my life. Jun and I used to discuss the different classes that the Thousand Worlds had produced, and I'd forgotten some of the old ones that were no longer in production, that had long ago been destroyed or cashiered.

That silhouette, though, told me this was indeed the dreadnought *Sejong-Daewang*, named after one of the legendary kings of the lost homeworld, from the days before humans and supernaturals dispersed to the Thousand Worlds and beyond. Daewang Sejong, or the Great King Sejong, had invented the Hangeul alphabet. Before that, the people of his land had used a completely different writing system, one based on logographs, which required years to master. The new alphabet, said the yangban officials who resisted the king's innovation, was "so easy even a woman could learn it." My family had had to explain to me that in the very old days, scholarship was mostly the province of men. As foxes, who usually chose to be female, we thought this very silly.

Only three dreadnoughts like the *Sejong-Daewang* had ever been built, and all of them had been lost, or so Jun had told me when we were both fox kits on Jinju dreaming of a better life. One ship had been lost to treachery; one had self-destructed in battle and no one had survived to report where it took place; and the last, this one, had been resting on Jasujeong in the aftermath of a great and terrible war.

Starships took all sorts of shapes, but this one reminded me of nothing so much as a cannon. It bristled with gun turrets.

Although it rested aslant, it looked like a great wedge built around the central core of its engine.

Jun and I met each other's eyes. For once my brother didn't look sad or regretful. He glowed faintly, and although I couldn't smell him, I knew he shared my enthusiasm for the technological beauty of the ancient ship.

Then he frowned. "We're not alone," Jun said in a low, tense voice.

I sniffed the air. He was right. It wasn't the smell that alerted me. It was the change in temperature.

This was midday. We'd endured the sun on our backs, the blinding glare of its light reflecting off water and leaves. I'd grown inured to the suffocating heat, the way mirages of an inferno danced in front of my eyes, and learned to trust my nose over my eyes.

Now the heat had evaporated, replaced by a cold wind like the one that accompanied Jun wherever he went. Only this wasn't his usual small breeze. It was as though winter was invading the marsh. I could even see that the water was icing over . . . *toward* us.

"Maybe we had better get out of here," Jun said uneasily.

"We can't," Miho said. Was that a whiff of frustration I detected from her?

I frowned at Miho, not liking the sense of anger. But she was right. "We need that ship to get off-planet," I said. "We can't turn tail and run."

"Then we're going to have to get past the ship's guardian ghosts," Miho said grimly. "Sebin, stay back. I don't think your strength and fighting prowess are going to be of any help against the intangible."

Sebin growled in agreement.

At first my dazzled eyes suggested that we were surrounded by ghosts in every direction, a horde of translucent white spirits with telltale long, ragged hair, like Jun's. I did a quick estimate and there weren't quite as many as my senses had initially suggested, more like fifteen or twenty.

The longer I studied them, however, the more I was able to pick out differences . . . and similarities. All of them wore uniforms, although they didn't look like the ones that Sebin and Jun were wearing. Instead of modern buttons, they had fancy ties that must have been a pain to do and undo quickly, and way more ornamentation than we had nowadays with the sleeker braid and lack of tassels. It hadn't occurred to me that military fashion would change over time, but of course it did.

None of them had donned spacesuits, an interesting detail. It suggested that the ship had made a controlled landing and that no one had feared suffocation in vacuum or poison gases from a hostile atmosphere.

The uniforms didn't have color as such. The ghosts appeared in variations of white and gray, like afterimages when one stared too long at an ink painting. Their glares conveyed a distinct sense of menace. We were not welcome here.

The ghosts kept their distance, which I found interesting. What did the dead have to fear from us?

As much as I disliked shamans, I wished we had one now to lay the ghosts to rest. I didn't know how *many* ghosts a shaman could deal with at once—that probably depended on the individual. But it didn't matter. We didn't have a shaman with us.

No, we'd have to rely on Miho's power . . . and mine, if hers wasn't enough.

I'd Charmed ghosts before, on a planet of ghosts. And now, like then, I had the magic of the Dragon Pearl to back me up. But I wasn't sure that *these* ghosts wanted the same thing as the ones on the Fourth Colony.

"Maybe we can negotiate with them," I said in a low voice, raising an eyebrow at Miho.

"Only after we've softened them up," she said.

We marched toward the ghosts, despite the way my heart pounded in my chest. The specters receded from us like mirages of wind and omen. The breeze whispered curses at us, and *"Go back, go back."* The dreadnought seemed to grow no nearer.

This dance continued for some time, us walking toward the ship, the ghosts drawing back, refusing to engage with us.

"This might be a trap," Sebin said, voicing what we were all thinking.

Miho stepped ahead of me and stopped. "We're here to make a bargain," she said in a voice whose confidence I envied.

I stifled a sneeze, not for the first time.

From the throng of ghosts, one floated forward to speak with her. My nose itched: Miho was focusing all her Charm on the apparent leader. It made sense that ghosts from a military ship would acknowledge some kind of hierarchy.

This ghost hadn't stood out from the crowd earlier: a short person, shorter even than me, with their hair asymmetrically shaved and a round face. But I quickly changed my evaluation when I looked into their white-gray eyes. This was someone used to giving orders and being obeyed. The kind of person, if I was completely honest with myself, I didn't always get along with.

I didn't have a choice now. It wasn't just a matter of *getting along with*. We had to convince this ghost to let us pass. I suspected that if this one caved, the rest would comply.

"You do have a way of turning up in the strangest places, Miho," the ghost said. "How did you escape detection this time? By bribing someone? Oh wait, you don't need to rely on bribes like ordinary people."

Jun and I exchanged startled glances. Sebin was standing off to the side, their expression baffled.

"Miho," I said, "you've been here before?"

"Yes."

I didn't want a *yes*. I wanted an explanation.

The ghost laughed unkindly. "Miho's sister was a member of the crew. She went on to the spirit world, unlike the rest of us."

Now Sebin turned to stare at Miho. "How . . . ?"

"I have a supernatural heritage," Miho said without specifying, although I couldn't see why it mattered whether or not Sebin knew she was a fox if she was going to Charm the memory out of them anyway. "My kind can live not just for years, but centuries, under the right conditions."

An ugly suspicion unspooled in my brain. "So, you have a history with this captain?" I eyed the head ghost.

For the first time, I saw Miho wince. "That's . . ."

The ghost straightened, to the extent a ghost can do that while hovering in the air. Suddenly they didn't look so short anymore. "I'm *Admiral* Paik Sumin," they said, "and I landed the *Sejong-Daewang* on Jasujeong, in fire and ruin, rather than continue to fight a disastrous war with the Sun Clans."

"My request has nothing to do with the Sun Clans," Miho

said quickly. "We are stranded on this world, and we'll perish if we can't get back into orbit to call for help. We need your ship."

I stopped myself from narrowing my eyes just in time. Miho was lying about the Sun Clans. Did ghosts have a sense of smell? I'd never thought to ask that of Jun, and I couldn't right now. Jun was watching the other ghosts, his expression inscrutable. Did he feel a sense of kinship with them?

If I remembered correctly, Miho had told me that resurrecting this very ship would threaten the delicate balance of power between the Sun Clans and the Thousand Worlds. . . . For all I knew, the peace talks had ended with the space station disaster, and we were at war again. I hadn't allowed myself to think about that possibility the whole time we'd been making our overland trek.

"I'm sorry," the admiral said, "but I can't permit that. Frankly, Miho, you're the last person who should be allowed access to this ship."

The admiral and their crew of ghosts resumed moving. As though hypnotized, we followed them. The wintry cold, the ice . . . For the first time since the encounter had begun, I took my eyes off the ghosts—an action that made me incredibly nervous—and looked around.

We'd been drawn into the heart of an artificial winter. I couldn't even tell that we were in a marsh anymore. The ground underfoot was frozen solid. I thanked heaven that fox magic had provided me with socks and shoes, but even so, the cold nipped at my toes and fingers, my nose and ears. The fact that I'd come this far without paying heed to the chill or the dangers it posed worried me.

It wasn't just winter, either, but a winter *labyrinth*. We stood in occluded archways of ice beyond which we could only glimpse the starship in kaleidoscopic fragments. Cold wind breathed uncanny laments, and icicles glistened like grinning teeth. I couldn't imagine this environment was good for Haneul especially. The transfigured landscape was beautiful, but it was going to be our doom.

That's it, I thought dreamily. *In a thousand years they'll find us frozen like icicles. If only we'd hauled our spacesuits with us! They would have offered some protection from this chill.*

Miho's voice rang out again, coaxing, confident. "We just need to go up long enough to use your comms to call for help. Surely you wouldn't want to be responsible for more deaths."

The admiral laughed harshly. "Plenty of people have died on Jasujeong. Why should you be any different?"

Miho seemed to be glowing incandescently. I sneezed into my elbow as power gusted from her. But it wasn't focused on the admiral, as I had expected, but on Jun!

"You can't do this!" I screamed as I launched myself toward Miho, hoping I could knock her over and break her concentration.

She dodged more swiftly than I had imagined possible, as though she were made of wind and whispers. I landed roughly. Ghost luck, always bad.

I began to shout at Miho, my blood seething with fury. I swiped at her, unsuccessfully. It was difficult to focus on anything when I was trying to avoid sneezing and giving my true nature away.

A persuasive inner voice told me I should go along with Miho's plan, whatever it was—she was the adult in the situation, and surely she knew what was best. Miho would be able to get us out of this pickle.

That brought me up short. When had relying on adults ever worked for me?

Brute strength wasn't the answer. I had to persuade Miho to stop.

I looked up at Miho, only to see the others at her side. The twenty ghosts, especially the admiral. Sebin, Haneul, even my brother Jun, whom I had thought immune, like me. All of them were united against me.

She'd Charmed them.

EIGHTEEN

Sebin

"I have need of you," Miho murmured, so softly that only I heard her. "There is an enemy keeping us from getting to the ship—and rescue. A wretched magician."

I believed her. Why wouldn't I? She'd done right by us ever since we had the good fortune of running into her on Jasujeong. I wasn't sure what the threat was, since I didn't remember our group including a *magician*, but I growled and nodded my shaggy head to let her know she could count on me.

I was already in the shape of a tiger, fortunately, which would make it easier for me to fight. And it was clear that a fight lay before us.

Next to me my comrades waited: the ghost Jun and the dragon spirit Haneul. I widened my eyes in amazement. Not only did Haneul look recovered, but she also smelled healthier beneath the miasma of sweat. She swayed back and forth in her human form, as though to the beat of an unseen drum.

Before us a teenage girl stood defiantly. That must be the magician. I wasn't fooled. I knew that magicians had tricks of their own, and this one posed a threat. Especially if Miho said so.

The magician-girl shouted angrily at us. She didn't *look* particularly dangerous, but I knew better. I hardened my heart against her unimposing appearance.

Miho resumed speaking: "She has turned the ghosts of this place against us. We must bring her down so we can escape this planet."

Indeed, ghosts crowded us on every side, breathing without breathing. Winter blasted from their presence until I could no longer remember the scent of spring flowers, or the warmth of summer. Their eyes were blizzard-white and full of menace. I didn't want to know what they wanted to do to us.

Haneul shimmered, then reared. Her head broke through the ceiling of the ice passages that had sprung up around us. Above us blazed a discordantly fierce sun.

In a matter of moments, however, storm clouds gathered, blotting out the sunlight. It went from light to dark so swiftly that I couldn't help snarling in instinctive fear. I remembered how Haneul had stopped the river in its tracks, even if only for the space of minutes.

The wind swirled wildly around us, like a miniature hurricane. Miho, Haneul, and I were sheltered in its eye. The magician, on the other hand, crouched low to keep from being blown away.

"Well done," Miho said to Haneul, and I bristled with envy, wishing her warmth was directed toward me. "But we need to capture her and neutralize her magic."

Determination flared in my heart, even though we didn't have the aid of a friendly shaman or magician. I was guessing that a magician's powers took some degree of concentration to use, and they would cease to endanger us if the wielder herself was unconscious. I would have liked to question Miho on that point, but there was no time. We had to deal with the magician as soon as possible.

The girl darted to the side, making for one of the icy archways that led away from the collapse that Haneul had caused. The dragon roared, but the gust of wind that accompanied the noise only had the effect of pushing the magician *toward* the passage, the opposite of what we wanted.

Jun started after the magician, then stopped, confusion written over his features. "Min . . . ?" he asked. Then his expression firmed, and he vanished in a puff of cold vapor.

I didn't know what Jun was struggling with, but I did know that cutting off the magician's retreat was now up to me. I leaped after the girl, following her scent and sound. She fled, surprisingly swift for a human.

My senses went into overdrive. I exulted in the joy of the hunt. Thoughts of duty, of doing my best to live up to Miho's expectations, were erased. All that existed was the age-old work of the predator. *This* was what I had been made for.

My feet, covered as they were in fur and tipped with claws, gripped the ice securely as I chased the magician. What was her name? *Min*, whispered the human corner of my mind. I paid it no heed. An insignificant detail.

I could smell the magician's fear, like a rich spice. It blew off her like a wind out of the south, like a promise written in the language of meat. The patter of her shoes against the ice was loud, so loud. I could have heard it from miles away in the vastness of the labyrinth.

I should have figured that magicians were not easy prey. It wasn't like I'd ever had the chance to practice against the real thing before. My family had staged hunts, of course, but we'd only pursued rabbits, voles, deer. Creatures that were fleet of foot but not necessarily magical, or cunning.

I was sure I'd had a run-in with this particular magician before, although I had trouble bringing the details to mind. They dispersed like fog in a high wind.

The scent drifted away into more of the icy archways, and I realized that I could no longer pinpoint the source of the footsteps, that I'd been hearing echoes and not the real thing for some time.

I was lost. Worse, I was separated from Miho and Haneul, my allies.

I skidded to a halt and put my head to the ground, rather than looking up and around me. As far as I could tell, I was deep within the ice labyrinth that the ghosts had created. I had no idea how far I had gone from the dreadnought that was our ultimate goal.

Priorities, I reminded myself. Miho had said that the magician and her army of ghosts stood between us and the dreadnought. I had to deal with the magician first.

I sniffed the ground carefully. Mostly I smelled traces of minerals and salt in the ice, and my own tiger scent. Nothing of the magician's sour human reek, or her fear.

I closed my eyes and huffed, annoyed with myself for failing Miho when she had been depending on me. I'd lost the trail. It bothered me that the magician had outwitted me so easily.

I sniffed the ground again. Still no scent.

A memory stirred in my mind. Maybe magicians, like foxes and tigers and dragons, had the ability to change their shape. Or cloak themselves in illusions.

I straightened, resisting the urge to yowl my revelation, not that the others understood the language of tigers anyway. I hadn't lost the scent because the magician had evaporated. Rather, the magician had changed her shape—and thus her scent.

The only animal smell in this area was my own. This, I thought, was a small blessing. The ghosts had frozen the labyrinth solid, so that no animals ventured here other than fools like me.

Not fools, I told myself. Desperate people, under Miho's guidance. Aliens to this planet, just as this planet was alien to us.

That gave me an idea. I didn't know the limits of a magician's shape-shifting or illusions, but surely whatever she'd turned into, it would have a newness to it. A freshness at odds with the rest of the labyrinth.

I allowed myself a quick glance around. Nothing stood out, and I doubted that the magician had turned herself into ice. All the ice smelled the same, anyway: that same tang of strange minerals and salts. I hoped I wouldn't have to *taste* it.

Then I lowered my head to the ground and sniffed yet again, spiraling outward. This time, instead of concentrating on nuances, I allowed my mind to drift. *Something that doesn't fit*, I chanted to myself as I meandered. *Something that doesn't fit.*

Gradually my heart rate slowed. I forgot about the urgency of our mission. I forgot that I was trapped on a planet with dive-bombing raptors and inedible plants. I even forgot about Miho, strangely enough. All that mattered was getting to know my environment, and what didn't fit in with it—besides myself.

I had a faint awareness that I might be wasting time. With each passing moment, chances were higher that the magician would get away. That might have been her plan all along—to entangle me in this foolish search while she secured her escape.

No. I couldn't afford to second-guess myself. I had to commit myself to the search. Finding the magician was the most important thing. I had to trust my instincts, passed down from a long line of tigers, however dubious their ethics.

Ethics, said another whisper, but I shoved it out of my mind as irrelevant. I had a task. All that mattered was completing the task.

Eventually I came to a halt before . . . a tree. I huffed, watching the steam that my breath formed in the frigid air.

I stood at the edge of the labyrinth. I'd left behind the passages of ice, the barricades of icicles. Here grew trees, all shorn of their leafy plumage. Most of them were tall, like abandoned giants, left to brood over a decrepit kingdom and dream of a long-vanished spring.

Most of them were tall, but not the one I had stopped before. It was no taller than I was as a human, the height of a leggy teenager or your average Thousand Worlds adult.

I observed other anomalies. Botany wasn't my strong point, but even I had noticed that the trees here differed from the maples and ginkgoes and acacias I'd grown up with. These grew in grotesque shapes, as though carved by some forgotten disaster.

The magician-tree (or so I had already begun to think of it) didn't resemble any of Jasujeong's trees. It stood straight, as though not yet bowed down by the hands of wind and winter. Its bark had no blemishes. Most of all, it looked and smelled exactly like a sycamore sapling . . . hardly native to this planet.

Still, I had to double-check. I pawed at the ice, broke its surface, and dug down to the tops of the roots, pale and stringy. The tree trembled as though it could read the suspicions in my skull. Then I found it: the merest trace of the magician's scent. I roared my triumph three times. Excessive, maybe, but after the initial frustration of losing the magician's trail, I couldn't help myself. The tree shook again, and fragments of ice and bark rained down on my thick pelt. I was too determined to allow that to affect me.

The magician knew the game was up. In a flash of condensation and swirling light, the tree changed into the form of a human girl. Still smaller than me, but not to be underestimated. She shivered in the cold, despite being clad in a conjured rabbit-fur coat and boots and a fox-eared knitted hat. But she glared at me insolently, unwilling to be cowed.

"Sebin," she said urgently, biting off each syllable as though it might freeze in her mouth, "you've got to listen to me. Miho isn't your friend! She's controlling your mind. *She's a fox, like me!*"

I narrowed my eyes and growled, wondering why she was wasting time making ridiculous accusations instead of using *her* wicked powers. Maybe she was a magician *and* a fox? Was this some kind of complicated trick? I crouched and gathered myself, ready to pounce.

The magician's face scrunched up in frustration. I could smell it pouring off her. Any more of it and she would have collapsed into an inkblot-shaped black hole.

"Sebin—"

Listening to a magician, or a fox, or a magician-fox, was a bad idea. I pounced.

The magician vanished in a swoosh of air. No, not vanished, I realized as the scent walloped my nose a fraction of a second later. She'd combined her dodge with a shape-change, this time into a hawk.

Still, she hadn't accounted for tiger reflexes, or the fact that I could rear on my hind legs like a horse. With a mighty swipe of my paws, I batted her out of the air. She fell with a squawk that sounded more like an offended chicken (ironic, for a fox) than a bird of prey.

The magician wasn't done trying to escape, as much as I wished she would give up and face justice. I batted at the downed hawk—and missed as she turned into a shiny beetle. My attempt to squash the beetle with my paw failed as she scuttled behind a rock covered with dead moss.

I yowled as my claws dug into an unexpectedly soft patch of dirt, which I'd expected to be frozen solid, and got stuck. I wasted precious moments pulling my paw out. I'd failed again. The magician was surely long gone by now.

I heard footsteps approaching behind me. Two sets of them were lighter and more rapid, one set slower and more assured. I knew the latter belonged to Miho.

The magician's words nagged at me. *She's a fox, like me!*

Why would a fox need to trick me like this instead of using her powers?

Why, indeed, unless *another fox* had magic more potent than hers?

The old stories about fox spirits always portrayed them as solitary villains. The dangerous foxes of legend didn't work together or come in families, although I knew they didn't just spring up from the ground like mushrooms after the rain. It had never occurred to me that two foxes would be *adversaries*.

I whined in confusion, not knowing what to believe. The smaller fox could have taken advantage of my hesitation to escape. If she'd done that, I would have *known* she was my enemy, as Miho had said.

But the magician-fox hadn't done that. She reappeared after a few moments, standing warily out of reach. Her breath misted the air in front of her face. She was still wearing that ridiculous fox-eared hat.

Miho caught up to us. "Sebin," she said warmly.

I wanted nothing more than to listen to her say my name over and over. To do what she wanted of me. At the same time, a spark in the deep heart of me had been roused by the magician's warning.

"Knock her out, Sebin!" Miho cried in a commanding voice.

At the same time, the magician said, "I can counter her magic—but only if you let me. I won't force it on you."

Miho stood on one side of me, the magician on the other. I hunkered down exactly at the midpoint between them.

Miho muttered a curse under her breath—but my hearing was good. Then she said, "Don't listen to Min!" My head turned involuntarily. I had a hard time tearing my gaze away from Miho. Wasn't sure I wanted to. It was as if she had turned into the sole star in an infinite night sky.

The magician—Miho had called her Min—didn't say anything, only continued to stand there, as upright as a calligraphy stroke, looking at me with a mute appeal in her eyes.

Maybe Min was simply more subtle.

I smelled a flare of triumph from Miho as my muscles tensed to pounce.

That would have been yet another perfect moment for Min to flee. But she didn't.

She stood her ground, and if she was using her magic on me, I couldn't tell. Which was the problem with foxes, wasn't it? But I was sure of one thing: Min had been correct that Miho was up to something.

My mind was made up now. The world blurred around me as I leaped toward Min—

—and executed a 180-degree turn the moment I landed, launching myself again, this time at Miho.

The older fox, overconfident of her control over me, was taken by surprise. But she was an experienced and devious fox, and I was overconfident in my own right. Before I could reach her, she pulled a blaster out from nowhere. The last thing I saw was a corona of migraine-colored light.

NINETEEN

Min

Sebin lay stunned between Miho and myself, returned to human form.

I'd lost my one ally. Tears pricked at my eyes as I contemplated Jun, standing next to Miho as though she had leashed him. Haneul had resumed her human shape at some point and stood to the other side, seemingly unaffected by the wintry chill—or the poison.

In fact, Haneul looked radiant. Her skin glowed with good health. I'd seen Miho offer her an arm after she'd stumbled earlier. Had the assistant minister used fox magic on her?

Then the truth hit me like a blow to the stomach. Nausea knotted deep in my belly. "Haneul was never poisoned," I said. "You lied when you claimed you didn't have special medical skills. You used them to *make* her sick. So she'd be one less obstacle standing in your way."

Haneul showed no sign of having heard my accusation. Her head was turned slightly to face Miho. Her eyes were wide and glassy, and she was smiling as though someone had just announced that she could celebrate seven birthdays a year.

Miho's mouth thinned. "If you want to put it that way, yes. I had to weaken her before Charm would affect her the way I needed it to. She's surprisingly strong-willed."

I wanted to turn into a fox and bite her ankle, except it probably smelled like old socks. *Tasted* like old socks. Even fox magic couldn't save Miho from sweat and grunge.

"So much for using your magic to *do good*," I said bitterly. Her weight shifted, and I felt the pressure of her magic increase. I wanted to sneeze but couldn't, which is a pretty awful feeling, but not as awful as being surrounded by Charmed friends.

Miho studied me intently. "I know something of your record," she said.

My heart sank. How had I forgotten that Miho was a *government official?* When she'd talked a good game about all she could do for foxes and other renegades, it hadn't occurred to me that she might have *dirt* on me.

I thought back to something Seok had said during my orientation forever ago. I hadn't been paying attention at the time, mainly because I was more interested in figuring out how to hack the coffee dispenser. But he'd mentioned something about the fact that records relating to my earliest adventures and how I'd obtained the Dragon Pearl were classified as top-secret. And that should have been that . . . except Miho was high-ranking enough that she could have walked right in and ordered herself a copy.

She must have seen the realization dawning on my face. "It's curious how tightly sealed your records are, Min," she said. "But a magician of your precocity and age? Immune to a gumiho's magic? No wonder. Unfortunately, I didn't have enough time to track down a cryptographer I could Charm into breaking highly confidential ciphers."

Apparently, she hadn't been able to access my records after all. One point for me.

Miho took a step toward me. I tensed but didn't turn tail. What good would it have done? I couldn't abandon my friends to her control.

I must have muttered the thought under my breath, or else it was easy enough for an experienced fox like Miho to divine.

Miho kept speaking. "Foxes have always had to use trickery to survive, Min. A magician should be aware of that. Could *you* ever have obtained the Dragon Pearl without using your own special abilities, I wonder?"

She'd gone too far. I could feel myself shaking with rage, or maybe shivering from the cold, or quaking with guilt at the memory of how I'd disguised myself as Haneul and Sujin's friend Jang. . . . I couldn't differentiate my conflicting emotions. It didn't matter, anyway.

What could I safely reveal? "I was on a quest to clear my brother's name," I spat out. "Because they'd accused him of deserting, and it wasn't his fault!"

It crushed my heart to see Jun floating at Miho's side, apparently insensible to anything I was saying. He was my older brother. I'd always relied on him looking out for me.

Maybe it was my turn to look out for *him*.

"So how do you know," Miho returned, "that I don't have an important reason of my own?"

I scowled at her. "You Charmed my friends!"

I squirmed inside at the hypocrisy of the accusation. I'd done the same thing to get where I needed to go. I hadn't possessed the money to buy passage to Jun's ship, and I'd had no information about where he had disappeared to. I hadn't had a choice.

It had made sense at the time. It wasn't as though I'd run away from home and deliberately set out to make friends with the people I was deceiving. I'd improvised my way out of one problem only to land in another.

Still, all these sounded like excuses in my head. *I* knew I'd had the best of intentions—clearing my brother's name, or coming to his rescue—but no one else did. I doubted that the government's dossier on me was particularly flattering on that point, not that Miho had gotten a chance to read it.

"All right," I said, trying not to sound defensive and failing, "what's *your* excuse?"

"I need the ship."

I waited for more, but that was it. I scoffed. "We all need the ship. Or are you"—fear gripped me in cold claws—"planning on leaving us all behind while you swan off?"

Miho's eyes narrowed. "If we are to win the war against the Sun Clans, we need control of the dreadnought. 'Peace' with them was only ever going to be an illusion."

"You *want* there to be a war?" I asked, appalled.

Her silence was answer enough.

I grimaced. "So you *are* going to abandon us. Why join us in the first place, then?" That was the part that didn't make sense. She could have beaten us to the starship—or knocked us out in our sleep and raced ahead. Why wait until now?

Her eyes went opaque. She was deciding whether or not to tell me the truth. "Because the ship's ghosts will only negotiate with one of their own," she said. "I found that out a long time ago."

I was in big trouble. The only reason she'd tell me the truth—and I was pretty sure that had, in fact, been the truth—was if she no longer saw me as a threat. Which meant she was about to—

I waited for the sneeze that would signal she was redirecting her Charm against *me*. It didn't come. I looked around in confusion.

Miho's mouth twisted. "I can tell what you're thinking. Charming you *would* be easier if I could manage it, but you're annoyingly immune to my best efforts. Sometimes a fox has to do things the hard way. Tell me, Min, besides your brother, how much family do you have?"

I didn't understand the change in subject. Maybe they should have let her read my dossier after all, to save me this conversation. But I decided to humor her, on the grounds that any distraction from her walloping me with Charm was a good distraction.

Keep her attention. Talk for everything you're worth.

Fortunately, talking was one thing I was good at. "I used to live with my mom and aunties and cousins and brother in a dome house on Jinju," I said. I thought of ways to elude the fact that we'd all been foxes in hiding. "The adults were very strict with us. They didn't want to get in trouble with the authorities, who always took the side of the richer people on the planet. We had neighbors, if by 'neighbors' you mean inhabitants of other dome houses you had to ride the scooter to get to. Did *you* grow up in a dome house?"

"I know of them," Miho said. Who didn't? She smelled now of melancholy, at odds with the tranquil, almost blissful expressions on Haneul and Jun. "I was among the last generation of foxes to leave the Old World behind. Even we knew our time was up."

I didn't take the claim seriously. After all, who better than a fox to know that another fox was probably a liar? Especially since—I thought with a pang of guilt—I'd told my share of whoppers in the past.

"The Sun Clans and the Thousand Worlds have been warring with each other since before they colonized planets in space," Miho said.

Once I was moving in higher circles, as opposed to being stuck on a half-terraformed planet in the middle of nowhere, I'd started hearing about the intermittent conflict between the two nations. Maybe the news on the holo set had mentioned it from time to time, but to be honest, as a child I'd been too busy with chores and resentment to pay attention to anything as abstract as interstellar politics. I made an assenting noise to encourage Miho to keep talking.

Something nagged at me, though. I didn't consider myself savvy enough to be able to discern whether Miho was *really* telling the truth or not . . . but anger was rising off her like radiation. Contemplating the dried-up bones of the past, which I normally would have considered boring ancient history, made her mad.

"There was a war so long ago that even the historians lost its name," Miho said softly. "A war between the Sun Clans and the Thousand Worlds. The Sun Clanners of today deny it, and even our own people have swept the details under the rug, but the Clans' warships destroyed many of our early colonies."

"If even the historians have forgotten," I asked skeptically, "why does it matter anymore?"

Her eyes flashed. "You don't remember how you were born, but surely you consider the fact of your existence important. The present is born from the womb of the past."

She looked away from my face, into a history that she didn't, and couldn't, share with me.

Turns out I was wrong on that point.

"I come from a long line of foxes," Miho said quietly. "We have tricked queens and kings, scholars and peasants, all manner of people. One of my ancestors was known to debate philosophy with the Dragon King Under the Sea. Another story for another time, perhaps. In all that time, we have eaten livers and played with hearts, but we never, ever forgot that we, too, are Korean."

I was shamed into silence by the ancient word, one that I hadn't heard since one of my childhood history lessons. *Korean*, derived from the name of the ancient kingdom of Goryeo. To be honest, it was a struggle to remember any details beyond that. History hadn't been my favorite subject. I'd always had more of an affinity for technology.

But I remembered nights on Jinju when Jun and I had climbed onto the rooftop and stared past the blurred haze of the dome. He'd wanted to see every one of the Thousand Worlds—some mess we'd made of *that*—and been determined to be the first fox spirit to serve in the Space Forces. To show that a fox could be capable of duty and honor.

Things had gone awry in ways that I didn't want to recount, and which Miho would discover if she ever Charmed her way into the records. But the fact that Miho and her family felt this same loyalty to our people shamed me. For the longest time I'd been aware that the people of the Thousand Worlds reviled my kind, for things that . . . Well, okay. *Originally* I hadn't been guilty of anything but being born a fox, but if I explained my adventures to your average citizen now, security clearance aside, they would have reinforced my family's belief that we should hide meekly.

"You fought," I said, understanding dawning.

Miho laughed bitterly. "You think *I* signed on to fight? Oh, no. I had other plans for my life. Even as, one by one, the others of my kind served and died. But my sister—" Her voice caught on the word. "My *sister* served on the *Sejong-Daewang*. Served, and died, like the others, in an attack by the accursed Sun Clans."

I gulped. Her distaste for the Sun Clans wasn't casual. She really, really hated them. The Minister of Defense's hopes for peace had been doomed from the start. "Uh, but you said that was a long time ago. . . ."

"I never had a chance to give her the burial rites!" Miho snarled, all smoothness gone. Nothing was left but feral grief. "Her body was abandoned to space. And Admiral Paik wasted my sister's sacrifice instead of blowing away the Sun Clanners, even though the *Sejong-Daewang* had the capability. It's now up to me to destroy the Sun Clans for all the Koreans they've killed!"

I looked away, uncomfortable in the face of her anguish. First at Haneul, whose expression had shifted to one of sympathetic listening. Then at my brother Jun.

Without changing *his* expression at all, Jun winked.

The gesture shocked me so much, coming as it did in the middle of Miho's anguished confession, that I froze. Just as well, too, because I had a chance to gather my composure before Miho's attention returned to me.

Jun wasn't being controlled by Miho. He'd been faking it, biding his time. A ghost couldn't strike her physically the way

I could . . . but he had powers of his own. Supernatural ones.

My heart lifted, and it was with effort that I kept the corners of my mouth from turning up. It wasn't that Miho's personal tragedy or her patriotism struck me as funny. Rather, it was my relief and joy at discovering that Jun was still on my side.

I knew from hard-won experience how horrible it was to lose a sibling. I'd been lucky in that Jun clung to the mortal plane. But I had some idea of what she had gone through. The awful thought struck me that Miho and I weren't so different.

But I wouldn't reignite a war to get revenge, I told myself. I had to believe that.

Jun must have been immune to Miho's Charm because he was a fox like me, and death hadn't changed that fact. If only I'd realized earlier!

The other ghosts, alas, were not so lucky. They crowded behind Miho, their eyes white and blank, a wind like wintry death rising from their pale forms. I couldn't afford for Miho to remember that she had an army of ghosts to do her bidding. They couldn't overpower me physically, but I feared the prospect of being haunted forever.

Miho was still talking about funerary customs and what they meant to foxes. Part of me wished I'd been paying attention. History wasn't my favorite subject, but it was different when it involved people I knew.

Even people like Miho.

Making sure she was still monologuing, I twitched my left eyelid in response to Jun: *DO IT NOW.*

He understood the signal.

Unfortunately, so did Miho, who hadn't been as lost in her speechifying as I had hoped. She whipped toward me with terrifying speed. I stumbled to the side, bracing for the impact.

However, Jun was even faster. He passed *through* her, accompanied by a freezing wind, and she staggered.

I ran for the ship. I couldn't think of anything else to do.

Miho came after me. If I'd entertained any hopes that Jun could impede her in a ghostly way, they evaporated when I saw how rapidly she moved. And, like a fool, I was looking over my shoulder at her instead of sprinting faster.

A hard lump formed in my throat, as if I needed the distraction while running for my life. I had to get to the dreadnought first.

A hysterical laugh almost escaped me. I had started to reconcile myself to the way things were on this world. Even admire the untamed beauty of its wilderness, so unlike anything I had experienced on my own homeworld. Too bad I'd brought the real threat with me.

Miho shouted a command and the ghosts surged forward. As a fox, I might be fast, but spirits aren't constrained by the limitations of a physical body.

I increased my pace, fumbling at the pouch that contained the Dragon Pearl as I did so. *Help me*, I thought frantically. Surely the Pearl didn't want to wind up in the hands of someone as consumed with bloodlust as Miho!

Even mountains couldn't stop the ghosts from pursuing me . . . but on the other hand, Miho herself didn't enjoy the advantages of being insubstantial. An idea sparked in my mind.

I got the pouch open and clutched the Pearl to my chest. It would be a disaster if I dropped it as I ran! Its iridescent light washed over my hands and created gleaming highlights on the rocks, the ice, and the grasping branches of the trees that stood between me and the dreadnought.

The Pearl, reading my intentions, raised up craggy hills and rocks behind me, rough terrain that would impede Miho, if not the ghosts. The earth rumbled and shook as it reconfigured itself. Hoping Sebin and Haneul were on safe ground, I risked another glance over my shoulder. To my dismay, Miho was so agile that the barriers had done little to slow her. She and her ghosts were gaining on me.

I had to face the possibility that Miho was going to defeat me. That I wouldn't be able to reach the dreadnought in time, or free my friends from her Charm. That even Jun's assistance, or that of the Pearl, wouldn't be enough to save me. My heart seized at the prospect of failing when we were so close to our goal.

I could have turned the world itself against Miho in a bid to save myself. But I had to think bigger than that. The whole point of this mission had been to restore peace between the Thousand Worlds and the Sun Clans. Both my government and theirs expected me to use the Dragon Pearl to terraform Jasujeong—to transform it into a planet brimming with non-threatening life, one that both nations could settle together in peace.

Perhaps the surest way to combat Miho's plans didn't involve my personal survival, but rather my completing the mission I'd been sent here to accomplish.

I only had moments before Miho reached me. It was now or never.

I skidded to a stop and cradled the Dragon Pearl in my hands, marveling anew at its sea-shimmer beauty. Had circumstances been otherwise, I would have lost myself in contemplating its radiance. But I had a job to do.

Closing my eyes, I whispered my wish to the Pearl. Its

glow intensified, beating against my eyelids with a pulsing like a heart's. A warmth as of the sun's smile and the moon's mercy rose from it.

My eyes flew open. Miho was only ten yards away. Any moment now she'd pounce on me.

Then the Dragon Pearl's magic swirled outward from the artifact, changing Jasujeong as it went. Trees straightened and reached toward the sky, their branches suddenly forming tender green leaves and fragrant blossoms, from plum to quince to cherry. Grasses and wildflowers sprang up over the ground, carpeting it in a glory of bright colors.

The ghosts under Miho's command stopped short. The cold wind that normally wafted from them diminished to a brisk spring breeze, refreshing rather than deadly. Perhaps they recognized a supernatural power greater than their own—and Miho's.

Birdsong and the humming of insects rose around us. Earlier, the creatures of Jasujeong had sounded ominous. Now the sounds struck me as cheery and welcoming. The tension inside me eased. Even if Miho took me down, at least I'd go out to a spring serenade.

"You think this will bring peace," Miho snarled, "but I'll see this whole planet torched before I allow our people to suck up to the Sun Clanners!"

Miho leaped for me. I was slow to react, entranced as I was by my communion with the Pearl. *This is it*, I thought. *This is the end of me.* I wondered if Jun and I would wander as spirits together, an oddly comforting thought.

Then Jun lunged *through* Miho again. She tripped and fell to the ground, where she lay groaning and cradling her ankle.

I couldn't believe my eyes. The smart thing to do would have been to redouble my efforts to reach the starship. Leave her behind.

But, I thought now, that would mean leaving my friends behind as well, and that I couldn't do.

The Pearl pulsed warmly in my hands, as if in agreement. I shoved it back into its pouch and snatched up a hefty fallen branch. Lifted it, ready to swing it down on Miho with all my might. To rid the world of the threat that she posed—to make sure she couldn't work toward her ruinous war.

"Min, no!" It was Jun. "This isn't the answer. One ghost in your life is enough, don't you think?"

I stared at him. He couldn't stop me from getting rid of Miho. And, if I wanted to go through with it, he *wouldn't* stop me. I could tell from the anguished look in his eyes.

But Jun was right. Murder would make me just as wicked as she was. Besides, I could only imagine what it would be like to be haunted by the ghost of someone I had killed and who bore a grudge.

I lowered the branch without letting go of it. After all, I needed a way to defend myself if Miho attacked me again. "We can't go on like this, Assistant Minister," I said. "Call off your ghosts."

Miho was breathing raggedly. She stared up at me, then looked the branch. "You almost had me," she whispered.

"The Sun Clans that you remember *failed*," I said vehemently. "The current government wants peace with us, not war! The only thing that will happen if you carry on like this is more people getting killed. Including . . . including other foxes."

"All the foxes are gone!" Miho cried. "I'm the last one."

I gaped at her, sick at heart. All this time she'd thought she was the sole remaining gumiho? That's why she had jumped to the conclusion that I was a magician.

I'd hidden my real identity from her . . . because I didn't trust her. To be fair, she hadn't exactly been particularly trust-*worthy*. But if she'd been more reliable, and I'd been able to talk to her honestly, all this could have been prevented. Instead, I'd followed my family's teachings, that foxes should hide in plain sight. Who knew how long Miho had plotted and schemed in the belief that foxes were extinct when my entire family was proof otherwise?

Granted, that didn't make Miho a good person. I was pretty certain now that *she* was the one who'd orchestrated the station's explosion. But had I . . . had I missed the chance to talk her out of those plans?

"Actually, you're wrong about that," I said. "There's something you don't know about my family. You would have found it out if you'd gotten into my dossier." I let go of my human form— the one I'd been using to make people think I was older—and condensed into my truest shape, that of a red fox.

"I'm not falling for your magician's illusions," Miho snapped. She didn't believe me . . . or did she? I caught a whiff of uncertainty from her.

"I'm sure magicians can do many things," I said, "but Charm is unique to foxes."

For the first time since we'd met, I directed my Charm at Miho. Not because I expected it to work on her, but because I knew she would recognize fox magic. At least, I assumed that was one thing she'd never mistake for anything else.

Indeed, Miho sneezed into her elbow, not once but twice.

Her eyes widened and she sat up. "*That's* not allergies," she said. She sounded shaken. "You really *are* a fox," Miho breathed. "With two tails." She looked at me, slack-jawed.

Wait, two *tails?* I'd only had one before. I turned my head to look at them—twitched one, then the other, experimentally. Did this mean I was growing up? Would I someday get *more?* If we ever got off this planet, that is.

To reinforce the point, Jun's shape flickered, and he became a fox as well, albeit a translucent white-and-gray one. "We're both gumiho," he assured Miho.

"Yes. My family is all foxes, including Jun." I gestured toward him, and he swished his tail, ears pricking. "There's even a city fox on Jinju who knew my mother. There might be more of us elsewhere, survivors who went into hiding."

Miho stared at me, still coming to grips with the truth. "If only I'd learned of your family earlier . . ."

I thought she might be realizing the error of her ways, the insanity of all the violence, but then she said, "We could have worked together to bring down the Sun Clans!"

I growled at her. "We would never have joined you." I certainly couldn't imagine my mom and aunties, or even my annoying cousin Bora, going along with Miho's murderous plans.

"All that planning . . ." she said, as if she hadn't heard me, "just to be *literally* outfoxed by one of my own kind. Truly, the universe has a sense of irony." She got to her feet, favoring one leg, and I tensed.

"It's over, Miho," I said. "Admit it. If you kill me, my brother and I will haunt you forever. We'll tell everyone about your plot. You won't be able to keep your position as assistant minister."

For a long moment Miho's face was inscrutable as she digested my threat. Then, slowly, she transformed into her own nine-tailed fox shape, condensing into a blaze of russet, silver, and black fur. I had to admit that, in appearance alone, she was an impressive representative of our kind. She crouched before us, her tails down on the ground. At first I thought she was in pain, but then I realized what she was doing—making a display of submission. The fight had gone out of her—for now.

"Come on," I said. "We need to collect Sebin and Haneul."

Miho stood up. "Perhaps I haven't failed completely," she noted, which made me shiver. "If the government has accepted a *fox* as the Bearer of the Dragon Pearl, there might be a place for other foxes, too. Maybe even me someday, after I've served my penance."

Not if I have anything to say about it, I thought grimly. I couldn't imagine anyone trusting Miho ever again.

On that ominous note, we resumed our human shapes and started walking back to my friends.

TWENTY

Sebin

I woke an indeterminate length of time later to the sound of a thunderstorm. I was wet. For a moment I thought I had traveled back in time, to the river whose crossing had almost turned into a disaster.

But the water here was cold, colder even than the river had been. And it came from above, not all around me. I lay on my side, shivering violently, as hail pelted me.

"Ouch!" I exclaimed, then winced at the throbbing in my temples. I remembered now that someone had knocked me out with a stunner. Miho.

I struggled to my feet. The headache made it difficult for me to concentrate, and I knew better than to attempt to shape-shift into my tiger form in this state, as it would only make my head hurt worse. As a small cub I'd been afraid that shifting while ill would result in my melting into an amoeba-shaped blob, but even my strict family had been quick to reassure me that the worst that could happen was temporarily being stuck in my current shape, whichever it was.

Miho, whom I had originally identified as the immediate threat, stood like a wraith nearby, dignified but silent. Someone had bound her wrists behind her, quite securely. Jun floated at her side in a way that struck me as angry. I sensed that, at least at the moment, neither posed any danger to me.

Jasujeong had changed. The very air smelled different, fragrant with familiar blossoms and fruits. Around me grew the hectic leaves of spring, and trees like the ones I had grown up with on the world of Yonggi. Min must have used the Dragon Pearl to carry out her mission after all—and I hadn't even been conscious for the occasion!

Now I beheld Min, in her human shape, confronting a dragon. A very angry one I'd seen twice before.

"Stop, Haneul!" Min was shouting. "You can't!"

The dragon's only response was a roar and a hammer-stroke of lightning that landed not far from Miho. It scorched the earth, melted the ice, and left rivulets of hot glass amid the ash. Miho jerked back.

I'd misjudged this situation. Miho wasn't the threat—Haneul was. But this wasn't a problem that could be solved with a tiger's brute strength. A tiger's cunning, maybe, but how could a tiger be more cunning than a fox? Never mind that Haneul didn't look like she was in a mood for words.

"Excuse me for missing out on the prologue," I said, raising my voice to make myself heard and wishing that the drumbeats of hail didn't hurt so much. It had been a long . . . I'd lost track of time. The point was, Haneul wasn't the only one having a lousy day. Maybe a lousy *year.* "What's the matter now?"

Haneul opened her mouth, revealing knifelike teeth, bigger even than a tiger's fangs. This wasn't the first time I'd faced an angry dragon, but I hoped it would be the last.

"She used her magic to make me sick," Haneul hissed, her

head and neck weaving back and forth like a serpent in front of the cowed form of Miho.

At this point a cold wind stung my face, and I noticed the ghosts standing in a circle around us. More accurately, around Miho. Each one stared directly at her. Even if she made a break for it, I doubted she stood a chance against twenty angry ghosts and their admiral.

"You can't chomp her, Haneul," Min said reasonably. "She'd probably taste like socks."

So I wasn't the only one who'd noticed that we were all smelly from our time in the wilderness, and the attendant physical exertion.

The dragon did not seem convinced by this argument, though it would have persuaded *me*.

"C'mon, Haneul," Min tried again. "She needs to stand trial. To face true justice for the things she's done."

"She must pay for her crimes," intoned one of the ghosts. It was Admiral Paik. "Tempted as I am to let the dragon spirit have her way with the nine-tailed fox."

"A trial." The sneer came from Miho like a thin, sharp thread. "Why bother? You think the worst I've done is a little artificially induced coma? Who do you think blew up the space station?"

Haneul's blue-green scales went pale. The air around us grew chillier, which I assumed was Jun's reaction. "Silhouette . . ." Min whispered, the smell of grief wafting from her.

I studied Miho, both intrigued and horrified. How could someone be capable of blowing up *her own side*? "Why admit this now?" I asked.

"It would have come out in the investigation anyway,"

Miho said bitterly. "Not that it matters. For all we know, the Thousand Worlds and the Sun Clans are *already* at war because of the attack. Your terraforming magic was pointless." She grimaced, looking at the circle of ghosts, and added, "You'll never get off-planet. There's no hope."

"We can't let that happen," I said, and Min nodded agreement.

"C'mon, Haneul," Min said. "Preventing a war has to be our priority. Once that's done, we'll make sure that Miho faces justice for her actions."

We still had to persuade the ghosts to let us board the dreadnought, but one problem at a time.

Haneul appeared to consider this, her eyes slitting.

I was worried at first, but eventually the air calmed. The clouds that had shadowed the sky gradually dispersed. After several moments, the brilliant sun shone overhead. The crisis had passed—the first one, anyway.

"I have to tell you two something," Min said to Haneul and me. "I stood by while Miho Charmed you both and did nothing. I thought she was doing it to keep us together. Now I realize she was plotting against us the whole time."

Haneul looked at Min and sighed a gusty dragon-sigh. "She was very persuasive, wasn't she?" the dragon said, and I knew Min was forgiven.

"She really was," I added, so Min knew that I didn't blame her either. Tentatively, I clasped her shoulder.

Min sagged in relief, leaning into the touch. "I hope this never happens again."

Haneul nodded in emphatic agreement.

"If we survived this together," Min said, holding her hand out in appeal, "we can survive anything."

Haneul nuzzled Min's fingertips, then gently bumped my cheek with her snout for good measure. The intimidating dragon-shape evaporated into the only slightly less intimidating form of a teenage girl in her cadet uniform.

I eyed Miho suspiciously. "Now we just have to make sure this one doesn't stand in our way."

"I swear on my nine tails that I won't," Miho said. She shuddered after the words left her mouth. For a second I saw her as a doubled image, one of them the woman I knew, the other a nine-tailed fox, her tails waving like snow-tipped banners, which had to be her true form. "Do your best, children. It will be interesting to watch."

"You're very clever with your words," Min said. "If you take one step in the wrong direction, I'll let Haneul do what she wants with you."

Miho's lip curled, but she didn't talk back.

We confronted the twenty ghosts and Admiral Paik. Beyond them rested the dreadnought, painfully visible in the clear air, as though a veil of mist and mirrors had been ripped away. Its flanks were partly encased in ice rising from the ground.

The spirits hadn't fallen upon us, which might have been a good sign. But Admiral Paik's expression was forbidding, and my heart sank. It was harsh to have come so far only to have our way off-planet barred to us.

I summoned my courage and addressed the admiral. "Sir, I respectfully request that you allow us to pass," I said. "We came here on a mission to secure peace between the Thousand Worlds and the Sun Clans. Please let us use your ship to find out if there are any survivors and tell our government what happened."

Paik remained an impassive, immovable stone.

I tried a different tack. "You're from the Thousand Worlds," I said. "Surely you remember the oath that you swore when you joined the Space Forces."

Paik's eyes flashed. "How many battles have you seen," they countered, "that you can lecture me on my oath?"

Min and I exchanged looks of dismay.

"Could we at least use the ship's comm system to—" Min started.

"I've noticed you travel with a ghost of your own," Admiral Paik observed, looking at Jun, not Min. "Most unusual."

"He's my brother," Min said simply. "I couldn't save him, but we've sworn to visit the Thousand Worlds together."

"You were traveling with Miho," the admiral said sharply. "How do I know you're not collaborating, and this isn't some complicated trick of hers?"

"As if," Miho muttered, but no one looked at her.

Jun was the next to step up, and he spoke with unusual clarity. "Miho, Min, and I are all foxes," he said earnestly, "but not all foxes are alike. Didn't you mention that Miho's sister was once a member of your crew?"

"That's true," Admiral Paik conceded. "Jiho was brave and fierce, and she was always honest about her heritage."

"These days people distrust gumiho," Jun said. "I joined the Space Forces hoping to prove that my kind can serve just as honorably as humans or tigers, dragons, and goblins. I may be a ghost now, but that doesn't mean I can't continue to serve alongside my sister."

"I had wondered about that," the admiral said. "She's clearly the one you're haunting, but it isn't revenge or anger that binds you to her—it's family. Most unusual."

"Family *and* duty," Jun said. His features almost had color to them, and his form was more distinct than usual. For once the wind that accompanied him carried a hint of spring warmth.

If I hadn't known better, I would have mistaken him for one of the living. The fact was, however, that his ghostly nature was the only reason Admiral Paik was willing to hear us out.

"Min and I may be foxes," Jun continued, "but we're still citizens of the Thousand Worlds. Even if you don't let *us* use your starship, *someone* should make sure that a war doesn't break out and result in more deaths—on either side."

Admiral Paik listened intently. "Well spoken, ghost Cadet," they said. "We have abided here for centuries with the hope that the conflict would simmer down. But perhaps . . . perhaps it is time for us to involve ourselves in the mortal realm again. Perhaps this is the duty we've been waiting for all this time."

My breath caught. "You'll help us?"

Admiral Paik's gaze met mine. I felt as though they could see all the way into the crevices of my mind, all my fears and doubts and torments . . . all the things I hoped for and didn't know if I could achieve.

"We will," Admiral Paik said, and smiled. They gave Jun a brisk nod. "Welcome aboard."

Paik and the other ghosts withdrew into the ship. I wondered if that meant our mission would be plagued by even more bad luck. For a panicked moment I thought the admiral had forgotten that we couldn't follow them through walls—except for Jun, who hesitated, glancing uncertainly at Min as if wanting her permission.

Then the ship's boarding ramp came down from the ship's underside, one of the few areas clear of ice. I expected it to creak, given that it must have been centuries since anyone had last used it. But the mechanism operated smoothly, almost silently, as though someone had been maintaining the ship and its equipment all this time. Min and I walked up, each of us holding one of Miho's arms.

I didn't know what to expect of the dreadnought's interior. I'd assumed it would look like that of the *Haetae*, dignified but functional, all struts and polished metal surfaces and right angles.

Instead, the *Sejong-Daewang*'s docking bay more closely resembled the antechamber to a throne room, not that I'd ever seen a throne room except in historical dramas. Landscape paintings on slightly yellowed silk hung on the bulkheads, depicting vanished forests and mountains. Masks and knotted maedeup talismans occupied their own nooks. Even the supplies, mysterious as they were, rested in lacquered boxes inlaid with abalone rather than the more utilitarian crates I had become accustomed to in the Space Forces.

"Come this way," said the admiral with a polite nod.

I gulped, not knowing how to interact with an admiral, especially one I had offended earlier. But it didn't seem like Paik bore a grudge, and despite their high rank—I could see the insignia now that I looked more closely—they spoke to us in a disconcertingly normal tone.

Faint lights illuminated the interior. I wondered how long they had been burning. The air smelled sterile rather than stale.

I tried to take in our surroundings, but Admiral Paik was moving at a swift pace. Any faster and I would have had to break into a run. I slanted a glance at Min and discovered that she was cheating! Ordinarily she was somewhat shorter than me, but she had lengthened her legs so she could keep up. I supposed that made sense, since she didn't have to hide her fox identity anymore.

At last we arrived at the bridge. If I'd thought the docking bay was grand, the bridge glowed with bygone splendor. In contrast to the *Haetae*'s sleek but industrial-looking furnishings and workstations, each chair, each metal object, appeared as though it had been hand-forged by a master smith, engraved with words of praise and battle-glory. I sobered as I considered the phrases. I had been raised to be a soldier, but having met people like the Sun Clans ambassador from the other side, I couldn't imagine being ordered to fight and kill them.

Aside from the lights, however, none of the bridge's workstations were lit up. That seemed like a bad sign.

"Will the ship still work after all this time?" Min asked, frowning as she surveyed the bridge. I remembered that she had a knack for technical matters. "The engine, for instance..."

"You are correct," Admiral Paik said. "The engine is indeed dead. It can only be sparked into life again by a sacrifice ... and a promise."

"Haven't we sacrificed enough already?" Miho spat.

"A sacrifice from us?" I asked warily. All my instincts were telling me to turn tail and run, but we were trapped in this space by a circle of twenty ghosts. Besides, that wouldn't look very dignified. I stood up straighter and awaited Paik's answer, but I couldn't help wincing a little in anticipation.

"No, the sacrifice must come from myself and my crew," the admiral said. "We are bound to the ship and must become one with it to bring it back to life."

My jaw dropped in what I was sure was an unbecoming

manner. *They* would be the power supply? I was ashamed of not having taken more notice of the other ghosts before now. I studied each of their faces, committing them to memory. How long had they kept company with each other, trapped on this planet? And did they want to leave it this way?

"Are you sure?" I asked.

"As I said earlier, Cadet, it is our duty."

"And also your promise?" I asked.

Paik shook their head and pierced me with an intense gaze. "The promise must come from *you.*"

I heard Min's sharp intake of breath. Or maybe it was mine.

"This ship wants a living hand at its controls," Admiral Paik said. "A living crew to make sure it is used only for honorable causes, not monstrous ones as this saboteur planned. She will have to be confined so she can do no harm." The admiral didn't even look at Miho when he spoke of her.

We cadets nodded, anxious to hear what the admiral was going to say next.

Paik's eyes were serious as they met each of ours in turn. "Are you willing to be that crew?"

I was positive that if we agreed to this, the ghosts' influence over the *Sejong-Daewang* would make sure we kept our promise. For all I knew, if we died, we would still be bound to this very ship, and to each other, as ghosts ourselves. Strangely, though, the prospect filled me with more eagerness than dread.

"My handler is going to make me fill out four million forms once he finds out," Min said. Her eyes shone. "But it's a tremendous opportunity. Let's do it."

Haneul looked faint. "This isn't exactly what I envisioned when I decided I'd rather stay in the Space Forces," she said.

"We have a mission, though, and this is the only way to fulfill it. I'm in."

My heart lifted as I contemplated the bridge. I missed the people from the *Haetae*, but after everything Min, Haneul, and I had been through, the prospect of sharing a ship with these two excited me. "Yes," I said softly. Then louder: "Yes."

"Remember your bargain, no matter what befalls you," Admiral Paik said.

A blast of freezing air swept through the bridge, and I shivered violently. A fierce white light flashed before us. Then all the ghosts except Paik and Jun were gone, and the workstations lit up in brilliant colors.

"Someone will have to take the captain's seat," Min said in a hushed voice.

I looked at Haneul, who had been a cadet longer and thus outranked me. She shook her head and smiled. "Go ahead. *I'm* keeping an eye on Miho."

I had no doubt that if Miho so much as twitched funny, she would face a wrathful dragon. Since I had no desire to find out if flooding the ancient bridge would cause an electrical short, I hoped for all our sakes that Miho wouldn't trigger Haneul's stormy temper. If Haneul could smell my apprehension, she kept it to herself. As for Miho, she gave off an air of offended haughtiness.

"I'm only a cadet," I said to the admiral. Not in apology, only explanation.

"It is up to you now," Paik said.

"You have to start somewhere," added Min.

I acquiesced then and took the captain's chair. Min and Haneul buckled in Miho, who was still tied up, and then themselves. I allowed myself a moment to study the control panel. At first I worried that I wouldn't know how to launch the ship, that the controls would be as unfamiliar as Jasujeong itself. The embellishments in the dreadnought, in their every detail, told me that the past was just as alien as another planet.

To my surprise, once I got past the superficial decorations, the controls weren't so different than the ones that I had trained on aboard the *Haetae*. The colors were the same. The shapes were the same. Sure, it seemed extravagant that the status lights shone from literal crystals and the buttons were labeled in calligraphy rather than a plainer font, but the basic design had been preserved through the years.

"Blue for heaven," I said aloud, and began the preflight checks. One by one, each crystal glowed blue. I thought I could hear a faint humming, and I knew that the spirits infusing the dreadnought approved.

"Time to fly," the admiral said.

I powered up the engines, and—miracle of miracles—the ship lofted. Min and Haneul cheered. As for me, I stayed focused, hoping it wouldn't suddenly fall to pieces and crash back down. But I heard no groaning, felt no shuddering.

At first all I saw on the front viewscreen was a symphony of ice, the unnatural winter wrought by the ghosts' former presence.

Then the ice shattered as the ship broke free of winter's grip. Shards flew in every direction, yet I had no fear. I was sure the admiral would have told us if the ice posed a threat. The ship's shields were also status blue. We were going to be fine.

Whether that would still apply once we reached orbit was another story.

We soon left behind the flurry of ice shards and false snow. The ship pointed its nose heavenward. The viewscreen went deep purple swirled with lavender clouds, then the green-purple of Jasujeong's glorious atmosphere, and then deepened inexorably into the black of space. Stars shone like brilliant riddles of light and pattern in that darkness.

I would have lingered, lost in wonder, for some time, except a new sound intruded on my awareness: a communications alert, similar to the ones modern ships used.

"It's a distress signal," Haneul said. "Are we too late?"

"Let's hear it," Admiral Paik said.

"Min, could you . . . ?" I asked. I was concentrating on getting the ship into a stable geosynchronous orbit, at least until I figured out what was going on.

One thing, at least, was clear from the sensors, which I had rerouted to my seat since we only had so many living crew: I didn't detect any other active ships in the area, only one of the station's escape pods, whose inhabitants I hoped were still alive after two weeks. If the Thousand Worlds and Sun Clans were at war again, it wasn't happening here.

Min hit some buttons. A holo snapped into focus, and I almost gasped. It was the Sun Clans ambassador, Tanaka Sakura, rather the worse for wear. Her hair looked as though she hadn't brushed it in days. For that matter, I hadn't combed *my* hair in weeks, so I couldn't judge her.

". . . ambassador, requesting aid from any Thousand Worlds or Sun Clans ship in the area. I speak for refugees from Station Asa-Achim, including Captain Chaewon of the *Haetae*. We are about to go into the sleeper units and hope that you will rescue us before our power runs out in three months. There has been an attack on the station and the saboteur may still be in the area. . . ."

"It's a recording from just after the attack. Or . . ." I said reluctantly, "it could be a trap."

Miho scoffed. "What, you think there's a *second* saboteur?"

We all looked at her, and she clammed up. Haneul retrieved a rag from a supply locker and gagged the assistant minister so we wouldn't have to listen to any more of her remarks.

"Bring up the location of the escape pod," I suggested. "We can scan it more closely."

Min did so. "It looks real," she said. "The sensors say there are ten people aboard that one, and . . ." Her breath hitched. "It's not alone. There are a few more escape pods in orbit. In *decaying* orbit."

"How do we recover them?" I asked, looking around for Admiral Paik, but they were nowhere to be seen.

"I bet there are instructions," Min said. After she dug around in the computer system for several moments, she brought up a manual on how to use the dreadnought's waldoes: robotic arms that enabled it to retrieve objects floating in space.

I cleared my head, despite a sincere desire for a yearlong nap in a nice warm sunbeam, and followed the instructions. First, I maneuvered the ship closer to the ambassador's escape pod. "She's the highest priority," I said. "Her first, then the others."

"That makes sense," Haneul agreed. "I imagine a peace treaty would fizzle out if the Sun Clans' ambassador got killed."

I didn't want to smash into the pod, small speck that it was. Fortunately, the proximity sensors warned me when I got too close, and I was able to correct our trajectory in time, matching our vector to the pod's.

Then I activated the ship's robot arm. I soon got the hang of the controls, maybe because they reminded me weirdly of a puzzle video game I'd become obsessed with when I was a cub. Carefully, carefully, I approached the pod . . . and gripped it in the arm's pincers. For a second I was terrified that I'd used too much force and crushed the capsule, but the arm's own feedback mechanisms prevented that from happening.

I withdrew the arm into one of the cargo bays. "Are they all right?" I asked anxiously.

"Let's recover the rest and see to them all at once," Min said. "If the sleepers are any good, the passengers will keep for the time it takes."

I retrieved a second pod, then a third, and a fourth. And there were still more. I was amazed—and grateful—that so many people had survived the explosion.

The motions blurred into one another. After a time, there were no more distress signals, and I wondered what I was supposed to do now. Once again I looked around for the admiral, hoping they could give me some guidance.

Jun guessed what I was doing. He shook his head. "Admiral Paik is gone, Sebin. Once they saw that you had everything under control, they joined their crew."

"And became part of the ship?"

Jun nodded.

It wasn't a surprise, but it still stunned me. I wondered if I would ever be a leader who could make that kind of sacrifice for the greater good.

Min laid her hand on my arm, and I blinked up at her.

"It's done," she said. "We kept our promise."

"All life signs are stable in the pods," said Haneul. "The evacuees are safe now. Let's go wake them up."

EPILOGUE

Min

"This is Station Ssangyong," a voice came over the comms. "Please identify yourself and state your business."

Sebin and I exchanged glances, and I couldn't help grinning. The voice had definitely sounded intimidated by the sheer size of the *Sejong-Daewang*, which dwarfed any modern battle cruiser.

"Station Ssangyong," said the captain, "I'm Captain Chaewon, speaking for the dreadnought *Sejong-Daewang*, restored to service. We have refugees on board from the recent peace talks at Station Asa-Achim. We need to transfer them stationside for medical care."

Brief silence, then: "Did you say the *Sejong-Daewang*? But that crashed centuries ago!"

This time it was the adults' turn to exchange glances, and exasperated ones at that. "Listen," Captain Chaewon said, "you can debate history with me, or you can deal with people who need medical treatment *right now*. Including diplomatic representatives from the Sun Clans. Unless you *want* there to be a war?"

"Not at all, Captain," the voice said in a much more respectful manner. "Ah—there are Sun Clanners aboard?"

Ambassador Tanaka rolled her eyes.

"Of *course* there are," the captain said. "Or did you think we were going to leave them behind? That would be an even better way to start a war."

The adults who had taken over the bridge had tried to warn Sebin, Haneul, and me away from hanging out there with them, but even they couldn't deny that we'd *rescued* them, or nullify the bargain we'd made with Admiral Paik. Captain Chaewon and Sebin had come to the agreement that she would handle administrative matters on their behalf until the Space Forces figured out how to deal with the situation. Nevertheless, the *Sejong-Daewang* was *our* ship. We were now bound to it by our promise and our friendship with one another.

Still, Ambassador Tanaka and Captain Chaewon were in charge of Sun Clans and Thousand Worlds personnel respectively. Both of them looked much better after spending some time in sick bay and eating some of the magic tangerines Haneul had managed to bring aboard. Fortunately, one of the evacuees was a medic who knew how to treat sleeper sickness.

After some more logistical discussions I didn't pay attention to, the station permitted us to "dock." It turned out that the dreadnought was too large for a standard berth, so they were going to use one of the bridge extensions to ferry people over.

"I admit I'm going to miss my crewmates on the *Pale Lightning*," Haneul admitted as we watched the proceedings.

Sebin nodded. "I know what you mean. Excited as I am, life on the *Sejong-Daewang* will be very different from life on the *Haetae*."

"At least we can take comfort in the fact that all three ships are still intact," I added.

I would have killed to eavesdrop on Haneul's last conversation with Dragon Councilor Gwan, who was one of the survivors. All I knew was that Haneul had told Gwan that she didn't want to be their protégée anymore, no matter how prestigious the position. The councilor had stopped speaking to her, and the sentiment seemed to be mutual. Haneul wasn't so worried about disappointing her mothers now. Even they would acknowledge the importance of keeping an oath to an ancient admiral.

Unfortunately, Silhouette hadn't made it to an escape pod. I had grieved for her privately, and once asked Jun, "Why didn't she linger in the area as a ghost?"

"Because she made her sacrifice willingly," he'd said, "she was able to move on to the afterlife."

That made sense. Unlike Jun, Silhouette hadn't had anything binding her to the world of the living. I would never forget her selflessness. Perhaps someday I might even learn what her real name was.

For their part, Sebin had made a point of checking in on the two youngest cadets from the *Haetae*, Dak-Ho and Yui. Their good behavior impressed me, especially after all the stories I'd heard of their mischief. Maybe seeing a real disaster up close had frightened some sense into them.

"I wish we could be in control again," said Sebin now, looking begrudgingly at Captain Chaewon.

I said "Shh," to my friends and nodded at the adults. I wasn't going to use Charm, but I'd learned—from Miho, of all people—that simple persuasion sometimes worked just as well.

"We'd like to come along, please." I used my politest voice to address the captain.

"All right," she said with a sigh. "I suppose you've earned that privilege."

"They're going to hand Miho over," I said to Haneul and Sebin. "Wouldn't you like to watch?"

Haneul hesitated, then nodded.

Sebin looked for a moment like they were about to object, then subsided, their expression thoughtful.

We accompanied Captain Chaewon and Ambassador Tanaka like a line of friendly ducklings. I knew they would have preferred us to stay "safe" on the dreadnought, where *safe* actually meant *out of the way*. But we'd proven ourselves—hadn't we?—and we deserved to witness this one last event.

An elevator decorated with paintings of bamboo and carp conveyed us to the docking bay. It even played music, far removed from the bland ambient sounds I'd heard in the Ministry of Domestic Security. I'd rapidly learned that the dreadnought's soundtrack was typically the kind of old-fashioned instrumental music that I associated with historical dramas, except it hadn't been "historical" at the time it was programmed in. I was going to have to introduce the ship to some modern tunes.

We emerged into the cargo bay, where a holo showed the bridge extension being hooked up to the dreadnought. I longed to run over and study how it worked, but I had a promise to keep. Besides, I would probably have plenty of opportunity to learn such things later.

"There she is," Jun said in a low voice. He pointed.

We all turned as one to face the figure standing at the far

side of the cargo bay, next to another of the entrances. Miho was clad in a hanbok of modern but dignified cut . . . and handcuffs. I doubted the two guards who accompanied her could have stopped her if she suddenly shape-shifted and made a break for freedom. On the other hand, this was space. It wasn't like she could run off into vacuum.

I spotted a third figure trailing the guards. . . . Aha! A shaman in full traditional garb. *She* would be able to keep Miho from doing anything devious.

Miho caught my eye, began to mouth something, and sneezed instead. Not for the first time I was grateful that the general public didn't know about this fox trait.

The guards herded Miho toward the exit that led into the station. They stopped for a moment when they reached the ambassador.

"We ate at the same table," Ambassador Tanaka said to the assistant minister. Lines of grief and regret around her eyes and mouth made her look even older than she was. "We exchanged gifts. We worked together on the treaty. Were you really so determined to see people like me die?"

To her credit, Miho didn't turn away or make excuses. She merely said, "I did what I did, and I will carry that shame for the rest of my days." She looked straight at me when she said that.

"That's something for the courts to decide," Captain Chaewon said. She sounded as if she wished she could deliver a summary verdict then and there. But Miho was a government official, and protocols had to be followed.

The guards escorted Miho to the exit. A door opened; a door closed. Just like that, she was gone.

I stared after her as though her silhouette had burned itself onto my retinas. I thought I would see her image for the rest of my life, a shadowy reminder of the bad decisions I might make if I wasn't careful. After all, I'd used a lot of Charm in my adventures. At least it hadn't been to *kill* people. Despite what I'd been taught all my life, I didn't think Charm was good or evil. But it could definitely be used for good or evil *reasons*.

Then Sebin tapped my shoulder. "They'll be a while with all this," the tiger cadet said. "Let's get some food. They might have some more of that raw-fish sashimi stuff from the Sun Clans."

"Good idea," Haneul agreed, looking relieved. Then she gave my brother a wry smile. "I'm sure you're hungry, too, right, Jun?"

"Always," Jun said solemnly, and we laughed as we headed to the mess.

We had so much to celebrate. We'd completed our mission and no longer had to worry about war—at least for the time being. Thanks to the Dragon Pearl, the terraforming process had begun on Jasujeong, and it could no longer be considered a death planet. The *Sejong-Daewang* had been recovered and would not be used as a threat. Sebin would later be confirmed as captain, just as they had wished, and Haneul would continue to be part of the Space Forces as one of the crew. Now nothing could prevent Jun and me from journeying to every one of the Thousand Worlds . . . and returning to Jinju so we could transform it into a paradise with the Pearl.

We had a ship of our own now, and the ship had us.

PRONUNCIATION GUIDE

(Pronounce all syllables with equal stress)

Ajin: ah-jeen
Asa-Achim: ah-sah-ah-cheem
baduk: bah-dook
Baektusan: behk-doo-sahn
Baik: behk
biwa: bee-wah
Bora: boh-rah
Chaewon: cheh-wuhn
Cheonggeumseok: chuhng-goom-suhk ("oo" as in "good")
Dak-Ho: dahk-hoh
gayageum: gah-yah-goom ("oo" as in "good")
gimchi: geem-chee
Goryeo: goh-ryuh
gumiho: goo-mee-hoh
gwaemul: gweh-mool
Gwan: gwahn
gyoza: gyoh-zah
Haetae: heh-the
Hak: hahk
hanbok: hahn-bohk
Haneul: hah-nool ("oo" as in "good")
Hangeul: han-gool ("oo" as in "good")
Hasun: hah-soon
Hokusai: hoh-k'-sai
Hwan: hwahn
Jasujeong: jah-soo-juhng

Jee: jee
Jiho: jee-hoh
Jinju: jeen-joo
Juhwang: joo-hwahng
Jun: joon
katana: kah-tah-nah
Kim: geem
maedeup: meh-doop ("oo" as in "good")
mandu: mahn-doo
Min: meen
mugunghwa: moo-goong-hwah
Nihongo: nee-hohn-go
Paik Sumin: behk soo-meen
piri: pee-ree
pungsu jiri: poong-soo jee-ree
Sakura: sah-koo-rah
Sapsali: sahp-sahl-lee
sashimi: sah-shee-mee
Sebin: seh-been
Sejong-Daewang: seh-johng-deh-wahng
Seok: suhk
Sooni: soo-nee
Ssanyong: ssahng-yohng
Tanaka: tah-nah-kah
wakizashi: wah-kee-zah-shee
Yang Miho: yahng mee-hoh
yangban: yahng-bahn
Yi: ee
Yonggi: yohng-ghee
Yui: yoo-ee
yutnori: yoot-noh-ree

ACKNOWLEDGMENTS

Thanks to my wonderful editor, Steph Lurie, and to Rick Riordan, both of whom made this book possible. Thanks also to my amazing agent, Seth Fishman.

Thank you to my delightful alpha readers, Ellen Million and Mason Rounds.

Thank you to my lovely beta readers, Yune Kyung Lee and Ilana Stern.

Thanks to David Gillon for his support and help, and to Becca Syme and Terry Schott for their coaching.

Last but not least, thank you to my husband, Joseph Betzwieser; my daughter, Arabelle Betzwieser; my sister, Yune Kyung Lee; and my long-suffering catten, Cloud, for putting up with me while I was writing this. 힘내!